Hmm... Marr

Wouldn't i

Wouldn't *he* be wonderful....

He'd be rich and handsome. Passionate.

And he'd be madly in love—with *you!*

Torrey, Emily and Millie have their own
reasons for wanting—*needing*—
to marry money.
And they each have a plan.

But they hadn't *counted* on love.
Or on three dashing and sexy millionaires
with plans of their own!

Watch it happen in these three delightful new
stories by your favorite authors!

ABOUT THE AUTHORS

Suzanne Forster has written twenty novels to critical raves and has been the recipient of numerous awards, including The National Readers' Choice Award. She's also received recognition from Waldenbooks and Bookrak for outstanding sales. Her recent title *Blush* hit the Waldenbooks' Mass Market Top Twenty in the first week of its release, and was on the *USA Today* and Barnes & Noble bestseller lists.

Muriel Jensen, the award-winning author of almost thirty-five novels, began writing romance fiction in the ninth grade. She realized she'd found her niche in life when her classmates started gathering around her desk every morning for the latest installment. Muriel is a mother of three and lives in Oregon with her husband.

Judith Arnold is the bestselling author of almost sixty romance novels and has fans worldwide. The winner of numerous awards, including *Romantic Times*'s Best Series Romance Novel of the Year, Judith makes her home in Massachusetts with her husband and two sons.

How to Marry a
MILLIONAIRE

Suzanne Forster
Muriel Jensen
Judith Arnold

Harlequin Books

TORONTO • NEW YORK • LONDON
AMSTERDAM • PARIS • SYDNEY • HAMBURG
STOCKHOLM • ATHENS • TOKYO • MILAN
MADRID • WARSAW • BUDAPEST • AUCKLAND

HARLEQUIN BOOKS
225 Duncan Mill Road, Don Mills,
Ontario, Canada M3B 3K9

HOW TO MARRY A MILLIONAIRE

Copyright © 1997 by Harlequin Books S.A.

ISBN 0-373-83326-1

The publisher acknowledges the copyright holders
of the individual works as follows:
RICH MAN, POOR MAN
Copyright © 1997 by Barbara Keller
FAMILY WEALTH
Copyright © 1997 by Muriel Jensen
ONCE UPON A HUSBAND
Copyright © 1997 by Suzanne Forster
PROLOGUE and EPILOGUE
Copyright © 1997 by Suzanne Forster

CONTENTS

Prologue

"IF I FOLLOW your Mercedes home, will you keep me?" Torrey Benson read the breezy pickup line for the benefit of the studio audience, then closed the cover of her brand-new best-seller, *How to Marry a Millionaire,* and flashed the crowd of mostly women a sparkling smile.

"If you want to marry a millionaire," she told them, "first you have to get his—or her—attention. This book has a line for every occasion, from hobnobbing at Ascot to skiing in Vail."

The studio lights were blinding, but so was Torrey's desire to succeed. Turning up the wattage of her smile, she swept the small auditorium with her gaze, encompassing everyone. She even remembered to include the woman at the other end of the couch from her, Babs Randazzo, host of the number-one daytime talk show in the nation.

Babs's show was the highlight of Torrey's ten-city book tour, and it was crucial that Torrey make the most of her opportunity. There couldn't be a slipup. Not even one. Torrey came from a retail-sales background, and this was the first book she'd ever written, much less promoted, but today was about more than selling a book. She was salvaging a life and a future. *Her own.*

Ignoring cue cards that said it was time to take questions from the audience, Torrey spoke to the camera with total conviction. "Never settle," she counseled viewers. "If your dream mate is wonderfully wealthy and wildly successful, you won't be happy with the boy next door—unless you live in Bill Gates's neighborhood!"

"Don't you love her enthusiasm?" Babs broke in. "We all want our own well-heeled honey now, don't we?" With the wink that had become her trademark, Babs gracefully turned her blue-eyed sunny countenance to another beckoning camera. "We're going to tell you how to meet Mr. Fortune 500 right after this commercial break, so stay tuned for our version of the Millionaire Mating Game."

There was a flurry of activity as the camera's red light went out. Babs patted Torrey's hand, congratulated her on being a natural and rushed off to consult with a hovering assistant producer. A makeup man appeared to powder the shine from Torrey's nose at the same time Torrey tried to take a sip of water *and* consult her notes. Droplets dribbled down her chin and sprinkled her slacks.

A stack of napkins sat on the coffee table. Torrey reached around the makeup man and grabbed one to blot her pants, thankful the camera wasn't going to be pointed at her lap. The Tower Books publicist had advised soft colors and lines, so Torrey had chosen a powder blue pantsuit and lace camisole. Image was crucial when you were selling a book like hers. She'd discovered that most Americans were proud individualists and staunchly traditional. They'd grown up with The Dream, and they didn't look kindly on someone trying to take shortcuts.

More than once on the tour she'd been accused of encouraging her readers to sacrifice love for money, a notion that always startled her. "I'm not suggesting for a moment that anyone sacrifice love," she would assure them. "Millionaires need love, too!" And if that didn't sway the ambivalent crowd, she would add, "Don't despair if Donald Trump and Bill Gates aren't your type. There's a mogul out there for any woman who wants one."

She was used to ribbing from the audiences and took it good-naturedly, addressing concerns with humor and what she hoped was common sense. "There's nothing wrong with money," she pointed out, "only what people do with it. Once you get your millions, do good works. Think of the opportunities you'll have to make the difference you've always wanted to."

Fortunately she'd been gifted with a friendly smile and pleasing looks. Her publicist had told her that her freckles and fresh-scrubbed appearance challenged the notion of women who married for money. How could a woman who looked like Betty Crocker's kid sister possibly be a gold digger?

"My staff wants you to take some audience questions first," Babs announced as she scurried back to Torrey. Babs was short, plumpish and a fireball. An ex-comedienne, she'd taken daytime television by storm, partly because she was as adept at making her guests look good as she was at wisecracks.

Torrey held back her concerns. She didn't want the contest to get bumped, but she didn't want to make waves, either; it had been difficult enough getting a spot on the show. But Tower Books had come up with the idea to pick volunteers from the audience and send them out into the world to test Torrey's tips. There would be a follow-up spot five weeks later to announce the results.

Babs made a beeline for the audience, waving at the camera as the show resumed. "You've been dying to ask Torrey some questions, haven't you, folks? Go ahead, ma'am," she said, helping an older woman to her feet and offering the mike.

"Are *you* married to a millionaire, Torrey?" the woman asked.

"Not currently," Torrey admitted. A buzz

rose from the crowd and Torrey quickly explained. "My husband was killed in a freak accident only a few months after we were married. He owned several luxury-car dealerships, but it was his zest for life that will be sorely missed by those who loved him."

What she didn't share was how freakish the accident had actually been. A disgruntled customer returned an expensive lemon by crashing it through the showroom window at the very moment that Norbert Wakefield Benson III was closing a "killer" deal, to use his favorite term. She also didn't mention the mountain of debt poor Norbert had left. He'd had a million all right—a million in assets and two million in loans and bad debts. Torrey was flat broke. Every penny she made on this book would go to pay bills.

The next guest expressed her condolences and asked Torrey how she'd met her late husband.

"It's in the book," Torrey told her. "The chapter entitled 'When All Else Fails' has some tips for the daring and the desperate among you. For example, you could kidnap your millionaire, hold him for ransom, then don't give him—or the money—back. And if that doesn't work, there's always his dog.

"Norbert and I met when I mistakenly dognapped his prize borzoi, thinking it was my neighbor's missing Afghan hound. The dog refused to go home without me, leaving poor Norbert no choice but to take me along.''

She lifted her shoulders in a shrug and waited for the chuckles to subside. When they did, Babs took a few more questions, then much to Torrey's relief, asked the volunteers to stand.

Torrey was surprised to see that one of the volunteers, a tall dark-haired guest standing near the back, was a man. Even though the house lights were on, she couldn't see him well enough to make out details, but she felt an uneasy sense of recognition. Did she know him from somewhere?

Babs announced the rules over a flourish of fanfare. ''Each of our lucky volunteers has agreed to search for his or her own millionaire and try out Torrey's tips. The person who brings one back will be featured on our fabulous follow-up show, where we'll hear all about his or her excellent adventures. How's that sound?''

The swell of applause thrilled Torrey. Apparently she'd won this crowd over. Now all she had to do was pray that the contestants were good sports and nothing went wrong.

The first volunteer was a slim dark-haired young woman whose smile conveyed a mixture of excitement and panic.

''Torrey, meet Emilie Storrs,'' Babs announced. ''Why did you volunteer, Emilie?''

"I'm broke," Emilie said with a refreshing candor that sparked more laughter.

"No problem," Babs told her, "just prepare yourself for a close encounter of the seven-figure kind."

The second volunteer didn't look quite as promising. In fact, she looked ready to bolt as Babs approached. She reluctantly introduced herself as Camille Brown, but said she went by Millie, and she seemed more than a little apprehensive.

"Are you sure you want to do this?" Babs asked, echoing Torrey's sentiments exactly.

Millie managed a smile. "My sisters need the money for college."

"But what about you?" Babs pressed. "You must need...something."

A dreamy look transformed the woman for a moment, and she made a sound that might have been a sigh. "Well, a little romance would be nice," she admitted.

"You'll do fine," Torrey promised her from the stage, confident that she would—with a little help. "I'll personally coach you and the other volunteers in the art of attracting the opposite sex. Give it a try?" she coaxed. "You've got nothing to lose."

Millie nodded shyly, and the audience broke out in another round of applause.

By the time they got to the male volunteer,

Torrey's eyes had adjusted to the houselights. But they'd also nearly bugged out of her head. Worse, her temples had begun to drip with sweat. She could see him clearly now—his sexy smile and direct unavoidable gaze. That was the problem. Not only could she see him, she knew him. She knew him in every sense of the word.

He was her ex-husband.

"Your name?" Babs asked, clearly as taken with Christopher "Kit" McGrath as every other woman in the audience. He *was* devastating. Torrey had fallen in love with him on sight, but that was back in high school when she'd been young and ridiculously impressionable. She'd spent the past fifteen years trying to repair the damage he'd done. Kit McGrath had taught her not to trust men, ruined her for love and sent her on a mad quest in search of life's other compensations. He'd made a bitter woman out of her until she'd realized there was more to life than his gotta-have-you-baby blue eyes and her own wild uncontrollable yearnings. She hadn't loved him. It couldn't have been love, not that agony.

"Wait a minute. Aren't you Kit McGrath, the hockey player?" Babs queried, peering at him. "Why did a handsome devil like you volunteer?"

"Because I've got nothing to lose," he said softly.

His voice registered in every cell of Torrey's

brain, and his vibrant blue eyes transfixed her. This was no coincidence. He had come for her. It had never occurred to her until now that her television appearances would allow him to track down the child bride who'd run away from him.

She blinked, realizing she must look like a suspect in a police lineup. Her mind began to race, searching for an escape, but there didn't seem to be any way out of this. She was on national television and the success of her book was at stake. She couldn't let her publisher down. They'd spent a fortune on the tour and the contest.

"Torrey!" Babs called out, "you said you'd work with the volunteers, coach them personally. Mr. McGrath wants to know when he can start."

Never! Kit McGrath needed no personal coaching on how to attract women—especially from her. But she could see from the look in his eyes that he was going to want it.

He was probably going to want private lessons.

RICH MAN, POOR MAN

Judith Arnold

Chapter One

WELL, ALL RIGHT, Emilie thought to herself. *I'll give this nonsense a try. I'll see if I can snag myself a rich man. But I'll bet there isn't a rich man on earth as sexy as that bartender.*

She tried not to stare at him, but she couldn't help herself. The resort's elegant cream-colored buildings, its mosaic-inlaid patios and walkways, its emerald lawns and ruby-blossomed rhododendrons and pearl white beach faded into a background blur. All she saw was the bartender.

He was tall and lean and lithe. His skin glowed a rich golden color, no doubt the result of hours spent in the tropical sun, and his hair was long and wavy, the honey-colored locks streaked with blond. His eyes were bluer than the Caribbean Sea that swept out from the shoreline to the horizon, and his smile was punctuated by deeply etched dimples. He moved gracefully, and he filled his white cotton polo shirt and khaki shorts with a stunning arrangement of bone and muscle and high-octane testosterone.

They didn't grow men like him in Chicago.

They didn't cultivate his breed in the dreary projects where her former clients lived, or in the stagnant halls of the city-run bureaucracy where she'd occupied a cubicle until the politics of tax cuts and downsizing had cost her her job four months ago. The men Emilie knew back home were like her—pale, hardworking and chronically broke.

But she wasn't in the Windy City now. She was at the Golden Key Caribbean Resort, situated on a tiny island two miles west of St. Thomas, supposedly to find herself a rich husband. She'd read *How to Marry a Millionaire* and received personal coaching from its author, Torrey Benson. One of the chapters had explained that if you wanted to meet millionaires, you had to hang out where millionaires hung out. They hung out at the Golden Key, but the only way Emilie could gain entry to such a place was to take a job as a cocktail waitress.

Yet how could she spare the resort's wealthy guests a passing thought when there was a man like *him* standing in her line of vision? Even if he was a bartender...with looks like his, who cared about his bank account?

Actually the marry-a-millionaire idea was her sister Corinne's, not Emilie's. Corinne had married her own millionaire years ago, but she'd met him in college and they'd fallen head over heels in love. That he was the scion of one of

Chicago's wealthiest families hadn't been a factor in Corinne's decision to marry him.

Of course, once they'd settled into their penthouse high above Lake Shore Drive, and Corinne had learned the joys of never having to count pennies again, she'd advised her younger sister to aim for the easy life, too. She'd even tried to set Emilie up with some of her husband's rich single friends, but they'd seemed superficial to her, blithely unconcerned with the downtrodden folks with whom she worked.

"You're very noble, and I know you're making a difference in people's lives," Corinne had said. "But you can make a difference in people's lives with money, too. Look at how much I raised at that silent auction for the homeless. And the charity ball for children with cancer. And the fund-raisers for the Red Cross."

It was true. Corinne raised lots of money for those in need—and had a blast doing it—while Emilie had spent the past four years as an underpaid caseworker in the Department of Social Services. And then she'd gotten laid off.

"Read this book," Corinne had urged Emilie when they'd met for lunch one afternoon. "You're broke, Em. You're unemployed. You've been wearing sackcloth long enough. If you marry someone rich, you can still be a do-gooder, but you wouldn't have to live in that seedy little tenement with the cockroaches anymore.''

Emilie had glanced warily at the book Corinne nudged across the table to her. "*How to Marry a Millionaire?* Yeah, right.''

"Why not? It's as easy to fall in love with a rich man as a poor one.''

"Who says it's easy to fall in love?''

"Read it, Em. You might learn something. What have you got to lose?''

So Emilie had read the book, and Corinne had finagled some tickets to a talk show on which Torrey Benson, as part of her cross-country promotional tour, was a guest; and somehow, Emilie had been selected as one of Ms. Benson's test cases. Ms. Benson had boasted on national television that if Emilie followed the strategies outlined in the book, she would meet and marry a millionaire.

Emilie had gone through a bit of private tutoring—which mostly amounted to pep talks, beauty tips and reassurances that landing a rich husband was a worthwhile goal—and now she was here, following the strategies outlined in chapter seven, which recommended positioning yourself in an environment conducive to mixing and mingling with the elite. But at the moment, the only person she wanted to mix and mingle with was the bartender.

She hovered just beyond the patio of the open-walled cabana that housed the poolside bar. The midday sun beat down on her shoulders; she had twisted her thick brown hair into a knot and pinned a gardenia into the twist. If she had a prayer of attracting an eligible resort guest, she would have to look magnificent, which in her case wasn't easy. Unlike her ravishing sister, Emilie was moderately pretty, with narrow shoulders, a sharp chin, a sharper nose and a drab complexion courtesy of Chicago's chronic smog. She considered her butt too big and her bosom too small.

She felt absurd in her skimpy uniform: a floral-print bikini bra and a matching wraparound skirt that exposed a shameful quantity of pallid skin. Thank heavens she had a good mind and a pleasant personality—although she doubted they would be much use when it came to captivating the resort's rich bachelors. She couldn't even hope to captivate the bartender. He was evidently much too fascinated by the banana he was slicing into his blender to notice the new waitress gaping at him from just outside the cabana.

"He's something else, isn't he," Kim whispered in her ear. Kim was her neighbor in the employee residence on the far side of the resort. Like Emilie, she had journeyed south to work at the Golden Key for the glamour, the excitement, the chance to earn some money—or to marry it. Like Emilie, Kim was dressed in a bikini and wraparound skirt, but her body was the stuff of centerfolds, and the outfit made the most of it.

"Yes," Emilie murmured, continuing to stare as the bartender poured a generous splash of rum into the blender. "He's something else, all right."

"His name is Tyler Weston," Kim went on, digging her fingers into her lush hair and shoving it back with practiced nonchalance. "He's a major hunk."

"Oh, yes. Major," Emilie concurred.

"He's only been working at the poolside cabana a week. I heard he was tending bar in the Crystal Room, but then management transferred him out here. Lucky for us, I'd say."

Emilie nodded, watching as he emptied a scoop of ice cubes into the blender and turned it on. He poured the creamy concoction into a tall piece of stemware, balanced a notched strawberry on the rim and glanced up in search of a waitress. His eyes met Emilie's and his brow dipped in a frown. Then a slow smile curved his lips.

"That's my 'dack,'" Kim said, sauntering across the patio, her hips swaying sensuously in her tightly wrapped skirt. "Come on, I'll introduce you."

Emilie followed Kim out of the glaring sun and into the shade of the cabana. The closer she got to the bartender, the better he looked. Truly, the working class was fine with her. Absolutely peachy keen. As long as the working-class man in question had a build like the bartender's and killer eyes and big strong hands and a heart-stopping smile....

"Tyler Weston, this is Emilie Storrs," Kim announced briskly, lifting the tray on which the bartender had placed the banana daiquiri. "She's new, so be nice to her." With that, Kim pivoted on her sandaled heel and set out to deliver the drink to a man basking near the pool.

Left alone with Tyler, Emilie suddenly felt overwhelmed. Usually she was dauntless in the face of a challenge, whether that challenge entailed the tough young punks loitering at the projects or a television talk-show audience hooting and cheering when her name was announced as one of the three people chosen to put Torrey Benson's theories to the test. Yet Tyler wasn't like a boisterous audience or a street thug. He was merely a man with more in-your-face sex appeal than anyone she'd ever met.

And he was staring at her bikini bra.

"As I understand it," she said, deciding to ridicule her appearance before he did, "if you wear one of these silly outfits, you get bigger tips."

"Bigger *tips?*" he enunciated.

His voice was as smooth and cool as the drink

he'd just prepared, and it carried just as subversive a kick. Emilie felt her cheeks burn.

She opted to ignore his joke and behave like a professional. "I'm not sure what I'm supposed to do. The beach is practically empty. One waitress can handle the entire area."

"It'll start hopping soon," he assured her. "Most guests are having lunch right now. But on an afternoon like this—" he craned his neck to peer past the thatched overhang to the cloudless sky "—the place'll fill up. Enjoy the peace while you can." His gaze drifted back to her. "So, is this your first day?"

Her anxiety began to ebb. If punks couldn't intimidate her, this blue-eyed stud with his powerhouse smile couldn't. Why should she care about making a good impression on him, anyway? The only people she had to make a good impression on were rich bachelor guests. "I just arrived on the island the day before yesterday. And you heard Kim—you're supposed to be nice to me."

His grin widened. "I can be nice if I have to."

"You have to," she said, playing along. It was hard standing so close to him and not gawking. She considered taking a stroll and scoping the entire area served by the bar so she would be ready when the afternoon crowd—full of prospective husbands, she hoped—arrived. She ought to be focused on them, not on Tyler.

Before she could leave the cabana, he asked, "Where are you from?"

It was only small talk, but she appreciated his effort—and of course, if he was going to make the effort, she couldn't very well abandon him. "Chicago," she said.

"You've come a long way." Despite their size, his hands were agile. Even as he wiped down the bar with a damp cloth, he kept his gaze on Emilie. His eyes were more turquoise than blue, she realized. Gazing into them scrambled her memory of Corinne's claim that it was as easy to fall in love with a rich man as a poor one. As far as Emilie was concerned, it was as easy to fall in love with a poor one as a rich one.

Still, she had no intention of falling in love with a bartender, no matter what color his eyes were. She could fall in *lust* with him maybe, but not in love. For all she knew, he might be working at the Golden Key for the same reason she was: to find a rich sweetheart. He had a better chance of succeeding than she did, too. Emilie could imagine debutantes and dowagers lining up for the privilege of ogling him.

"Chicago," he repeated, tossing the cloth under the counter and grinning. "The Virgin Islands must be an adjustment."

"I'm not complaining." How could anyone

complain about being in the tropics after a life-time of sooty streets and blustery winds?

"So," he inquired, "what brings you to the Golden Key?"

He must be awfully bored to continue talking to her when he could be hunting for rich women—or voluptuous waitresses like Kim. "It's a job," Emilie said. "It sounded like fun."

"Were you waiting up in Chicago?"

"Waiting?" Sure, she'd been waiting. Waiting for the city to provide her agency with adequate funding. Waiting for her clients to straighten up and fly right. Waiting for the landlord to pay an exterminator to rid her kitchen of cockroaches. Waiting for her life to get a little less stressful.

After a moment she understood his question. "Waiting on tables, you mean? Actually...well, yes, I did some waitressing." She'd earned money during college as a waitress in an ice-cream parlor—which wasn't exactly the same thing as serving drinks at a Caribbean resort, but what the heck. She wasn't going to reveal her true reason for being here. If she did, Tyler would dismiss her as a gold digger.

He'd be correct, she admitted with a pang of distaste.

"So how'd you wind up here? No jobs in Chicago?"

She laughed. "If you've ever spent any length

of time in Chicago, you'd know why I'd rather work here. It's so beautiful! So warm! Actually I would have been happy to work at any of the Golden Keys.''

''Really?'' He leaned against the bar and studied her closely, as if what she said actually mattered to him.

If he was willing to listen, she would keep talking. ''The employment agency told me there were Golden Key Resorts in Vail, in the Adirondacks and outside Phoenix, and they were all hiring. This one was my first choice, though.'' She dragged her gaze from Tyler long enough to survey the sublime vista of beach and sea and sun-bright sky. Even if the millionaire-husband plan didn't work out, she could never regret having come here. ''What about you?'' she asked, figuring it was his turn to answer some questions. ''How did you wind up at the Golden Key?''

He gathered a knife and a bowl of oranges and busied himself slicing the fruit into circles for garnishes. ''I was doing the restaurant scene in New York,'' he said. ''I guess I was ready for a change of pace, too.''

''New York?'' she blurted. She would have guessed California. He had the coloring and the athletic physique of a surfer or maybe one of those beach-volleyball players. He had a volleyball player's hands, too, she thought, admiring the deft skill with which he wielded the knife.

"What's wrong with New York?" he asked.

"Nothing. You just..." She scrambled for a way to explain her surprise. "You don't talk like a New Yorker."

"Well, Emilie, you *tack* like someone from *Chi-caaa-go*."

She had relaxed enough to join in his laughter. "Give me a few weeks down here and I'll lose the accent, I promise. Is the weather always this perfect?"

"It rains sometimes. I haven't been here during the hurricane season, so I don't know how bad it can get. But this time of year, hurricanes aren't a problem. I don't think you'll have much to complain about climate-wise." He set aside the plate of sliced oranges and rinsed his knife in the sink behind the bar. "What are your hours?"

"Two to ten. I thought I should come out a few minutes early to get a feel for things." Once again she surveyed the area beyond the cabana. Kim was chatting with the man who'd ordered the banana daiquiri. He was paunchy and balding. Emilie wondered whether he was a millionaire in the market for a bride.

Looks weren't everything, of course. Bell-ringing gorgeousness had its place, but in the grand scheme of things it wasn't what defined a good husband. Far more essential were intelligence, compatibility, kindness, maturity...oh yes, and money, if Torrey Benson could be believed.

"Business really starts picking up at around two-thirty," Tyler told her. "The pace doesn't let up until around six or seven. In the evening you get the honeymooners, but it's not as hectic."

Honeymooners? Probably more of them than single men on the prowl, she acknowledged grimly. Probably the place was full of happily married folks, and she would never meet any bachelors.

But she might befriend someone who knew someone who knew someone. The importance of networking was explored in another chapter of Ms. Benson's book. Emilie might make a good impression on an older wealthy couple who had a son, and they would set her up with him, and—

Honestly! Thanks to Torrey Benson and her book, Emilie was going to turn from a professional do-gooder into a conniving vamp! But who could blame her, really? Corinne was right: she might as well try falling in love with a rich man.

"My shift starts at noon," Tyler said, breaking into her thoughts and reminding her that rich men weren't necessarily the only creatures worthy of her notice. "It's supposed to end around eight, but I usually stick around till ten to help out Bill, the evening bartender. At ten we shut down for the night. Then I can sneak some time on the tennis courts. Do you play?"

She laughed. "I try. But I stink at tennis. I have trouble finding anyone patient enough to play with me."

"I'm patient," he said bluntly.

Bemused, she shot him a quick glance. Was he actually implying he would be willing to play tennis with her, or was it just idle flirting, a way to occupy himself until someone better came along? "Doesn't the management mind employees using the courts?" she asked, refusing to entertain the possibility that Tyler could be coming on to her.

"Not if they're empty—and by the time we get off, the courts are almost always empty. I understand the previous owner of the resort wouldn't let the help anywhere near the courts. But the new management is a lot more flexible."

"That's nice." She tidied a stack of cocktail napkins emblazoned with the Golden Key logo—a gold skeleton key in the shape of the letters *G* and *K*. "The management doesn't mind if we cross paths with the guests? Outside work, I mean."

He eyed her quizzically. "Don't tell me you're hoping to hitch up with a guest?"

She nearly flinched at the accuracy of his

guess, but managed to return his grin without giving herself away. "Now why would I want to do that?"

"Beats me." He shrugged. "After all, the guests here are usually rich and ready to party."

"Rich and ready to party, huh?" she echoed. "That'd let me out. The last thing I'd ever want to do is have fun with rich people."

He chuckled. "It's none of my business. I suppose you can find staff fraternizing with guests at any resort—especially young pretty staff in sexy uniforms." He glanced down at her bikini bra again, and then at the below-the-navel waistline of her skirt and the above-the-knee hem. "I've heard rumors some of the waitresses get to know guests by working with Marty Boyce over at the fitness center. Have you met Marty?"

Emilie shook her head.

"He runs the gym. He's always looking for pretty waitresses to help him out during their off-hours."

Emilie laughed. "He wouldn't want me. I don't know the first thing about fitness training."

"I'm not sure he has them working as trainers. In fact, I don't know what's going on, except that the waitresses seem to get up-close-and-personal with the guests through Marty." Tyler scrutinized her intently. "So tell me, Emilie, what's your plan? You want to get up-close-and-personal with the guests?''

Mild disapproval shaded his mocking tone, and that disapproval magnified her own doubts about this whole marry-a-millionaire plan. Why had she let Corinne talk her into it?

But Tyler was awaiting a response. ''I came here to work,'' she said lightly. ''If I make some friends while I'm here, so much the better.''

A young couple strolled past the cabana. They were clad in beach attire, their eyes hidden behind dark glasses, and plush white resort towels hung around their necks. As they passed the cabana, the woman dug a bottle of sunscreen from her wicker tote.

Tyler flicked a gaze at them, then turned back to Emilie. ''I hope you've put sunscreen on. You haven't got a base tan.''

She opened her mouth and then closed it, disconcerted. Sunscreen seemed like a terribly intimate subject. It made her think of skin, and lotion, and rubbing.

She smiled uneasily. ''I have a bottle of sunscreen in my room. I didn't think I'd need it while I was working in the cabana.''

He shook his head. ''You're going to fry to a crisp. This sun is much stronger than what you're used to in *Chi-caaa-go.*'' He rummaged around on a shelf under the bar. Straightening, he produced a bottle of sunscreen and planted it on the bar in front of her like a chilled mug of beer. "Here, help yourself."

She hesitated. "Whose is this?"

"Mine."

If thinking about sunscreen was intimate, using Tyler's sunscreen was even more intimate. She'd only just met him. She didn't want to think about his sun-bronzed skin, all slick and shiny with lotion.

But he was right. If she didn't use the sunscreen, her skin would sizzle like bacon.

With a sigh and a nod of thanks, she took the bottle and opened it. Tyler discreetly turned from her to stack clean glasses on a shelf, offering her a modicum of privacy. Once she'd coated her face, arms, chest and legs, she tried to reach around to apply some lotion to her upper back.

"Come here," he said. His voice held a clear hint of authority, like someone used to giving orders and being obeyed.

If he had commanded her to take a tray loaded with drinks, she might have considered him bossy, but she wouldn't have balked. This was different, though. It was *personal*.

"You can't reach your back," he said. "I'll do it for you."

Do her back? Touch her with those big sturdy masculine hands?

Well, he was right: she couldn't reach her own

back. And she couldn't ask for help from Kim, who was still hobnobbing with the paunchy fellow by the pool.

There was no need to overreact, she reassured herself. Tyler was simply offering to help.

Mustering her courage, she marched behind the bar, passed him the bottle and spun around, presenting her back to him. After a long breathless second, she felt his fingers on her, strong and firm, massaging the fragrant lotion into her skin. His palms glided along her shoulders, across her back, down the ridge of her spine from the nape of her neck to the bikini bra strap, beneath it and farther down to her waist, then outward to her sides, tracing the edge of her skirt.

His touch felt good. Better than good. It felt unbearably erotic. His hands were as potent as his smile, his gaze, his husky voice when he'd said, ''Come here.''

His fingers veered forward, lightly skimming her belly, and then withdrew. After another moment's delay, he stepped back. Only then did she remember to breathe. The length of her spine tingled as if he'd branded it. She was afraid to turn around, afraid he would see in her eyes how powerfully he had affected her.

''There,'' he said quietly. ''Now you've got some protection.''

From the sun, perhaps. But when at last she

did turn to face him and saw the seductive glow in his eyes, she understood that the tropical sun wasn't the worst threat she faced.

If there was anything she needed true protection from, it was Tyler.

Chapter Two

THE LAST THING he wanted was to get involved with a waitress at the cabana bar.

Except...he wanted *her*.

All afternoon he watched her roam the far reaches of the pool and the beach, her pale slender body on display in her beachwear uniform. He recalled the way her skin had felt beneath his fingers, smooth and silky, as he'd rubbed sunscreen lotion on her shoulders and back. He admired her legs, her midriff, her tantalizing belly button exposed above the edge of her skirt. He noted the gentle sway of her hips, the arch of her throat, the defiant angle of her chin...and her eyes. Definitely her eyes. Dark and wide-set, they communicated an intriguing blend of intelligence and innocence.

Putting sunscreen on her had turned him on. It made him want to rub her entire body with some sweet gooey liquid—a banana daiquiri would do—and then lick it off one square inch at a time.

He wasn't sure why she appealed to him so much. She wasn't exactly a raving beauty, and she didn't seem to advertise her availability the way some of the other waitresses did. He watched her move around the patio and then meander across the beach, taking orders, smiling at the patrons, delivering wine coolers and margaritas and smiling some more. In spite of the sunscreen, her shoulders were turning pink.

He shouldn't be staring at her shoulders—or any other part of her anatomy. Yet he couldn't stop thinking about her. He couldn't stop wondering what had brought her all the way from Chicago to the Caribbean for a waitressing job. He couldn't stop remembering how she'd arched against his palms when he'd touched her, the way her narrow waist had fit his hands.

He would be at the resort only for another week or so. Then it was back to New York, and from there to the Golden Key in Phoenix. He had no time to get up-close-and-personal with anyone here. Besides, Emilie was probably just like all the other pretty young waitresses at the resort: on the prowl, hoping to hook herself a sugar daddy. That was reason enough to keep his distance from her. He couldn't afford to let the staff learn the truth about him, not if this stint in the cabana was going to be useful.

Bill joined Tyler behind the bar at four o'clock. They worked well together, mixing drinks and sharing the cramped space in a smooth choreography. At five Marty Boyce from the fitness club came out to the cabana for a light supper. The fitness club was closed from five to seven, and Marty usually spent his break at the beach bar, shooting the breeze with Tyler and Bill while he ate.

Actually Tyler suspected that what brought Marty out to the Cabana Club was not the scintillating company of the bartenders but the scenery. Specifically, the waitress scenery. He ogled them with an openness Tyler found almost repulsive. But he suspected there was more than boyish lust in Marty's inspection of the women. Trying to get a bead on Marty helped to distract him from his thoughts of Emilie for a few minutes.

"I brought you guys some sandwiches," Marty said as he pulled up a stool and settled at the bar. Dressed in a pair of white drawstring shorts and a white polo shirt like Tyler's and Bill's, Marty had a physique that proclaimed his devotion to weight training. His neck was thick, his biceps bulging, his chest a tapering sculpture of muscle and his calves alarmingly well-defined. Tyler had always prided himself on being in shape—but the shape he was in was a hell of a lot less brawny than Marty's. Tyler looked like what he was: a tall lanky guy who enjoyed recreational sports but didn't make an obsession of his body.

Of course it was Marty's profession to be obsessed with bodies—not just the waitresses', but his clients' and his own. His job entailed knowing the equipment in his gym and the needs of the hotel guests who made use of it. He liked to say his primary goal was to make sure the Golden Key guests didn't leave the resort looking like blimps, even though the chefs in the resort's restaurants and cafés were hell-bent on undermining that goal with every meal they served. In fact, he liked to say it often enough to make Tyler wonder what he was trying to prove.

"Thanks for the sandwich," Tyler said, passing Marty his usual—a bottle of nonalcoholic beer—and entering the drink onto Marty's account in the computer. "How's life in Sweat City?"

"Sweaty." Marty unwrapped his own sandwich. "I've been working with this lady who thinks she's going to leave here on Saturday looking like Cher," Marty went on. "I told her it took an army of plastic surgeons to create Cher's physique, but she doesn't want to hear it. Sheesh. The men are much easier." He bit into his sandwich and washed down the food with a slug of fake beer. "They don't work out in the gym to look better. They do it because they want to feel good."

"That proves they're smarter than women," Bill piped up from the far end of the bar. The waitress whose tray he was loading with margaritas gave a snort.

"The men who come to the gym want rubdowns. That's the main request," Marty reported.

"I don't blame them," Tyler said. "I wouldn't mind a rubdown at the end of the day."

"I'd prefer a rub-up," Billy joked, grinning lecherously.

Tyler rolled his eyes and turned back to Marty, who was surveying the activity beyond the cabana's circle of shade. "New waitress?" he asked, pointing his sandwich at Emilie.

Tyler gazed into the mauve evening light. Emilie was collecting empty glasses and beer bottles from an abandoned table. Her back to the cabana, she leaned over to reach across the table. The men at the bar enjoyed a tempting view of her rear end.

Cringing at his reflexively male response to the sight, Tyler directed his attention back to Marty and nodded. "Her name is Emilie. Today's her first day on the job."

Marty appraised her thoughtfully. "Nice buns."

Tyler suppressed the urge to punch him. After all, Marty had only put into words what he himself had been thinking. For some reason, though, he didn't want any other men noticing her bottom.

"I wonder if she'd like to come work for me

during her off-hours," Marty pondered aloud. "She could earn herself a little spare change."

Tyler shoved aside his irrational possessiveness about Emilie and leaned forward. He'd been struggling to figure out Marty's game ever since he'd arrived at the resort. The whiff of rumors about Marty had been enough to compel Tyler to change assignments, from tending bar in the Crystal Room to working the cabana bar where Marty tended to hang out. Marty Boyce and his arrangements with the waitresses troubled Tyler, but he hadn't yet discovered exactly what those arrangements were all about.

"How would Emilie earn spare change with you?" he asked carefully.

"I just told you—the men want back rubs. We've got one licensed masseuse on staff—excuse me, massage therapist. That's what she likes to be called." He pulled a face. "Thing is, she can't handle everyone. She can only do so many clients a day. So, I have waitresses fill out the staff. It's not like you need an advanced degree to give a back rub."

"What do you need?" Tyler asked.

"A pretty face and good hands."

If those were the only requirements, Emilie was more than qualified. "How do you pay the waitresses? Do you have room in your budget for that?"

Marty laughed. "They get paid. The money's there."

Tyler peered into Marty's opaque eyes and saw nothing, no emotion, no reflection, just a flat hard gray that reminded him of concrete. He made a mental note to find out whether fitness-club massage therapists were supposed to be licensed. He made another mental note to keep even closer tabs on Marty.

Emilie sauntered into the cabana, and her mere presence tossed all his mental notes into a musty corner of his brain. The tip of her nose was pink, a rosy shade that made him think of winter's bite. She smelled of sun lotion—*his* sun lotion, which reminded him of the unexpectedly erotic pleasure of putting the lotion on her. Talk about back rubs—he'd had quite a fine time giving her one. He wouldn't mind having her return the favor.

She set her cluttered tray on the bar, and the empty glasses clinked and rattled like chimes. Relieved of the burden, she let out a weary sigh.

"Tired?" Tyler asked with a smile.

She sighed again and rolled her shoulders to loosen them. Once more he found himself remembering the curve of those shoulders against his hands, the delicate bones of her neck and back. "I'm absolutely exhausted," she announced, actually sounding full of energy.

Marty started humming Roy Orbison's

"Pretty Woman." When Tyler missed his cue, Marty stopped and said, "So, what does it take to get an introduction to this beautiful lady?"

Emilie's smile lost some wattage as she turned to Marty. She obviously didn't trust his palaver—another sign of her intelligence, as far as Tyler was concerned. "This is Marty Boyce," he said. "He runs the fitness club. Marty, Emilie Storrs."

Emilie gave Marty a brisk handshake, sliding her hand from his as quickly as she could. "I need a piña colada, a screaming monkey and a Perrier with lime," she said, glancing at Bill.

"I got the Perrier," he shouted from his end of the bar.

Tyler grinned. Ordinarily he would have sniped at Bill for taking the easy drink and leaving him with the elaborate ones to fix. But the longer he took preparing Emilie's order, the longer she would loiter near the bar, near him.

"So, sweetheart," Marty said, obviously not discouraged by her reticence. "You interested in making a little extra income on the side?"

She sent him a quizzical glance. "Doing what?"

"Come see me after your shift."

"I can't," she told him. "I've got a tennis date." Her gaze held a plea as it intersected with Tyler's.

This cue Tyler didn't miss. "That's right," he

told Marty. "Emilie and I are going to whack some balls around." Her eyes flashed at his choice of words, and he grinned.

"Come see me tomorrow, then," Marty suggested. He popped the last of his sandwich into his mouth, swallowed and wiped his hands on a cocktail napkin. "I hear we're going to be hosting a convention. Some investment company is sending all its top-level executives down here on a retreat."

"Investment bankers?" Emilie's brows twitched up. "How lovely that they'd have a retreat here."

Marty guffawed. "Retreat, my arse. It's a boondoggle, but who cares? The place is going to fill up with lots of men with time to waste and money to burn." He shoved away from the bar. "We're all going to line our pockets on these guys. They'll tip like there's no tomorrow. And they love massages." Sending Emilie a knowing smile, he waved and strode out of the cabana.

Tyler dumped a scoop of ice cubes into the blender, gathered a pitcher of pineapple juice and a bottle of coconut cream, and then glanced at Emilie. She'd been staring after Marty, but she turned and met Tyler's gaze as if she'd sensed his eyes on her. "What did he mean about massages?"

"He hires waitresses during their off-hours to

give massages to the fitness-club clients,'' Tyler said, then shrugged. ''That's what he says, anyway.''

''What do you mean, that's what he says? Do you think something else is going on?''

''I have no idea.''

She considered Tyler's statement. ''People pay a fortune to come here. They come to be pampered. Why wouldn't they want massages? If I was a guest here, I'd want a massage.''

Tyler didn't want to verbalize his suspicions—he wasn't even certain what his suspicions were. ''I don't know. It's just the idea of waitresses giving back rubs. You'd think they would earn enough serving drinks without trying to pick up some spare change after hours.''

She shook her head. ''Waitresses never earn enough. Even with tips. Even in these silly outfits.''

He almost argued that the outfits weren't silly. But then, until he'd met Emilie, he hadn't paid much attention to the outfits, although he'd heard the waitresses liked them. They covered everything they had to, they were tropical enough to fit in with the island ambiance and, as Emilie damned well knew, they led to big tips.

''I hope you don't mind that I put Marty off by pretending we have a tennis date tonight,'' she said.

"Were you pretending?" He poured the piña colada into a frosted glass and skewered a wedge of pineapple on a toothpick. "I thought we did have a tennis date."

"It was nothing definite, Tyler. We only just—"

"Ten-thirty. I'll meet you at the courts," he said. "It's definite."

"But...I really do play terribly."

He pulled a clean blender toward him to prepare the screaming monkey. "Great. I'll win," he said.

"Are you sure you don't mind?"

"Don't mind?" He threw back his head and laughed. There was something indescribably appealing about the way she could turn in an instant from self-righteous—complaining about the pay and the uniforms—to insecure. More than appealing, it was exciting. At least as exciting as rubbing her skin with sunscreen. "Never in my life have I minded winning, Emilie. And I sure won't mind tonight." He held her gaze just long enough for her to understand that he wasn't only talking about tennis. Then, before she could back out of the date, he got busy with the screaming monkey.

THEY PLAYED two sets. Tyler won both—no surprise there. To equalize the game, he'd suggested that she play within the singles lines while he used the doubles lines, but the handicapping didn't help much. After her long shift at the cabana, Emilie was too tired to charge the net.

Too tired, and too distracted by his broad shoulders, his sinewy arms, the glint of perspiration on his upper lip, the competitive fire blazing in his eyes. Too dazzled by the sight of him loping gracefully around the clay court, his hair flopping onto his forehead and his long legs carrying him from one sideline to the other.

"I don't know about you, but I'm wiped out," he announced after acing his final serve. He tucked his racket under his arm and pulled off his wristbands. He looked far less wiped out than Emilie felt, but she appreciated his tact.

"Do you play every night?" she asked, scooping up the stray tennis balls and approaching the net.

"Only when I find someone I want to play with." He held out an empty can and she dropped the balls in. "How about a cold drink?"

She would love one. She knew the waitresses weren't supposed to visit the various cocktail lounges and pubs around the resort, but there were vending machines in every building where they could buy chilled cans of soda.

To her surprise, Tyler didn't lead her to the nearest vending machine. Instead, once they'd zippered their rackets into their cases, he escorted her back to the cabana. Closed for the night, the bar stood in the deep shadows cast by the moon above the water. Although the cabana itself was just a large thatched roof supported by wooden poles, the bar was shuttered and locked.

Tyler marched over to the bar as if he owned it and pulled a key from the pocket of his jeans. "Um…is this allowed?" Emilie asked nervously.

"Don't worry about it." He slid up one louvered shutter, reached around the bar and unlocked the door cut into the teak. "I'm not raiding the liquor supply. You want a cola or a ginger ale?"

"Ginger ale," she said, feeling a bit wicked. "Are you sure we won't get in trouble with the bosses? First we played tennis on the guests' courts and now—"

"Don't go blabbing that we were here. What the bosses don't know won't hurt them." He pulled two icy bottles of ginger ale from a small refrigerator, stepped in front of the bar and locked the shutters once more. After twisting the caps off the bottles, he handed one to her, then ushered her out of the cabana and onto the beach.

The beach chairs were all vacant. At midnight, apparently, anyone who wasn't already in bed was at one of the resort's nightspots, dancing or romancing or listening to the torch singer headlining in the cabaret that week. Tyler and Emilie had the beach to themselves.

He stacked their tennis gear in a neat pile, then dragged one chair over to another so they could sit side by side. Emilie dropped onto one of them, yanked off her sneakers and socks and dug her toes into the warm sand. Tyler took the other chair, touched his bottle to hers in a toast and drank.

Even drinking from a bottle, he looked remarkably sexy. She watched the way he pursed his lips around the bottle opening, the way his throat moved with each swallow, the way his long fingers wrapped around the glass.

The heat that infused her wasn't from the exertion of their game or the balmy night. She touched the cool surface of her bottle against her forehead and cheeks before sipping.

For a moment the only sound was the whoosh of the waves lapping at the shore, the papery whisper of the wind in the palms that lined the walkway—and the sound of her heart thumping at the thought that she was alone on a beach at night with the kind of guy that beauty queens, cheerleaders and girls like her sister, Corinne, usually wound up with. And he was acting as if he liked her. Chicago's Department of Social Services seemed in another galaxy, another lifetime. She closed her eyes and felt the moon rain its silver light onto her face.

"So," Tyler said, his voice a husky murmur in the peaceful night, "how do you think your first day went?"

"The best part was playing tennis—" She bit her lip before she could complete the sentence: *with you.* She didn't want him to think she was smitten with him, even though she was. "The work's okay. It wasn't really as busy as I thought it would be."

"It's going to get a lot busier when the investment bankers arrive. I bet they're planning to party hearty."

"I can handle them." More than handle them—maybe she could beguile one into marrying her. Investment bankers successful enough to be chosen for a company junket to the Golden Key had to be rich. This might be her best chance to meet a millionaire.

If only she wasn't so stuck on Tyler.

"I bet they'll be wanting massages," he said.

Emilie groaned. They probably *would* want massages. Signing on for massage duty with Marty Boyce could be a fine way to ingratiate herself with an eligible bachelor. But massages were so...*personal*. Like the way Tyler had massaged her when he'd put the sunscreen on her shoulders. And the small of her back. And the nape of her neck.

A tiny sigh escaped her. She turned to stare at the rolling waves, hoping their rushing rhythm would clear her mind. "Is Marty Boyce a friend of yours?" she asked, not wishing to insult Tyler by insulting his pal.

"I think he thinks he is."

She laughed. "I don't know if I'll work for him. I guess I'll see how busy things get at the bar before I offer my services at the fitness club."

"He's got other waitresses working for him. I gather Kim's one. You could ask her what it's like."

"Maybe I will." Emilie sighed again, this time not with lust but with indecision. "It's not like I want to…well, get that close to the resort guests. But the money would come in handy. The pay here isn't exactly exorbitant."

"You don't think so?"

She peered at him, surprised by his bemused tone. "I guess the bartenders get paid a lot more than the waitresses."

"We may get a higher base pay, but we don't get much in the way of tips."

"This is what drives me crazy," she said, happy to abandon the unpalatable idea of working for Marty and, instead, pursue a subject that interested her. "The waitresses are nearly all women, so they get paid a minuscule salary, and they're expected to make up the difference with tips. That means, of course, that they're getting paid to be sweet and cute and subservient, instead of just to serve drinks. Bartenders don't have to be nice to get sufficient wages. All they have to do is mix the drinks properly.''

"But I *am* nice," he insisted, smiling roguishly.

"You don't have to be. You're a man. Women always get the raw end of the deal. They get paid for their personalities and their looks, not their labor. I remember the waitresses I knew back in Chicago—" she was really gearing up now "—who struggled at below minimum wage and then were forced to pool their tips, so if some other waitress on their shift was in a bad mood that day, everyone suffered. Plus, the short-order chefs took a cut of the tips. The waitresses would work odd hours, trying to fit their jobs in around child-care needs and maybe some high-school equivalency classes. They worked until they were ready to drop, and even then they could barely make ends meet.''

She paused to catch her breath and realized Tyler was staring at her, frowning. "What kind of waitresses were these? Where were you working?''

"Well, I..." She saw no need to hide the truth from him. "I was a social worker back in Chicago. Those women were my cases. Many of them were on public assistance. All of them were desperate to support their families.''

"You were a social worker?''

Why did he seem so astonished? "Yes, I was a social worker."

"Then what are you doing here? Why are you serving drinks?"

"I got downsized out of my job. And I was ready for a change." And she'd appeared on a television talk show promising to give Torrey Benson's ploys a whirl to see if they worked. But none of that meant she had to forget where she'd come from. "I know the Golden Key hired me to be just a waitress and not a social worker, but I can't help getting angry about injustice. Some of the women working here are getting the shaft, just like my clients up in Chicago."

"They are?"

"Yes. Take the chambermaids, for instance."

"They get a good salary," he asserted almost defensively.

"They get a barely adequate salary. And unlike the bellhops, they *don't* always get tips. They're anonymous. They slip into the guest rooms and suites, clean up other people's messes, vanish as soon as they're done and hope someone will be kind enough to leave some money on the night table for them—as if they were hookers or something. They shouldn't have to rely on tips. They should make what the janitors make, at the very least."

"Emilie—"

"I moved into the employee residence two

days ago. I spent most of yesterday filling out employment papers, getting my uniform and all that, but I talked to some of the other women living there. It's nearly all women. The men live outside the resort.''

"There are some cottages off the grounds, yes.''

"It's like the army. The women live in barracks, and the men in officers' quarters.''

"Hey, some of the off-grounds cottages have three or four guys in them splitting the rent.''

"At least they're living like adults, instead of college students.''

"A lot of the girls working here *are* college students, or just out of school. This is their first job. They aren't planning to make a lifelong commitment to the Golden Key. They're just here to have some fun and enjoy the scenery. The residences work perfectly for them.''

"Sure. Like you said, they're kids, barely out of their teens. Maybe if this place hired more mature waitresses, they wouldn't be spending their free hours working for a sleaze like Marty.''

Tyler didn't speak for a minute. He sipped his soda thoughtfully, digesting Emilie's tirade. Finally he said, "You think Marty is a sleaze?''

Chastened, she lowered her voice. "I shouldn't judge him by first impressions. I'm sure he's very nice.''

Tyler chuckled and shook his head in disbelief. "Oh, sure, he's nice. Does that mean you're going to work for him?"

"I haven't decided yet." That was true. She didn't know whether Marty could help her to connect with a millionaire. And no matter how much she'd rather spend time with Tyler, she'd be a fool to waste the opportunity working at the Golden Key provided. When would she ever again find herself smack-dab in the middle of an upper-class playground? When would she have this chance to rub elbows with the rich?

Tyler reflected for a minute. "You've got some interesting theories, Emilie."

"I'm a firebrand with a big mouth. That's what my sister says." She shrugged and drank some soda. "Actually I'm usually a little more diplomatic."

"But...?"

"You're so easy to talk to." That she could admit it proved how comfortable she felt with him. But their instant rapport puzzled her. She wasn't used to passing an evening with a stunningly handsome man. This was not a normal situation. She ought to have been bashful or awkward.

Yet she wasn't. Something about Tyler opened her up, made her feel she could say anything, and he wouldn't hate her for it. Something about him made her not mind losing two straight sets of tennis to him. Something about him made her want to stay up all night talking to him.

She gazed at him across the narrow space separating their chairs. He was smiling, his feet planted firmly in the sand just inches from hers. And she knew, very suddenly but with a certainty that shook her from her scalp to her toes, that while he might want to stay up all night with her, talking wasn't all he wanted to do.

Chapter Three

"NO," SHE SAID, sounding flustered and frantic and wistful all at once. "No, Tyler—I can't do this."

Do what? he wanted to protest—but he knew damned well what. Maybe he hadn't consciously decided he was going to kiss her. But he'd been leaning closer and closer to her the entire time she'd been speaking, until he was so close her lips were within reach. And once he'd gotten that close, the idea of kissing her seemed almost inevitable.

Strangely enough, she looked sexier to him now, dressed in a pair of white shorts and a pale green T-shirt, than she had in her beach-bunny getup. He liked her hair loose, brushing past her shoulders and catching the sea breezes. He liked the way her eyes gleamed when she started speechifying. He'd heard what she said—he'd had to listen, because what she was saying was important to him. But while his brain had absorbed her words, his body had responded to other things. Like the flare of color in her cheeks, and the perfect shape of her mouth, and her intense dark eyes.

"You can't do this," he echoed, inching back.

"I hardly know you." Her fingers fluttered nervously in her lap, and he gathered her hands in his just to keep them still. She took a deep breath and let it out slowly. Gradually she relaxed, her fingers curving through his. Lowering her gaze sheepishly, she said, "Maybe I'm presuming too much—though you've probably already figured out that I'm presumptuous. For all I know, nothing was going to happen here. You probably consider me just a fellow employee, someone to play tennis with. I don't know why I would think you could take a special interest in me. There are prettier waitresses here, and I'm sure some of them play tennis, too, so maybe—"

"Did anyone ever tell you you talk too much?" he broke in.

Her eyes rose to meet his. "I'm sorry. I only talk a lot when it's something I really care about."

"In other words...you really care about me?"

She took a deep breath, let it out and groaned. "I am such a doofus. I don't know, my sister seems to have inherited all the charm genes in the family. She knows how to act in these situations. Assuming we've got a situation here. Which we probably don't."

He wanted to laugh, but that might hurt her feelings. "We do have a situation, Emilie."

"What's the situation?"

He closed his hands more snugly around hers. "You weren't being presumptuous. I'm attracted to you."

She swallowed, but didn't break away from him. "There are more attractive women working here."

"I haven't noticed any."

"Then you haven't been looking."

"You're right. I haven't." He stroked her hands with his thumbs. She had soft small hands. That she could lug heavy trays around the beach—or swing a tennis racket well enough to return half his shots—seemed miraculous. He imagined that the sensation of her hands gliding across his skin would be even more miraculous.

Maybe she was right; maybe other waitresses were conventionally prettier. Someone like Kim, with her startlingly blond hair and her abundant bosom, would probably appeal to most men. But Tyler wasn't most men. His tastes ran to smart, sharp women who spouted off at the mouth when they were excited and who played their hardest at tennis even though they didn't have a prayer of winning.

"Maybe I'm rushing you," he conceded, unable to stop caressing her hands. "But..." But he didn't have much time. He was supposed to be leaving here in a week, and if he explained that to her, he would blow his cover. Then she'd know he wasn't just a bartender and she'd hate him for his deception—to say nothing of what he paid the chambermaids.

"You *are* rushing me," she confirmed, sliding her hands from his and sighing. "Whatever I came here for, it wasn't romance." With a rueful smile she lifted her soda bottle from the sand and stood. "I'm sorry, Tyler. I just... This just wouldn't be right."

"I understand," he said. Sure, he understood—but he wasn't pleased. "I'll walk you back to your room," he offered, rising to his feet.

"No, that's okay." She seemed awfully eager to get away from him.

He used to think he had a smooth way with women. At least, he didn't usually get shot down with such speed. But Emilie Storrs—the Chicago social worker who could get more impassioned about underpaid hotel employees than about a man who might just go berserk if he didn't at least kiss her once before he left the resort—wanted to get away from him as quickly as possible.

Watching her dart across the sand and past the shadowy hulk of the cabana, he couldn't really say he blamed her.

THE INVESTMENT BANKERS started streaming into the resort the following day. They were easy to recognize: well-groomed men—nearly all of them were men—in pastel polo shirts and crisp khaki trousers, their faces as pale as Emilie's had been when she'd arrived on the island, and their hair meticulously coiffed.

Each time she spotted one, she thought of Tyler's unkempt untrimmed mop of hair and sighed.

Still, the bankers were her ticket to the life of ease. She checked each one out, trying to guess his age, his marital status, whether the abundance of monogrammed leather golf bags meant that whoever married him would wind up a golf widow, and whether being a golf widow was a good or a bad thing when one married not for love but for money.

By midafternoon, most of the new arrivals had found their way to the pool or the beach, where they kept Emilie and her sister waitresses on the go. She circled the patio, taking orders, smiling politely and surveying the selection of potential husbands. That the fellows by the pool had donned swim trunks gave her the chance to evaluate their physical assets, she reminded herself that she was supposed to care more about their liquid assets. Still, she made note of the younger ones, the better-looking ones...the ones wearing wedding bands, the ones not wearing them. She also made note of which ones tipped well—a sign of a generous nature, she reasoned—

and which ones smiled, which ones socialized with their colleagues and which buried their noses in books. She automatically disqualified anyone reading a book about finance or the economy. A man who didn't know how to unwind at a Caribbean resort would never be the husband of *her* dreams.

Then again, her dream husband would have longer hair than any of these financiers. He would have broad shoulders and eyes the color of the sea, and... No. She was not going to fantasize about Tyler. Nor was she going to waste any time or energy yearning for a dream husband. She was going to be pragmatic and organized, listening to her head instead of her unruly heart. If Torrey Benson's book was worth its cover price, Emilie would snare a financier, have herself a grand glorious wedding and settle down to a life of luxury and good works. No bartender could get her where she intended to go.

But it would be nice to say the hell with her sister and that stupid book, and go where Tyler Weston could take her.

Him, she thought, her gaze zeroing in on a prospect. *Forget about Tyler and concentrate on him.* The gentleman in her sights lounged in a chair near the pool. His body extended nearly the length of the cushions, so he was probably taller than average, and his physique, while not in Tyler's class, was passable. He had short dark hair with a few threads of silver highlighting his temples, and he was holding a John Grisham thriller open across his chest; Emilie couldn't tell if he was actually reading it, because he had on expensive-looking steel-rimmed sunglasses with extremely dark lenses. His legs weren't too hairy, and his feet...well, forget his feet. Men's feet were universally ugly. She wasn't going to disqualify the man just because he had knobby toes.

She approached him, tray in hand and smile in place. When she halted beside his chair he peered up and smiled.

"Can I get you something to drink?" she asked in her most winsome voice. She saw twin reflections of herself in his lenses and wished she looked as winsome as she sounded. The gardenia in her hair had wilted from the heat, and her modest bosom scarcely filled the B-cups of her bikini.

"Actually another waitress just asked me that very question," he said.

Oh, well. Someone had beaten Emilie to the punch. Someone who looked better in his lenses, no doubt.

"Funny thing—I wasn't thirsty when *she* asked me," he told her, still smiling; "but I'm thirsty now. What imported beers do you have?"

Of course he wouldn't want a domestic beer.

He was too classy for that. She listed the selection and he requested a Beck's dark ale. With what she hoped was a saucy grin, she turned and headed toward the cabana, twitching her hips as much as she dared.

Stepping into the cabana, she swallowed a groan. She wasn't cut out for flirting. Trying to tweak the man's interest was a real strain.

Yet he did have potential. He'd denied another waitress the opportunity to serve him, and he'd made sure Emilie knew that. Maybe she *had* whetted his thirst—for beer if nothing else.

Even so, one glance at Tyler Weston, reigning over the bar, reminded her of every reason she should abandon her silly marry-a-millionaire plan and listen to her heart. So what if Tyler was a working-class drudge? So what if he'd indicated no feeling for her more complicated than lust? So what if he was handsome enough to storm through the entire female staff of the resort like Sherman through Georgia, conquering and pillaging and then moving on without a backward glance? So what if he could offer her nothing she needed other than an imported beer for a rich guy with a ringless left hand?

She thought about asking Bill to get her the beer, but he was busy mixing a tequila sunrise for Kim. Reluctantly Emilie crossed to Tyler's end of the bar. "One Beck's dark," she said.

His eyes were too beautiful. Why couldn't *she*

have eyes that lovely? she thought petulantly. Why couldn't she have thick lashes like his, and dimples?

"Tennis tonight?" he asked as he lifted an icy brown bottle from one of the refrigerators below the counter.

"Me?" she blurted. "You want to play tennis with me?"

He laughed. "Is there anyone else here?"

"Bill and Kim."

He gazed over at them as if seriously considering inviting them to play tennis. Then he laughed again and turned back to Emilie. "I want to play tennis with you," he said.

"Nothing's going to come of it," she warned.

He stopped laughing, but his smile remained in all its seductive glory. "I'm glad that's cleared up. So, same time as last night?"

"Tyler. Are you listening to me?"

"Loud and clear. All I'm asking for is some tennis. If you don't want to play, say no."

She didn't want to play. She shouldn't want to. She couldn't want to.

"Yes," she said, annoyed with herself for giving in, not just to him but to her own treacherous longing. More than annoyed, however, she was thrilled. "Same time as last night. I'll be there."

IT TOOK TYLER a half hour to win two straight sets, but tonight Emilie knew better than to have a postgame drink with him. She knew what would happen if she did. She would become even more infatuated than she already was.

She must be some kind of idiot, passing more time with Tyler than she absolutely had to. Every minute spent in his company was a minute during which she grew more attached to him and more removed from her goal of finding a rich husband.

"No, thank you," she said when he asked her to join him for a soda. "This was great, but I've really got to get some rest. It's late and I—"

"I'm tired, too," he assured her, so pleasantly she couldn't find it in herself to tell him not to walk her back to the staff residence. Side by side, they ambled along the winding paths, past the main pool, the kiddie pool and the diving pool, past velvet-smooth lawns, past private bungalows and the sailboat marina, past a torch-lit nightclub and the central kitchens, past the maintenance barns and vehicle garages to the most remote part of the resort, where several nondescript two-story buildings huddled among the palm trees.

Neither she nor Tyler said a word during their moonlit stroll. Carrying her racket and a towel, she had an excuse not to hold his hand.

Not holding his hand or talking to him wasn't enough to immunize herself against him, though.

When the lamps illuminating the walkway spilled amber light across his face, she felt a shiver of desire in the pit of her stomach. When a breeze wafted across the lawn, she smelled not fresh-cut grass, flowers or ocean, but Tyler, his scent of soap and clean sweat and virility. His presence burned away her memories of the financier to whom she'd delivered a Beck's dark just hours ago. What was his name again? He'd told her…Stewart. Stewart Culpepper. He'd also told her he was from New York and specialized in mergers and acquisitions…and…

Tyler.

Tyler didn't specialize in mergers and acquisitions. At least not the investment-banker kind. Right now she was feeling so galvanized just being close to him she could easily imagine performing a merger with him. Mutual acquisitions seemed very much in the realm of possibility.

The light above the doorway to her building beckoned. Just ten more yards and she could break free of his spell, ten more yards and she could barricade herself inside and think about why she was at the Golden Key, what she was supposed to be after, what mattered in the long run. Not passion. Not this swirling, swooning, dazzling crush she'd developed on Tyler.

Just ten more yards—but before she could escape, he had her in his arms. She wasn't sure how he'd managed it, but suddenly she had dropped the towel and the racket and looped her arms around him. When he lowered his mouth to hers, it seemed as inevitable as losing to him in tennis, as natural as returning his smile. As simple as a man and a woman could make it.

KISSING EMILIE STORRS was so perfect, so honest, so *right*. Thank God she realized it, too, instead of fighting the obvious. Emilie and he were made for kissing each other. They were destined for this. There was no denying it.

Her mouth tasted sweet and salty. Her lips were soft and moist and welcoming. Her body nestled against his as if it had been designed just for him—and his own body grew hot and hard as if it had been designed just for her.

Asked to explain why he responded this way to Emilie, he would have drawn a blank. Yes, she was intelligent and cute, but why her and not anyone else? He didn't know, and it really didn't matter.

His entire life had been a journey of serendipity—a mediocre school career that concluded with his dropping out of college because money ran out and he wasn't scholarship material. Stints as a waiter and then a bartender at grungy clubs in SoHo, at ritzy cafés on the Upper East Side, until he knew the business well enough to set out on his own. He hadn't planned his career, hadn't expected to succeed, hadn't dreamed of coming as far as he had. Call it fate, call it luck, or call it the karma of a man with enough good sense to learn what he needed to know and enough ambition to make the most of that knowledge.

He hadn't planned on Emilie, either. He hadn't expected to find a funny, feisty woman at this elegant island retreat, and he hadn't dreamed of enjoying a kiss so much. But it had happened. It was happening right now.

He plowed his fingers into her hair and angled her head so he could deepen the kiss. He wanted to drink her in, absorb her. He wanted to make love to her, fast and hard. And then a second time, slow and gentle. He wanted to sleep with her in his arms all night long and then wake up with the sun and make love to her again. He wanted to take her back to his room and lock them both inside and never open the door again—because he knew that the instant his door opened and he and Emilie emerged back into real life, he would be leaving her. And he didn't want that. He didn't even want to think about it.

She moaned, a tremulous whisper of sound in the tropical night. Slowly she eased her mouth from his. She rested her head against his shoulder, hiding her face from him. He closed his arms tightly around her, pressing her close, feeling her breasts crushed against his chest, her nipples taut with arousal. He slid his hands down to her bottom and pulled her even closer. When she moaned again, he moaned, too, aching with desire.

He wanted her desperately, insanely—but a shred of decency reared up in his soul, silencing him before he could invite her into his bed. He couldn't spend the next few days making love with her and then kiss her cheek and say goodbye. No matter what might happen between Emilie and him in those few days, it would have to end with a goodbye. He couldn't stay here.

"I'd better go," she murmured.

Reluctantly he loosened his hold on her.

She took a step away. She was flushed and flustered, her eyes luminous and her lips still damp from his kiss. "I'm sorry, Tyler. I..." She sighed and lowered her eyes. "I'd just better go."

He watched her turn from him and take a step toward the door. Another step. Then another quicker one, until she was running. "Good night," he called after her, but he doubted she even heard him.

Chapter Four

"'IF YOU'RE SERIOUS about marrying a million-aire,'" she read, "'you must remain single-minded in your pursuit of your goal. Don't let a pretty face distract you. Listen to your brain, not your hormones.'"

Emilie took a long sip of diet cola straight from the can, reread the passage in the book and swore under her breath. She couldn't seem to listen to her brain, not when her heart and her hormones were clamoring to be heard.

What her heart was saying with every beat, every pulse, was that Tyler Weston was the man for her. What her hormones were saying was that no man had ever made her feel what Tyler could make her feel with one kiss, one admiring gaze, one touch. No man had ever turned her on so much. No man had ever made her yearn for him in a way that shortcircuited her brain completely. No man had ever made her want to forget everything that mattered in life because all that mattered at that one moment was the man himself.

This was not a good frame of mind to be in, especially when she was supposed to be following Torrey Benson's recipe for millionaire-marrying.

She gazed around her small room. It was probably about one-fourth the size of the least-expensive guest accommodations on the island, a twelve-by-fourteen-foot room with a single window, a compact refrigerator, a double bed and thin beige carpeting. The first floor of the residence contained a lounge and a small kitchenette. It really was like a college dorm, even to the female chatter and laughter that echoed down the corridor linking the rooms.

She heard footsteps in the hall approaching her room, then saw the shadow of two feet in the narrow space between the bottom of the door and the floor. A gentle knock was followed by Kim's voice: "Hey, Emilie, are you still awake?"

Emilie hastily stuffed her book into the drawer of her night table. "Come on in."

Kim pushed open the door and entered. Dressed in a meshy black lace outfit with what was either a bikini or black underwear beneath it, she looked almost chic, almost tacky. Her silver blond hair tumbled wantonly around her face, and she was grinning. "Hi," she said, flopping into the easy chair and slinging one leg over the upholstered armrest.

"Do you want a soda?" Emilie asked, gesturing toward the small refrigerator.

"No, thanks. Did you hear the good news?"

Emilie sat up straighter. She would love to hear some good news. Frankly she'd love to hear anything that would get her to stop thinking about Tyler for a minute. "What good news?" she asked.

"The chambermaids just got a raise. Dorena told me they all got hiked fifty cents an hour. That adds up to a thousand bucks a year."

"Wow! That's great!"

"It *is* great. If they get a raise, maybe there'll be a raise for us, too."

"Even if there isn't, the maids deserve it," Emilie asserted, recalling the fervent lecture to which she'd subjected Tyler the other night. The chambermaids worked so hard and got so little for their efforts.

"Granted, if you take tips into account, we earn more than they do. But compared to what we're worth..." Kim smiled. "No amount they paid us could possibly be enough."

Emilie shared her grin. "I know I've only been here a few days, but if my tips stay as good as they've been, I'll be earning as much as I was earning in Chicago. I might even be able to finish paying off my student loan before the end of the century." Of course, if she married a millionaire, her student loan would no longer be a problem.

Kim eyed her speculatively. "Do you have a big loan?"

Emilie answered by rolling her eyes and groaning.

"Because if you're really hard up for money, Marty Boyce might be able to help you out."

"What exactly is that all about?" Emilie asked, remembering the dark-haired trainer with the overblown muscles. "He's hiring waitresses for the fitness club or something?"

"Or something," Kim said vaguely. "He hears from lots of hotel guests who want to spend some time with pretty young women when they're down here."

"I thought he was hiring waitresses to give back rubs."

"That, too. I guess you set things up the way you want them with him. Some guests like back rubs. Others like other things." Kim shrugged. "Some just like pleasant company. It's a cool way to meet rich guys."

Emilie opened her mouth to protest that what Kim was describing sounded suspiciously like prostitution. But Kim's last statement made her rethink her response. She'd come to the Golden Key to meet rich guys, hadn't she?

Well, not *that* way.

Except that Kim hadn't exactly said Marty was demanding that the waitresses perform sex acts with the hotel guests. The guests were looking for company, that was all. Back rubs and conversation.

She flashed on a memory of Stewart Culpepper, the investment banker. He'd been nice-looking enough—not in Tyler's class of course, but then Tyler was in a class by himself. And she wasn't so obtuse that she couldn't detect a trace of interest in him.

What if he wanted a back rub?

She would rather rub Tyler Weston's back. She'd rather rub any part of Tyler... The thought made her blush.

"So, Marty's looking for more off-duty waitresses?" she asked, hoping Kim couldn't hear the tremor in her voice.

"As many as he can get. The place is crawling with investment bankers."

"Most of them must be married," Emilie said.

"Who cares? The idea is to earn some extra money."

That might be Kim's idea, but it wasn't Emilie's. Still, if she was going to find a husband, she was going to have to connect personally with a man. Marty Boyce's fitness-club-staff shortage might offer her an opportunity to do that. "I'll talk to Marty tomorrow," she said. "Maybe he can find something for me." Maybe he could find *someone,* she amended silently.

"He'll be thrilled to have you. There are big

bucks in working for him," Kim promised. "You'll see."

Long after Kim had bade her good-night and headed down the hall to her own room, Emilie remained awake, contemplating whether signing on with Marty was the way to go. She didn't have to agree to be pleasant company for just anyone; she could ask for Stewart, her dark-haired John Grisham fan. He might enjoy her company. He might be looking for a bride, someone who could make good use of the wealth he would bring to their marriage. With access to an investment banker's personal funds, Emilie could do all sorts of things: organize chambermaids to demand better working conditions, help welfare mothers get their children into safe and reputable day-care programs so they could finish their schooling and get decent jobs, attend charity balls with Corinne and feel terribly noble about it.

A rich man could open so many doors. What could a poor man like Tyler Weston do for her?

She had a damned good idea what he could do for her. And imagining it, filling in all the juicy details, recalling the long lean hardness of his body against hers, the hot hunger of his mouth, the demanding grip of his arms around her...

It was no surprise she couldn't fall asleep that night.

"MARTY BOYCE?" Tyler muttered when Emilie mentioned the fitness-club director the next day. "What do you want to talk to him for?"

"I've decided to work for him during my off-hours. He's looking for some extra help at the fitness club, right?"

Sure, Marty was looking for extra help. But Tyler didn't want Emilie anywhere near the guy. "I thought you thought he was sleazy," he reminded her.

"It's not fair to judge him on first impressions. I have nothing to lose by talking to him."

Tyler gnashed his teeth but said nothing. It wasn't his business if Emilie wanted to work for Marty. Just because he'd played tennis with her, and talked to her, and kissed her—and realized he didn't want any other man within ten miles of her, let alone lying on a massage table beneath her fingertips...

He had done some prowling through the records in his spare time. The licensing of massage therapists was apparently a state-by-state thing, and the standards in the Virgin Islands weren't terribly rigorous. Massage professionals were advised to take certain courses, and they or their employers had to have insurance coverage, but the fitness clubs at all four Golden Key resorts were insured to the max. And Joseph in the head office hadn't had any complaints about Marty or the fitness club, either from guests or from waitresses who'd worked with him. Tyler had no proof that Marty was doing anything wrong.

All he had were his instincts. And his instincts told him to keep Emilie as far away from Marty as he could.

Who was he kidding? Emilie was an adult, she was educated, she was perfectly capable of fighting her own battles, and she'd made it clear that, despite the chemistry bubbling to the point of explosion between them, she wasn't going to let that explosion occur. If she wanted to enlist in Marty's brigade, let her.

Still, the notion of Emilie hooking up with a slick operator like Marty just didn't sit right with Tyler. "Why do you want to work for him?" he asked, keeping his tone casual. "I thought this work—" he swept his arm in an arc to indicate the chairs lined up around the pool and scattered across the beach, half of them holding hotel guests and the other half sure to be occupied within an hour "—tired you out."

"Playing tennis with you tires me out even more," she said, then smiled to let him know she didn't mind being tired out that way. He almost complained that if she filled her spare time giving back rubs, she would have no time for tennis. But maybe that was what she wanted—an excuse to stop spending her off-hours with him.

"Did you hear? The chambermaids got

across-the-board raises,'' she said, setting a stack of cocktail napkins on her tray.

He nodded. ''Yeah, I heard.'' He'd listened to her the other night, had Joseph examine the pay scales, and saw to it that the right thing was done. Joseph had yammered about the region's prevailing wages, about what hotels on the big islands paid, what the chambermaids would be earning elsewhere—but Tyler had listened to Emilie a lot more attentively than he'd listened to Joseph. So now the chambermaids had raises. ''I guess it was the hot news over at the staff residence, huh?''

''People were celebrating.'' She nudged the tray closer to him so he could place two Bloody Marys on it. ''Oh, and I'll need a Beck's dark, too.''

''Uh-huh.'' He took a beer from the refrigerator, twisted off the cap and set it, along with a chilled glass, on the tray. ''The investment bankers are beginning to flood the beach, aren't they.''

''I hear they were in workshop sessions all morning,'' she said, pulling the tray toward herself. ''I thought this was a retreat for them. I didn't know they'd be sitting indoors talking shop all day.''

''I think they're just doing round-table discussions before tee time. And they were having some sort of private buffet lunch. It makes the whole shebang tax-deductible. They can pretend they're getting some work done, even though they're spending eighty percent of their time on the golf course.''

''Or by the pool,'' she said, hoisting the tray onto her right shoulder and sauntering out of the cabana.

Tyler watched as she paused between two lounge chairs to deliver the Bloody Marys, then moved on to another chair to serve the beer to a fellow in Ralph Lauren swim trunks, his face hidden half by his sunglasses and half by the John Grisham novel he was reading. Tyler observed the way Emilie leaned over the man, the way she smiled at him, the way he lowered his book and picked up his end of the conversation.

A bolt of jealousy seared him.

He must be insane. He had no hold over her. He *wanted* no hold over her, other than his body holding hers for a night or two. Let her flirt with the guests. Let her team up with Marty. What she did with Marty wasn't any business of his— except that he needed to find out what Marty was doing with the waitresses after-hours.

The truth might be benign, perfectly respectable. If it was, Tyler would let it go. Soon enough he'd be back in New York, and what Marty Boyce did with waitresses in their spare time would no longer be his concern.

But if the guy was involved in anything even

the least bit underhand, then it *was* his concern. It would be his concern for a million reasons, not the least of which was that Emilie Storrs might get herself caught up in something she couldn't get out of. As smart as she was, he still couldn't shake his sense that she was somehow naive.

She was talking to the Grisham fan for longer than it took to hand him his beer. He was talking to her, too. Even from a distance, Tyler could tell the guy's sunglasses were fancy designer shades, the sort that usually carried hundred-dollar price tags. The Golden Key Resorts didn't attract guests looking for bargains.

Tyler glanced at his watch. Kim approached the bar and requested two White Russians. Tyler mixed the drinks, sent Kim on her way and turned his attention back to the pool. Emilie was still talking to the Grisham fan.

It shouldn't matter. Waitresses played up to customers all the time. Flirting was at least as useful as sexy outfits in reaping big tips. Of course the waitresses at the cabana were chosen for their visual appeal, too. Older waitresses and waiters did nicely in the resort's numerous other eateries and watering holes, but out here, where the uniform showed off a lot of flesh, the staff had to look good. It wasn't exactly news that the guests noticed.

So why was Tyler steaming with resentment?

Why, when he had no chance of winning Emilie—and no desire to win her—did it infuriate him that she was making nice with one of the bankers?

Ten minutes later—the ten longest minutes of Tyler's life—Emilie moved away from the Grisham fan and returned to the cabana. Her smile tweaked his nerves. It wasn't the honest all-out smile he'd seen when they'd played tennis together. This was an introspective smile, tight and controlled, and it didn't reach her eyes.

"Did you make a new friend?" he asked, motioning with his head toward the banker.

She glanced over her shoulder. "You mean Stewart?"

Cripes. She was already on a first-name basis with the guy.

"He's very nice," she said. "He's one of the investment bankers."

"Surprise, surprise." Tyler rinsed a blender in the stainless-steel sink behind the bar and wished he didn't give a damn about Stewart, the nice banker.

"He said it was cold and rainy back in New York, but this weather is reviving him. He said he feels ten years younger since he got here."

"That would make him, what? Seventy?"

Emilie eyed Tyler curiously. She must have sensed the jealousy gnawing at him. "He's in his late thirties," she said. "Not much older than you, I'd guess."

"I'm thirty-one," Tyler said, then decided he was acting like a total jerk. He covered with a laugh and a shrug. "I just can't imagine anyone wanting to do something as boring as Wall Street banking when they're young," he rationalized. "It seems like an old man's game."

"From what Stewart's told me, I gather it *is* a game. One with major monetary rewards."

Now it was Tyler's turn to size her up. "So, are you the type of lady who gets turned on by major monetary rewards?"

She had the good grace to lower her eyes. "Given my current economic situation, I'm the kind of lady who gets turned on when I see a quarter lying on the ground."

"Meaning, you'll happily sign on to make some spare cash working for Marty."

"I intend to talk to him." She looked at her new buddy, Stewart, and then turned back to Tyler. "You must think I'm awful, Tyler, but..." She sighed. "I've been scrimping all my life. I've got a sister who married a wonderful man— and he also happens to be very wealthy. Her life is so much easier than mine. I'm not saying money is the source of her happiness, but..." Emilie sighed again. "Sometimes I fantasize what it must be like never to have to scramble for the rent."

"So, you're going after rich Stewart."

"No," she said a little too hastily. "That would be crass."

"But if he fell head over heels for you and asked you to go back to New York City with him...?"

"I'd think about it." She slumped against the bar and groaned. "Oh, God, I *am* crass. But it isn't just me, Tyler. It's...it's this book."

"What book?"

"I was on a TV talk show. The author of the book, Torrey Benson... Well, my sister gave me this book about..." Faltering, she anxiously searched his face. "Promise you won't tell?"

"Not a soul. I promise." He propped his elbows on the bar and leaned forward. His face was just inches from hers.

"It's called *How to Marry a Millionaire.* Anyway, I was in the audience of 'The Babs Randazzo Show' where the author of the book was a guest, and I think my sister must have pulled some strings—she knows the producer of the show from some charity or other, and she got us tickets, and there we were in the audience. The next thing I knew, my name was being called, along with two other supposedly random people in the audience. The author—Torrey Benson—claimed that if we followed the advice in her book, we would marry millionaires. Now I'm not sure I believe any of it, but...I mean, there I was, on daytime TV, agreeing to be a part of this experiment to prove her theories.''

Tyler sorted through Emilie's words. Her lecture on worker exploitation in the hotel business had made a bit more sense than this. ''You're part of an experiment?''

''I read the book and got some private coaching from Torrey Benson, and as a result I'm supposed to marry a millionaire. I don't know if I want to marry a millionaire. I want to meet Mr. Right and fall in love and live happily ever after, sure, but I got laid off from my job, and my kitchen had cockroaches....''

He definitely was having trouble following her. ''Cockroaches.''

''Promise you won't tell anyone?''

''About your cockroaches?''

She shook her head impatiently, then laughed ruefully. ''I took this job because I needed the work, but also because, according to chapter seven in the book, you can't meet a millionaire unless you locate yourself in a place they're likely to be. I figured the Golden Key was a place where millionaires were likely to be. I mean, I could have worked as a waitress in Chicago, but if I had, I would have met Bulls fans. Working-class heroes.''

''You don't like working-class heroes?''

''I love them. I'm a social worker, Tyler, remember? A blue-collar kid who grew up to pursue a career helping other blue-collar folks. But I'm tired of poverty. I'm tired of always being down to my last nickel, always having to budget before I can buy a pint of ice cream. I'm tired of wearing my sister's hand-me-downs. I'm twenty-six years old and I want to be solvent. Does that make me a bad person?''

No. Emilie wasn't a bad person. What she was was the most honest woman he'd ever met. Lots of women chased rich guys—and guys chased rich women, too. But most of them wouldn't dream of admitting it.

Emilie had admitted it. And although the last thing Tyler wanted to do was pull off his mask and reveal his true identity, he was very tempted to tell her the truth.

He was richer than Stewart and all his investment-banker cronies. He was probably the richest guy Emilie Storrs had ever met. As the owner of the Golden Key Resorts—to say nothing of two chichi restaurants in Manhattan and a partner's share of a theme-bar chain on the verge of going national—he was rolling in dough.

All he had to do was tell Emilie—and he could have her. In an instant, no doubt. She'd tumble into his arms, into his bed, and he could finish what he'd started with a hot steamy kiss the other night. All he had to do was tell her how rich he was, and she would be his for as long as he wanted her.

And that would make him even more crass than she was.

Chapter Five

THE FITNESS CLUB was a square, brightly lit room on the far side of the pool. The walls were mirrored, the floor immaculate, and every piece of chrome on every piece of exercise equipment had been polished to a blinding shine. Given the sparkling cleanliness of the place, Emilie almost felt as if she'd entered an operating room.

A woman in color-coordinated spandex was firming her thighs on a StairMaster, and a middle-aged man was grunting with exertion as he worked out on the Nautilus equipment, with a nubile young woman in a Golden Key polo shirt and shorts guiding him through each exercise. Emilie wondered whether the woman also gave back rubs. Maybe she was the official massage therapist—or a waitress filling in during her off-hours. She did seem fairly knowledgeable about how to use the weight machine, but then, waitresses spent a lot of their professional lives lifting heavy trays.

Turning, Emilie spotted Marty Boyce behind a sleek counter, chatting on the phone. His compact physique reminded her of a bull terrier's, broad-shouldered, bow-legged and ready to rumble.

As soon as Marty saw her, he grinned and nodded a greeting, then beckoned her to the counter with a wave of his fingers. He concluded his call, hung up the phone and beamed at her. "Emilie Storrs," he murmured.

She was surprised that he remembered her full name, but too wary to be flattered. "Marty Boyce," she said politely.

"To what do I owe the honor?" he asked with a cloying yet chilly smile.

She resisted the urge to bolt, reminding herself that to fulfill the promise of Torrey Benson's book, she was going to have to ingratiate herself with a millionaire. Right now the only potential millionaire she could bear to ingratiate herself with was Stewart Culpepper—and if anyone could help her to ingratiate herself with him, it was Marty Boyce.

Not that she was terribly keen to marry Stewart. She wasn't even sure he was a millionaire. But perhaps, under the right circumstances, he could turn out to be an interesting fellow to get to know. An interesting, *rich* fellow.

Emilie repeated Corinne's mantra for the umpteenth time: it was as easy to fall in love with a rich man as a poor one. Just because her stomach didn't twitter with nerves whenever she saw Stewart, just because her blood didn't run hot in her veins and her breath didn't grow shallow in his presence, just because she didn't feel so comfortable with Stewart that she could spout off about anything she wanted, whether it was the plight of the working class or the absurdity of agreeing to give Torrey Benson's theories a try... Just because her soul told her Tyler Weston was the most exciting desirable man she'd ever met, and who gave a damn that he was a bartender....

She was going to try to convince herself she had a chance with Stewart.

"I was wondering," she said to Marty Boyce, "whether I could give someone a back rub."

His smile grew predatory. "Of course you can. You know I can use you."

She decided not to weigh all the nuances of that statement. "What exactly would it entail?"

"Well, different clients want different things. It's up to you how far you want to take it."

Warning flags fluttered in her brain. "How *far?*"

"Some men want neck rubs. Some want neck and back. Some want full-body rubdowns."

Full-body rubdowns? She shuddered but refused to let her courage falter. She wasn't going to do anything with "some men." She was going to offer a back rub to Stewart, who seemed like a very nice, respectable, affluent fellow.

"Actually there's only one man I'd be willing

to work with," she explained, studying Marty closely, trying to fathom what he was thinking.

"Only one?"

"His name is Stewart Culpepper. He's one of the investment bankers."

"I see." Marty flipped through the pages of a schedule ledger. "Since you know him personally, why haven't you worked this out just the two of you?"

Worked what out? "I don't know him personally," she clarified. "I know his name. We've talked a few times when I served him a drink. I'm not interested in becoming a masseuse, Marty. But he's a pleasant guy and I wouldn't mind doing this with him. For some extra money," she added, sensing that Marty suspected her of ulterior motives, which she had but which were none of his business.

"Okay," he said slowly. "I haven't had any requests from him yet, but let me jot down his name." Marty scribbled Stewart's name onto a page of the ledger. "If he doesn't contact me, I'll try to contact him. How would that be?"

"Great." She felt oddly unsettled by the discussion, by Marty's refusal to talk in concrete terms. She decided to counteract him by being as concrete as possible. "How much will I get paid?"

"It depends on how much you're willing to do," he said blandly.

That was hardly a reassuring answer. "How does it work? Stewart sets up an appointment and I meet him here? Do you have a massage table or something?"

Marty's eyes narrowed on her, and his smile grew progressively less reassuring. "I do have a table here, but the massage room is very cramped and uncomfortable. Most clients prefer to have the ladies go to their rooms."

"Their rooms?"

"They feel more comfortable there, and it's more private. Is that a problem for you?"

"I—" She snapped her mouth shut before replying that, yes, it was a major problem for her. More than a major problem—what Marty was suggesting sounded illegal—and definitely immoral.

But she stifled herself before she could erupt in a lecture about exploiting women, arranging for them to engage in God knew what kinds of activities in the rooms of male guests. Before she accused Marty, before she reported him, she wanted to know exactly what sort of venality she was dealing with. "How much do *you* get paid if I give Mr. Culpepper a private back rub?" she asked, hiding her suspicions behind an impassive smile.

"I work on a percentage," he said. "The guest pays for whatever services you perform of course, and since I make the arrangements and it's all happening through this desk, I take twenty percent.''

She had learned from some of her clients back in Chicago that the standard street pimp took a lot more than twenty percent of a prostitute's earnings. But this didn't exonerate Marty in her eyes. It only made him marginally less greedy.

"Let me think about it." Her crusading social-worker genes quivered to full attention. She was going to unmask Marty Boyce if she could. She was going to bring him down for taking advantage of underpaid female workers—for running an exceedingly discreet call-girl ring out of the fitness club, if indeed that was what he was doing. "Perhaps in the meantime you could get in touch with Mr. Culpepper and see if there's any interest on his part," she said.

"If not him, can I add you to my list for other guests?''

"No," she said. There was a limit to how big a risk she would take in her effort to expose Marty. She'd chatted with Stewart a few times and felt she could handle him if she went to his room. She didn't know any of the other guests, though, certainly not enough to prance off to their rooms for a full-body rubdown.

Marty looked disappointed, but he only shrugged. "Whatever you say. I'll see what I can do.''

Emilie kept her mouth locked in a smile until

she left the fitness club. Then she slumped against the white stucco wall of the bathhouse adjacent to the pool and let out a sigh. She wasn't cut out for undercover work—or under-the-covers work, either. What had possessed her to agree to let Marty set her up with Stewart Culpepper?

Well, if Marty was doing what she thought he was doing, someone had to take him on. And if he *wasn't* doing what she thought he was doing, if off-duty waitresses really were only giving guests neck-and-shoulder rubs, why shouldn't she offer to give Stewart a neck-and-shoulder rub as a way to get to know him better? She wanted to marry a millionaire, didn't she?

Across the patio, she glimpsed Tyler ambling toward the cabana. And like a fist slamming into her gut, the answer to that last question knocked the wind out of her. She didn't want to marry a millionaire. She wanted Tyler.

Her gaze followed him across the patio to the thatch-roofed hut where he worked, and then her legs carried her along the route of her gaze, passing the upholstered lounge chairs, the glass-topped tables, the mosaic rendering of a mermaid inlaid into the tiles surrounding the pool.

By the time she reached the cool shade of the cabana, Tyler was already behind the bar, punching his code into the computerized register. When he glanced up and saw her, his smile brightened his eyes. "How's it going?" he asked. "Meet any rich guys yet?"

She cringed and approached the bar, grateful they were the only two people in the cabana. "I think Marty Boyce is doing something weird."

Tyler's smile faded, but he looked intrigued. He gestured her closer and leaned over the bar, fully attentive. "What do you mean?"

"Well, I can't prove it, but—"

Kim swept into the cabana, bristling with energy. "Buckle up, guys. The bankers just finished their last workshop of the day. They're heading in this direction. We're going to have to start working for a living."

Emilie peered out of the cabana. Kim wasn't exaggerating. When she'd left the fitness club a minute ago, no more than three or four people were lounging by the pool. Now it was teeming with swimsuited men, an army of bankers of every race, creed, color and age, but only one socioeconomic class, as best Emilie could tell.

"Meet me after work," Tyler murmured to her. "We'll talk then, okay?"

"Okay."

"And for God's sake, stay away from Marty."

She grinned. If there was anything she couldn't stand, it was an overprotective man. And yet, for some reason, Tyler's overprotectiveness made her blush with pleasure.

SHE DIDN'T STAY away from Marty. Tyler should have known she wouldn't. En route to the bar for his evening sandwich and nonalcoholic beer, Marty waylaid Emilie at the outskirts of the cabana, too far away for Tyler to hear what they were saying. They talked for a few minutes, Emilie smiled and nodded, and then she headed poolside to deliver a tray full of mudslides and margaritas while Marty settled himself on a bar stool and requested his usual drink.

"So," Tyler said casually as he poured the fake beer into a glass, "have you got Emilie lined up to work for you?"

"She's expressed an interest," Marty answered laconically.

Tyler kept his cool. He wanted to wrap his hands around Marty's throat and squeeze until Marty confessed—although Tyler still wasn't sure what Marty had to confess. He was going to have to remain patient until he and Emilie had finished their shift. Then she could tell him.

"She's hot for one of the bankers, you know," Marty commented before biting into his sandwich.

Now Tyler *really* wanted to throttle him. He sublimated the urge by hacking lemons into wedges with the largest knife he could find. "Hot for a banker, huh?" he muttered.

Marty eyed him curiously, then drained his glass and stood, rewrapping his half-eaten sandwich. "Gotta run," he announced. "The fitness club is jumping, what with all these bankers trying to stay in fighting trim. They like to think of themselves as financial gladiators, you know? Survival of the fittest and all—to say nothing of wanting to impress cute waitresses like Emilie." With a wink he strode out of the cabana.

Survival of the fittest indeed. Tyler lifted a lemon wedge and sucked on it, preferring its sour flavor to the bad taste left in his mouth by his conversation with Marty. If he could get anything on the guy, any grounds to have him fired, he'd be a happy man.

If Emilie could tell him anything he could use against Marty...

In a matter of hours he'd find out what she knew. He scanned the area around the cabana and spotted her on the beach handing a woman in a thong bikini a frosty margarita. The woman had the sort of body thong bikinis were designed for, but Tyler didn't spare her a second glance. It was Emilie who held his attention, Emilie with her unstyled hair, her wholesome features, her luminous eyes. Emilie, whose trust and ingenuousness came through in her smile, in her fervent words, in her desperate kisses.

Emilie, who had promised to meet him after work. Only four hours from now. Tyler was counting the minutes.

"WHERE ARE WE?" she asked.

He gave her hand a gentle squeeze. "Just another part of the resort."

They were on the far side of the golf course, a long pleasant hike from the poolside cabana. The full moon spread a silver sheen across the velvet-smooth grass, the rounded hills and neatly edged sand traps.

"I guess I've seen this area on the resort map," she said, gazing around her. The path they were on curved sinuously past several fairways, arching around small ponds, towering palms and gardens in full bloom. Light fell in golden circles from intermittent lampposts lining the path. "But I've never been up this way before. It's kind of far from the action." The remoteness didn't trouble her, though. She and Tyler might as well have had the entire island to themselves—it certainly felt that way, given that they'd last passed another human being ten minutes ago—but she trusted him. He could take her anywhere and she'd feel safe.

With his fingers woven between hers, strong and thick, she experienced his nearness in too many ways to count. She could smell his fresh male scent mingling with the tart fragrance of the dewy grass and the sea. She could feel his warmth like an aura, radiating from his body to hers. She could see the moonlit breeze toying with his hair, and she knew that the only danger she faced right now was her own reckless longing for him.

On the far side of the fourteenth hole, Emilie was able to make out the peaked thatched roofs of a dozen cottages. "What's over there?" she asked as they followed the path down toward the cottages.

"Guest villas."

"Oh, right." She recalled that area from her map. As they reached the villas, she saw that each was as large as a small private home and surrounded by a patio. Guests must pay a staggering premium for such privacy.

The patios were interconnected by more paths lit by lamps. A plank stairway led down to a secluded beach, and a roadway lined with golf carts circled the villas. Emilie assumed that people too lazy or weary to hike across the golf course could scoot to the main part of the resort on the carts.

To her surprise, Tyler led her through the cluster of villas to the farthest one, which sat on a small bluff overlooking the water. Still holding her hand, he ushered her around the building to the patio, which held several lounge chairs, a table and what had to be the most spectacular view on the island. The patio ended in a railing at the very edge of the bluff, and beyond the railing spread the ocean. Surf hissed against the pebbled beach below them.

"We shouldn't be here," she whispered as Tyler brought her right up to the railing so she could admire the vista.

"It's all right."

"But...but someone must be staying in this villa. If they find us here—"

"Don't worry about it."

"Tyler, we could get in trouble trespassing like this."

"We aren't trespassing."

"Yes, we are. I don't want to get fired."

"Don't worry."

She *should* worry, but he sounded so certain that they weren't breaking any rules. "Why did you bring me here?"

"We needed to talk, and this is a nice quiet place."

"But what about the guests staying here?"

"Emilie." He gathered both her hands in his and turned her from the railing. "There are no guests in this villa."

"It's empty?"

He gave her question more thought than it merited before repeating, "There are no guests here. Just...just sit. We need to talk."

He brought her to one of the lounge chairs, and she lowered herself onto the cushions. Instead of sitting on the other one, he perched on the end of hers, so that when she extended her legs they brushed against the small of his back.

It was too intimate an arrangement. There they were, using the deck furniture at one of the priciest accommodations in the resort, and...

And this was Tyler. And she wanted so badly to trust him.

"Are you sure we won't get into trouble?"

"Are you always such a Goody Two-shoes?"

"Yes," she admitted, "I am."

"Would you still be if I kissed you?"

His eyes were brighter than the moon. The honeyed aroma of flowers seemed to drug her. She and Tyler had come here to talk. He'd said so himself. If he kissed her as they sat here alone beneath the midnight sky, she still in her skimpy waitress outfit, he in his masculine splendor...

"I think," she said, deciding her best defense was to start talking immediately, "Marty Boyce is running a prostitution ring out of the fitness club."

That brought Tyler up short. "What?"

"He didn't come right out and say it, but he said the guests ask him to send young women to their rooms, and how much you get paid depends on how much you're willing to do."

Tyler gaped at her. "He said that?"

"He said different clients want different things, and the payment depends on how far you want to take it."

Tyler continued to gape at her. "Marty told you this?"

"Yes. He also said he gets twenty percent of the fee for setting everything up. Where I come from, that's called being a pimp."

"Oh, my God." Tyler no longer seemed interested in kissing her. He sat straighter, resting his elbows on his knees and frowning in the direction of the patio railing. "Did he actually come right out and say he expected the women to perform sex acts with guests?"

"No. He chose his words very carefully." Emilie sat straighter, too, drawing her knees to her chest and wrapping her arms around her shins. "He never exactly spelled anything out. But if it was only about back rubs, he would have said so, wouldn't he? The fee wouldn't be negotiable. It would have been X amount for a neck rub, Y amount for a neck-and-back rub, Z for a full-body rubdown."

"But he didn't actually come out and say he expected the women to have sex with the guests."

She didn't have to answer. He was obviously inferring exactly what she had. "Here's what I was figuring. I could get Marty to set me up with someone, go to the guy's room and see what he was planning to do with me."

Tyler swung back to her, aghast. "And then what?"

"And then I'd know what Marty was up to."

"And then the guy would expect you to follow through. You can't do that."

"Why not? I told Marty I wouldn't agree to give a so-called back rub to just anybody. I told him I'd do it only with one particular person—one of the investment bankers. I've talked to this man and he seems respectable. I know he wouldn't force anything—"

"Are you insane?" Tyler's eyes blazed with indignation. "I'm not going to let you go into some creep's room and sit around waiting for him to pounce on you—for a price! Cripes, Emilie! You can't do that!"

Once again she reminded herself that she didn't like overprotective men. But for some strange reason, seeing Tyler so upset at the mere suggestion that she would risk her safety—even if the risk was minuscule—made her feel special, almost beloved.

"How about if I talked to management first?" she suggested. "They could supply me with a backup. One of the security guards could be right outside the room. Maybe they could even wire me with a body mike."

"You watch too much TV," Tyler muttered.

"No, I think it could work. I could sneak in, undercover, and—"

"No," he declared. "No, I won't let you do that."

She laughed incredulously. "It isn't up to you to let me or not let me."

"You bet your ass it's up to me!"

"You're a bartender, Tyler. Maybe a few rungs higher than me in the hierarchy of the poolside cabana, but you can't stop me."

"Oh, yes, I can."

His seething anger intrigued her. Feeling daring, she pushed him. "How are you going to stop me?"

"Like this." He kissed her then. It began as a hard silencing kiss, a kiss meant to shut her up and shut her down. But the instant his lips found hers, his rage seemed to transform into something else, something equally fierce, equally protective, but much less angry and much more loving.

Her mouth moved with his, opened to him, and she sighed as heat swept through her. She'd been angry, too, she realized. Angry at Tyler for trying to stand in her way, angry at him for not having any faith in her, angry at him for refusing to let her take a risk.

Except that she was risking far more by kissing Tyler than she ever would have risked to uncover Marty. With Marty, she might have been risking her physical well-being. Now she was risking everything: her heart, her soul, her future.

Tyler wasn't the millionaire she'd come to the

Golden Key to meet. But he was a man, the only man she wanted, the only man who could mean so much to her, who could make her feel so much.

Then his hands were on her knees, nudging her legs down against the cushions, his body taut and heavy as he settled into her arms. Somehow he found the lever that released the back of the lounge chair, causing it to sink to a horizontal position so that they were both lying on the plush cushions, wrapped in each other's arms, kissing until she was certain all that existed in the universe was the sea and the sky, one man and one woman.

He twined his fingers through her hair as his tongue delved deep. His body arched above hers as if he was trying not to crush her, but she wanted his weight, his strength. Ringing her arms around him, she slid her hands up his back and then down past his waist to his hips.

He groaned. "Emilie," he whispered, lifting his face and peering down into her eyes. "I don't want you going undercover in some strange man's room. I don't want anyone touching you."

"You're touching me," she responded breathlessly.

Yes, he was touching her. His fingers feathered along her hairline, coiling through the silky tendrils there before brushing down her cheeks, behind her ears. His body was touching her, chest to chest, hips to hips. His gaze was touching her, searching, exploring, probing. Could he see what she was feeling? Did he understand that it took as much courage for her to open herself to his love as it would take for her to unmask Marty?

"I want you," he murmured, then shook his head. "I want you all to myself. I know that's greedy, I have no right—"

"Kiss me," she demanded, aware for the first time that she wasn't the only one who talked too much. She drew her hands up to the back of his head and pulled his face down to hers once more.

His kiss swamped her with sensation, telling her exactly how much he wanted her, exactly how greedy he could be. Whether or not he had the right to want her like this didn't matter. She wanted him, too, at least as much. Maybe more.

His kisses dazed her, dazzled her. His lips skimmed her cheeks, her chin, the curve of her throat. He slid the straps of her bikini top from her shoulders, wedged his hands under her back and plucked open the clasp. Tossing the bra aside, he pressed his mouth to the hollow between her breasts. She gasped and clung to him, loving each kiss, each caress. Loving him.

He savored one breast and then the other. Her hips surged beneath him, her legs shifting restlessly. When she clutched at his shirt, he reared back, yanked it off over his head and sent it sailing across the patio. She moved her hands over the warm satin-smooth skin along his ribs, tracing the lean muscles, combing the hair that dusted his chest. He groaned low in his throat, closing his eyes and letting her have her way with him.

Her way led from his chest downward, to his shorts, to his fly. She had never been particularly aggressive before, but this was different. This was Tyler, and she reveled in the greed he'd set loose within her. Why waste time lusting for a rich man? If she was going to be greedy, it should be for *this,* for a man like Tyler.

He tugged at the knot of her wraparound skirt as she tugged at his fly. She felt the skirt give way; she felt the strain of his arousal against the metal teeth of his zipper. And then, suddenly, the balmy night air and the thin silk of her panties were all that covered her.

He leaned back, gazing down at her, nudging away her hands so he could strip the rest of his clothing off. Her vision filled with the sight of him, hard and hungry, his body utterly beautiful, his face tense with need, his eyes shimmering with passion. She skimmed her hands lightly over his thighs and he moaned. His eyes seemed to grow darker, the color of the sea where it abruptly grows deep, mysterious shadows rippling beneath the turquoise surface.

She continued to gaze into his eyes as he reached down and removed her panties, as he slid his palms from her ankles up over her calves to her knees, to her thighs and higher. His hands were so large, so warm, as they moved her legs apart, as he covered her and stroked downward again and again, until she could no longer hold still. Her hips twitched as he bowed to kiss her breasts, first one and then the other, sliding his tongue over the tight flushed tips. His fingers stroked more deeply until she cried out, uncaring that they were on someone's patio, completely naked to the world.

"Tyler..." She reached for him.

He leaned over the edge of the chair and groped for his shorts. When he came back up he was holding a foil envelope. He tore at it and she wrested it from him, removing the sheath and rolling it down over him. He had touched her; she wanted to touch him, too.

She'd journeyed his length only once before he peeled her hands away and pinned them above her head. Then he settled over her, brushing her lips with his, entering her with a deep hard thrust.

His body swelled inside her, plunging, stroking, leading her toward ecstasy. Her flesh seemed to transform into sheer energy, burning emotion, the physical definition of love.

Nothing mattered but this. No guarantees. No life of luxury. No it's-as-easy-to-fall-in-love-with-a-rich-man. The only man Emilie could fall in love with was Tyler Weston. And the guarantee was right here, right now, in her heart.

"COME INSIDE," he said, a long time later.

She was still lying in his arms on the chair. Gradually she had come down to earth. The moon bathed her and Tyler in its glow.

God help her, she was in love. She was madly in love with this big bossy bartender, this guy who didn't want her to take chances or let another man touch her. She was crazy in love with Tyler, and she didn't want to move out of his embrace, not even for the few minutes it would take for them to gather their clothing and go indoors.

Indoors? Into the villa?

Startled, she pushed herself to a sitting position. "We can't go inside," she said, glancing frantically at the elegant cottage. "Do you want to get us both fired?"

"Emilie, you're not going to get fired. It's all right."

"We should get out of here before we get caught—"

"I'm staying here," he said quietly. His gaze

locked with hers; she could see no trace of teasing in his eyes.

"What do you mean, you're staying here?"

"This is where I'm living while I'm at the Golden Key."

She shook her head, sure she'd misheard him. When he didn't correct himself, she twisted to stare at the villa. How on earth could he be staying there, when the waitresses and chambermaids were relegated to those cramped dormitory rooms at the nether end of the complex? It wasn't fair, it really wasn't. Just because he was a bartender, a *man*, just because he had the most persuasive smile, didn't mean he ought to be allowed to live in a fifteen-hundred-dollar-a-night villa.

"How'd you manage that?" she asked dubiously. "Did you kiss up to Mr. Golden Key?"

He tucked his thumb under her chin and steered her face back to his. "I *am* Mr. Golden Key," he said. "I own the resort."

Chapter Six

SHE LOOKED STUNNED, stricken, frozen in shock. Her eyes were wide, her bare shoulders pale in the moonlight. Her nostrils flared and her mouth shaped a perfect little circle that turned him on.

Hell, everything about her turned him on. But his announcement seemed to have totally turned *her* off. Her reaction was something of a mystery, though. Hadn't she said she was in the market for a millionaire?

They obviously had to talk, and sitting naked outside on the patio wasn't the way to go about it. When he was naked with Emilie, talking was the last thing he wanted to do.

Partly because she appeared so vulnerable, stripped of her clothing and apparently unable to speak or move, and partly because he felt pretty damned vulnerable himself, he climbed off the lounge chair, snatched his shorts from the patio tiles and tugged them on. Then he padded barefoot to where his shirt had landed and carried it back to her. When he eased it over her head, she came to life enough to poke her arms through the sleeves. The shirt draped down over her, way too large for her slight build.

At least it hid her from him. Not that he had any difficulty remembering how her body looked, how it felt, how she'd felt when he was deep inside her.

She continued to stare at him, even as she ran her fingers haphazardly through her tousled hair and adjusted the drooping shoulder seams of the shirt. "Say something," he goaded, unable to stand the silence.

"I don't believe you."

"It's the truth."

She shook her head. For once she wasn't talking too much.

He really hadn't expected her to be upset. Surprised, maybe—but combine her goal of marrying a rich guy with the X-rated fireworks he and she had just experienced, and she ought to be thrilled, not horrified.

Sighing, he clasped her hand, hauled her out of the chair and led her across the patio, collecting their scattered clothing along the way. At the back door of the villa, he pulled his magnetic-card key from his hip pocket, inserted it into the lock and waited for the green light on the brass lever to flash. When it did, he opened the door.

Still she didn't speak. He led her through the marble-floored breakfast nook, where he tossed their clothing onto the table in a rumpled heap, and down two steps into the sunken living room.

He left her there while he returned to the kitch-enette and pulled a bottle of Riesling from the refrigerator. "Wine?" he called to her.

He saw her nod mutely, then turn to stare out the wall of windows at the night-dark sea.

He filled two crystal goblets with the wine and carried them to the living room. She accepted the glass he offered, took a bracing sip, and then glowered at him. "You lied to me, Tyler."

"When?"

"You told me you were a bartender."

"I *am* a bartender. That's how I got my start when I quit school. I just sort of parlayed things into this."

"You 'just sort of parlayed' bartending into ownership of the Golden Key Resorts? All four of them?"

"Plus a few restaurants and some other prop-erties."

She sank onto one of the low-slung leather sofas as if her legs could no longer support her weight. "I don't believe you! If you own this place, why are you mixing drinks in the poolside cabana? Surely you have more important things to do—papers to push, deals to make, politicians to bribe, workers to exploit."

"Hey." Anger built inside him, pressing for release. "I don't bribe politicians and I don't exploit workers. You told me you thought the chambermaids weren't getting paid enough—I checked it out and I agreed. What do you think? That it was just a bizarre coincidence they got a raise?''

She opened her mouth and then shut it. Fury burned in her eyes. ''I confided in you...''

''You sure as hell did. You confided that you wanted to marry a millionaire. Well, let me tell you something, sweetheart. With an attitude like yours, don't expect any millionaires to want to marry you.''

That got her. Her jaw clenched and her hands gripped the stem of her glass so tightly he thought she might break it. ''Why are you tending bar in the cabana?'' she asked, practically choking on the words.

''I completed the acquisition of the Golden Key Resorts about a year ago. Since then, I've been going from resort to resort, kind of undercover, so I can get a feel for things. The director of operations here knows who I am, and so do a few other people in the business department, but they've kept my identity a secret so I can mingle with the staff. If everybody knew I was the boss man, they wouldn't speak freely to me. You wouldn't have mentioned the underpaid chambermaids, for instance.''

''You're right. I wouldn't have.'' She sipped some wine, her gaze riveted to the pearl gray carpet beneath her feet. ''I probably would have set up a picket line, instead.''

"I don't like picket lines. I like people talking to me. So I immerse myself in the scene and keep my ears tuned. The first thing I picked up, while I was working the bar at the Crystal Room, was that Marty Boyce was pulling some shady moves in the fitness club. So I transferred out to the cabana to see what I could learn. What would have happened if I'd put on a suit and tie, marched into the fitness club and confronted him? He would have presented himself as Mr. Clean and denied all the rumors, and I'd have nothing."

She lifted her eyes to study him, then shook her head. "I can't imagine you in a suit and tie," she murmured.

With her seated on his sofa in nothing but his Golden Key shirt, he knew what he'd want to do if he was in a suit and tie—tear them off as fast as he could, and then tear the shirt off her and then go at it the way they'd gone at it on the patio. He willfully shoved that idea aside. "So I worked the cabana bar and got to know Marty. Got to know him enough to sense that the rumors had some truth to them."

"I'm the one who figured out what he was up to, not you. You could have stayed in your suit and tie."

"You're right," he said. "You're the one." Unable to stop himself, he set his glass on the coffee table, pried her glass from her bloodless grip and set it down beside his. Then he sandwiched her hands in his. "The fact is, there's no law that says consenting adult waitresses can't fool around with guests. But this deal with Marty's turning it into a side business with money changing hands, that part's flat-out wrong. And dangerous. I don't want you getting stuck in the middle of it."

"Oh, sure," she snapped, her fingers flexing against his palms. "You don't want me getting stuck in the middle of it. I'm just a helpless little slip of a thing."

"If there's a word I would never use to describe you, Emilie, it's helpless."

"But now that I've come this close to finding out what Marty is up to, you want me out of the picture. And you're the boss, so I have no choice."

He caught himself before retorting something equally sarcastic. He just couldn't fathom where all her bitterness was coming from. They'd made love, hadn't they? It had been fantastic, hadn't it? He was a millionaire, and she'd claimed to want to find herself a millionaire. What was the problem?

"Okay, I give up," he conceded, pulling her closer and peering into her face. "What did I do to make you so angry?"

Unexpectedly her eyes welled with tears. "Tyler..." Her voice broke and she averted her gaze. "I was prepared to give up everything for you. The strategies in that book, the life of ease..." She swallowed and blinked her eyes, jarring a few tears loose. "Marrying a rich man seemed like the answer to everything, but then I learned there were questions I hadn't even known to ask—and answers far more important than money. I got to know you, and I realized there were things I wanted more than a millionaire. I—I wanted you."

She swallowed again. One of her tears dropped onto his wrist. He wanted to pull her into his lap and hug her, wanted to kiss away her tears. But he knew she had more to say, so he waited patiently for her to say it.

"All my life," she went on at last, "I believed that money didn't matter. But then, when I was down to my last dollar, without a job, without a caseworker to help me the way I'd helped so many other struggling women, I thought, all right, I'll give money a try. But...but deep down, I never wanted money to matter that much. And when I met you, when I decided to toss aside the whole millionaire thing—" another tear skittered down her cheek "—you gave me the chance to go back to my old values. And I wanted that, Tyler. I wanted to be the sort of woman who could fall for a guy because he was down-to-earth and funny and sexy—and honest."

"Can't I be down-to-earth and funny and sexy and rich?"

"If you're rich, you're not who I thought you were. You're not just a guy—you're my boss. And if you were honest, you would have told me the truth before we...before we did what we did outside. You would have let me know who I was making love with." She sighed. "I don't think I can trust you anymore."

She broke from him abruptly, pushed away from the sofa and strode to the breakfast nook, where she picked through the pile of clothing until she found what was hers. Ignoring his presence, she peeled off his shirt and tossed it onto a chair, then donned her bikini top, her panties, her skirt. As he watched her, a strange pain gnawed at his gut.

Emilie had fallen for him thinking he was poor. In spite of her plans, in spite of her dreams and schemes, she'd fallen for *him*. Not his money, not his power, but *him*. And now, because he hadn't told her the truth about his wealth before he'd made love to her—because he'd deprived her of the chance to think she was better than the money-grubbing readers of that *How to Marry a Millionaire* book—he was going to lose her.

"I'VE GOT GOOD NEWS for you," Marty told her, snagging her by the arm and drawing her into the shadows by the bathhouse. She'd been on her way to the cabana to start her shift, but in all honesty, she was in no hurry to get there. Once she did, she was going to have to see Tyler, and the mere thought of seeing him made her stomach churn with nerves.

The only news she would consider good right now would be that Corinne had sent word for her to fly back to Chicago because the Department of Social Services was rehiring her at twice her old salary, and her apartment was fumigated and awaiting her return. But that was unlikely, so she smiled patiently and said, "Oh? What good news?"

"Your friend Mr. Culpepper wants you."

She tried not to cringe. At this point she didn't want to find out what Mr. Culpepper wanted her for, or how much he was willing to pay for her, or how much Marty was going to make from the deal. She didn't want to save the Golden Key from a major scandal. She just didn't care, not about Stewart Culpepper, not about Marty, not about *How to Marry a Millionaire.* How could she care, when last night she'd discovered that the man she'd fallen in love with had deceived her by letting her think she was too righteous to love a rich man, when he was richer than sin?

"He'd like you to go to his room tonight after your shift. Think you can handle it?"

"What do I have to handle?" she asked dully.

Marty grinned. "He's a gentleman. I'm sure there'll be no trouble. You can work out the arrangements when you get to his room. He's very taken with you, Emilie. You could turn this into something big."

"Oh, I'll bet," she muttered, freeing her arm from his grip and turning toward the cabana.

"He's in suite B-314—that's in the Bayside building," Marty told her. "Can you remember that?"

"I'm not an idiot." *Ha,* she thought sullenly. Only an idiot would abandon her principles, rediscover them and then lose them because of a creep like Tyler.

"He'll expect you there at ten-thirty."

"Fine." She stomped off, unwilling to spend another minute with Marty. Only when she'd reached the shade of the cabana did it dawn on her that she was expected to go to this banker's room and *do* something.

She might as well stick with her original plan. If Stewart Culpepper was truly a gentleman, perhaps they could talk. She could bring herself to massage his shoulders, she supposed, and she could chat with him, ask him about the Grisham novel he was reading, ask him about his life in New York, his hobbies—the sorts of things people asked each other on first dates. And if she liked him—and he didn't push her into an unpleasant predicament—she could pursue a friendship with him. She could woo him into wooing her. And she could sure as hell keep her clothing on.

If he *did* push her into an unpleasant predicament...she would run like hell, screaming at the top of her lungs. And then pack her bags and clear out of the Golden Key, declaring herself and Torrey Benson's theories failures.

She reached the edge of the cabana and faltered. Of all her failures, the worst was to have fallen in love with Tyler. How dare he turn out to be a millionaire? He didn't look like one. He didn't act like one. He'd fooled her. He'd convinced her to forget about her plan, to be the idealistic woman she'd always fancied herself, to follow her heart—and her heart had led to him.

The rat.

He was behind the bar, as she'd known he would be. He must have been watching for her, because his gaze zoomed in on her the moment she stepped from the sunshine into the shade of the thatched roof. His eyes were still that uncanny turquoise color, rippling with shadows. His devilish smile was nowhere in evidence.

She was tempted to climb onto a stool and announce to everyone within earshot that the guy mixing daiquiris behind the bar was none other than the head honcho himself. But just because she felt betrayed didn't mean she ought to betray him. He had his reasons for pretending to be a prole. Let him deceive the universe if that was what he wanted to do.

Her heart splintered into a million pieces as her gaze met his, as she saw the profound sadness in his face, as she remembered how close they'd been last night, how intimate, how blissful those hours had been. She and Tyler had hidden nothing from each other then. At least, *she'd* hidden nothing. The only thing *he'd* hidden was his identity.

Steeling herself, she strode into the cabana to grab a tray. Before she could escape, Tyler covered her hand with his, pinning it to the bar. "You're not going to work for Marty, are you?" he asked.

She glanced around, searching for an excuse to get away. Kim was out on the beach flirting with some sunbathing bankers. A couple of women were sipping what appeared to be colas from tall frosty mugs at a table near the cabana, but they weren't going to bail Emilie out, either.

If she could handle Stewart Culpepper, she could certainly handle Tyler. "None of your business," she said.

"Like hell it's not my business!" His voice was muted but simmering with anger. "It *is* my business."

"Oh, yes—of course. You own it."

"I meant *you*. Your safety is my business."

"I'm sure you've got insurance if anything happens to me. I promise I won't sue the pants off you." Bad choice of words, she realized belatedly. A vision of Tyler with his pants off caused her cheeks to grow warm.

"Emilie, listen to me," he said, stroking her wrist with his thumb. Obviously he knew that tenderness was more persuasive than force. "This has nothing to do with insurance and lawsuits." His voice was barely above a whisper. "It has to do with you and me. It has to do with last night, and the night before, and every day and every night since we met. It has to do with talking, and playing tennis, and talking some more. And sex. If anything were to happen to you, I don't know what I'd do."

She wanted to weep. He sounded so much like Tyler the bartender, the relaxed good-natured sexy guy who'd swept her off her feet simply by being himself—whoever that was. He sounded like a man whose wealth was measured not in dollars but in passion.

"Nothing will happen to me," she murmured because she didn't know what else to say.

He studied her for a long minute, then asked, "What room is the guest staying in?"

"Bayside 314."

"That's an expensive suite. He must be loaded."

"Like I care," she mumbled.

His hand relaxed. "Let me have someone from security outside the suite, okay?"

"Okay." For Tyler's peace of mind, she told herself, not for hers. "You can send a security guard. And give him a raise," she added for good measure. "Give the entire security staff raises, why don't you."

"I already did. They've got excellent contracts," Tyler said, almost smiling as he released her. She grabbed her tray and ran, unwilling to give herself a chance to do what she really wanted: vault across the bar and hug him for worrying so much about her.

HE'D NEVER BEEN so nervous in his life. Not when he'd quit college and set out for New York on his own, not when he'd scrounged for jobs, not when he'd negotiated his very first purchase of a business, applied for his very first loan, outmaneuvered adversaries with MBA's. Not when he'd first realized that women might love him for his money rather than himself. Actually that hadn't made him anywhere near as anxious as the thought that Emilie Storrs had loved him for himself, not his money.

He hovered just steps behind the security guard on the third floor of the Bayside building, his attention riveted to the closed door with the number 314 etched onto a small brass plaque above the knob.

Emilie was inside.

He reminded himself that she was tough, re-sourceful and smart. He reminded himself that before she came to the Golden Key she'd been working with city punks and equally perilous city bureaucrats. But still, he prayed that the banker would keep his freaking hands to him-self.

"How long has she been in there?" he whis-pered to the guard.

"Five minutes."

Too long. Too long for Tyler's peace of mind, anyway. If she was giving the guy a back rub of course, she might be in there for thirty minutes or more. If she'd decided to forget about last night and make a play for the banker...

He sent another prayer heavenward.

He'd put a second security guard on Marty Boyce's tail. If anything went amiss in suite 314, this guard would contact that guard, and Marty would get escorted directly to Tyler's office. The legalities of the situation were vague enough; Marty could claim that he'd hired the waitresses only to give back rubs, and that as free citizens, they were entitled to pursue whatever activities both they and the guests agreed to. But Tyler didn't need to have the law on his side to fire the guy. The employees of all the Golden Key resorts were obligated to behave with decorum.

Acting as a pimp for the waitresses was unacceptable.

Suddenly the guard pressed his ear to the door. Tyler sprang across the hall and listened. Through the thick oak panels, he heard Emilie's voice bellowing, "No, Stewart. I'm sorry, but no."

Stewart, Tyler thought angrily. She was using the guy's first name.

"I said no!" she repeated. Tyler heard a low male voice, too muffled to make out the words. Then another no from Emilie. Then a thud. Then a crash.

"Go in, go in!" he ordered the guard, who rammed a master-key card into the slot and shoved open the door, his walkie-talkie already off his belt. Tyler was so close behind, he barely missed bumping into him as he charged into the suite.

Like all the suites at the Golden Key, this one was opulent, with plush carpeting, elegant furniture and real art hanging on—not bolted to—the walls. The grandeur of the accommodations was diminished somewhat by the banker, stripped to his Calvin Klein underwear, sprawled on the floor next to an overturned Queen Anne chair, beside which lay a broken lamp and a John Grisham novel. Across the room Emilie stood, arms akimbo and chest heaving. She was wearing a clean white T-shirt and neat linen shorts. Tyler had never been so happy to see her fully clothed.

Ignoring Culpepper, he raced across the room to her. "Are you all right? What did he do to you?"

The banker pushed himself up to a sitting position and rubbed his wrist. "What are you worried about her for? *I'm* the one injured here."

"I threw the book at him," she said, pointing to the thick hardcover novel. "Literally."

"Look," the banker said to the guard, rubbing his other wrist and then inspecting his legs for damage. "The fellow at the fitness club came to me. He assured me Emilie was willing. It's just a terrible misunderstanding— Say, aren't you that bartender at the poolside cabana?" he asked, peering up at Tyler.

"Among other things," Tyler said, signaling the guard with a nod. "Tell security to bring Boyce in." He turned back to Emilie and scrutinized her. "Are you sure you're all right?"

She pursed her lips. "I'm perfectly fine. And I told Marty—" she directed her remark past Tyler to the man gingerly picking himself up from the floor "—that I would give Mr. Culpepper a neck rub. Period."

"As I said, it was just a misunderstanding."

"Did money change hands?" Tyler asked the banker. "Because if it did—"

"No," the banker said quickly.

"Not yet, anyway," Emilie chimed in. "He made me an offer."

"Marty said you wanted this."

"Marty was mistaken," Tyler declared briskly. "Go get dressed, Mr. Culpepper, and we'll straighten this whole thing out with Marty in my office."

"Your office?" The banker glanced quizzically at the security guard. "Isn't he a bartender?"

"Among other things," the guard said, unplugging the broken lamp and righting the chair.

Satisfied that the guard had matters under control, Tyler took Emilie's hand and led her out of the suite. He was glad she didn't resist, didn't question his presumptuousness, didn't start yapping at him. She simply went along until they reached the open-air stairway at the end of the hall then stepped out onto the landing, where they were greeted by a sweet sea breeze.

Emilie pulled to a halt and eased her hand from his. "Why were you a part of this, Tyler?" she asked, looking far from pleased. "I agreed to a security guard. You didn't tell me you were going to be coming along, too."

"I didn't tell you I *wasn't* going to be coming along, either."

"Typical. Just like you didn't tell me you *weren't* the owner of the Golden Key. *Not* telling the truth is as bad as telling a lie, Tyler. Sins of omission are still sins. How am I ever going to believe anything you ever—"

He kissed her, gently but firmly, and then drew back, his hands resting on her shoulders. "Believe this, Emilie. I love you. You drive me crazy, but I love you. I'm not *not* telling you anything. I'm *telling* you the truth. I've got money, yes, but I'm no fancy-dancy rich man. I'm just a guy who managed to climb to the top of the heap. And I need you to tell me who's being exploited, who's being overworked and underpaid—basically, who's doing what around here. If it wasn't for you, I don't know if I would have figured out what Boyce was up to."

"Plus, your chambermaids wouldn't have gotten themselves a fair salary," Emilie added.

Tyler laughed, then bent his head and kissed her again. "I'm telling you the truth now," he swore. "I love you, Emilie. I know you were trying to follow the instructions in that book of yours, but I'm the guy you won. Not one of the wealthy resort guests. Me."

"The hell with the book," she whispered, threading her fingers into his hair and pulling his face down to hers. "I believe you, Tyler." And then she kissed him back, kissed him deeply, kissed him with such conviction he knew he'd won her trust.

A long time later they came up for air. "I'd

say the book worked out okay," he murmured. "If it brought you here, it worked."

"We'll have to let Torrey Benson know. She wrote the book, so I guess she deserves the credit, even if I wound up with a bartender."

He laughed. "Fine. We'll invite her to the wedding."

"Just so long as it's clear I'm marrying you in spite of your money, not because of it," Emilie reminded him. "And I swear, Tyler, I'm going to check all your employee-salary scales. You really need to be aware of the inequities, especially with the female workers. How are things run at your other resorts?"

It occurred to him that he hadn't precisely proposed marriage to her. But he hadn't *not* proposed marriage, either. She'd jumped straight ahead to *why* she would marry him.

It occurred to him that they were back to their regular form, and he liked it just fine.

"Anything you want to know, just ask," he said, brushing his lips against hers once more. "All I've ever needed was a good woman to keep me honest."

She grinned. "Then you've got all you've ever needed," she promised, resting her head against his shoulder and holding him close.

Two stories below, Tyler noticed the guard ushering Stewart Culpepper from the main entrance of the Bayside building. Across the gardens, he spotted another guard leading a rather irate Marty Boyce from the vicinity of the pool. In a few minutes Tyler was going to have to go to his office, get a statement from Culpepper and remove Marty from his payroll. He was going to clean up the resort, because it was his and, as the boss, he got to decide how he wanted things to be.

But for just a few more moments he was going to hold the woman he loved, because holding her was exactly how he wanted things to be.

Dear Reader,

When I was creating the fictional Golden Key Caribbean Resort for *Rich Man, Poor Man,* I tapped into memories of my honeymoon in the Bahamas, more than sixteen years ago.

Our plan was to stay for a couple of nights in a modest hotel in Nassau, and fly from there to the Bahamian island of South Andros for a week at a resort. The night before we were scheduled to leave Nassau, we took a stroll along Cable Beach and came upon a magnificent hotel, old and elegant, with patios, lush gardens, cabanas and a glorious expanse of private beach. We decided to eat dinner at the hotel's restaurant, where we spent most of the meal lamenting that we couldn't afford to stay at such a classy place.

The next day we boarded a rickety little plane and took off for the remote island resort. We landed on a strip of tarmac carved out of a rain forest. The airport terminal—a small hut beside the tarmac—bore a sign that read: Welcome to San Andros. We gathered our bags, climbed out of the plane and located a cab driver. When we asked him to drive us to the resort, he guffawed. "You'll need a boat to get there," he told us. "You're on *San* Andros Island. That hotel's on *South* Andros Island, five hundred miles away."

We raced back onto the tarmac, and implored the pilot to let us back onto the plane. An hour later we found ourselves at the airport in Nassau, where a ticketing agent informed us that no planes were scheduled to fly to South Andros that day.

There we were, stranded in the Nassau Airport with no way to get to our reserved hotel room. My husband and I exchanged glances—and we realized that we both had the same idea. We summoned a cab and asked the driver to take us to the exquisite hotel we'd discovered on our beach stroll the night before.

Our tale must have touched the manager's heart; he agreed to charge us the hotel's minimum rate for the one vacant room he had—which just happened to be a fifteenth-floor suite with a balcony overlooking the Caribbean sea. We happily spent the rest of our honeymoon in the luxurious suite.

Our adventure proves that even a couple of newlyweds just starting out can live like millionaires for a few heavenly days, if they're lucky. Of course, the real measure of luck is finding true love—and if you find it, you possess a wealth infinitely more valuable than money. (But having money doesn't hurt!)

Sincerely,

Judith Arnold

FAMILY WEALTH

Muriel Jensen

To Ron
Solid gold in jeans and a sweatshirt

Chapter One

MILLIE BROWN pushed the videotape into the VCR and sat back on her heels, waiting for the picture. Behind her, her sisters squabbled.

"You buttered the popcorn!" Pru accused, her tone dramatic, her elocution perfect. In September she would be a junior majoring in theater arts. Provided, of course, Millie's plan worked.

"Yes, I buttered the popcorn," Amy admitted. "I know butter goes right to your hips, but Chatty and I don't have that problem and I see no reason why we should deprive ourselves because of you. And stop emoting. There isn't a producer or a director within a thousand miles of us."

Amy was a year away from her B.A. in English literature and the beginning of her career as a novelist. She intended to win a Pulitzer prize before her thirty-fifth birthday.

"I'd rather have a fat butt than a fat head!"

"How about a fat lip?"

"Don't call me Chatty!" Charity's voice joined the angry chorus. She'd just completed her first year at the Art Center of Design in Los Angeles and had the temperament to fit her calling. "I've asked you a million times not to call me Chatty! I'm not eight years old anymore. It's Charity! *Charity!*"

Millie pressed the pause button on the VCR and turned to her sisters. They were a trio of beautiful redheads seated on the sofa.

Their beauty, contrasted against her plainness, never failed to remind her that she was their half sister. But that acknowledgment was always instantly overpowered by the fierce love she felt for each one of them—even when they were being infantile.

They'd been away at school all year, except for the Christmas holidays, and the first few weeks of their summer reunion in Millie's apartment was always an adjustment process. She'd been dealing with their artistic egos ever since their mother had died, when Millie was fourteen, and she was usually able to take the task in stride. But she intended to implement her plan tomorrow and she was edgy. If it didn't work, their college careers were over, and she'd promised their father she'd see his girls graduate.

"Will you listen to yourselves?" she demanded. "Your father named you Amity, Prudence and Charity, and listen to you!"

"It's intimidating to be named after a virtue." Charity took the bowl of popcorn from Pru and filled the smaller bowl in her lap. "Everybody expects you to live up to it. Why couldn't he have named us after flowers?"

Pru rolled her eyes. "Because he was a minister, not a botanist."

Amy laughed wickedly. "He should have named us after three of the seven deadly sins. Pride, Envy and Gluttony."

"We know who'd have gotten to be Gluttony." Pru passed the popcorn bowl to her older sister with a smirk.

Millie rescued the bowl and caught Amy's arm midswing. She frowned sharply into one upturned face after the other. "I," she said with strained patience, "was not named after a virtue, so I have nothing to live up to. I could inflict physical pain on each one of you without a second thought."

The three young women looked at each other, then back at Millie and gave one common snort of disbelief.

"Yeah, right," Amy said. "So, what's this plan you have to tell us about, and what does a videotape of *Yanni at the Acropolis* have to do with it?"

Millie drew a breath and gave herself a minute to pull her explanation together. It was a little bizarre, and though she had artistic siblings, she was a left-brained accountant and much preferred things that added up and made sense.

But in the interest of acquiring enough money to keep her sisters in school, she couldn't ignore an opportunity, no matter how outrageous.

So she'd appeared on "The Babs Randazzo Show."

"This is Mrs. Magruder's tape," she said, pushing Amy's sneaker-clad feet aside and sitting on the edge of the coffee table. "I was on a talk show last week and she recorded it for me over Yanni." One had to know how enamored Mrs. Magruder was of the performer to appreciate the generosity of the gesture.

Three pairs of eyes the same shade of ocean blue stared at her. Finally Charity shifted, grinning. "You mean you actually went on television and talked about that time the alien impregnated you with twins?"

Pru's eyes widened dramatically. "How will we hold our heads up?"

Amy put the back of her wrist to her forehead. "Tell me you didn't mention how you sold the babies to pay for your sex-addiction treatments."

The girls dissolved into laughter. Millie waited it out, thinking wryly that persecuting *her* was the only activity the three could indulge in together without fighting.

"Are you through?" she asked at last.

"For now," Amity replied, scooting to the corner of the sofa and drawing Millie down between her and Pru. "How come you didn't tell us you were going to be on a talk show? We could have watched you."

"I didn't want you to be disappointed if I didn't win."

Charity leaned around Pru to look at her. "Was it 'Oprah'? Win what?"

Millie opened her mouth to reply, but found it all too preposterous to put into words. So she aimed the remote at the VCR and the tape came to life.

Her sisters watched in fascination as "The Babs Randazzo Show" titles rolled, then gasped in unison when Babs announced that her guest would be Torrey Benson, author of the outrageous new bestseller *How to Marry a Millionaire*.

"That's the book we bought you for Christmas!" Charity exclaimed.

The others shushed her. They listened as Babs stated that the show's producer had selected three candidates from the audience to take part in a contest sponsored by Benson's publisher.

"Torrey will talk about her book," she said, "we'll get acquainted with our contestants, and Torrey will take them away for some personal coaching. Then, on their own, our contestants will select their millionaire and woo him or her. Five weeks from today, the one who brings back a millionaire will be featured on our fabulous follow-up show."

The audience applauded wildly. Amy, Pru and Charity stared at the screen. When the contestants were brought onstage and Millie was among them, the girls' mouths fell open.

The show proceeded with an interview with Torrey Benson, who quoted passages from her book, listing what she considered the unique personality traits of millionaires and the equally unique traits required of a woman hoping to interest one in marriage.

As Millie's sisters leaned forward, entranced, Millie leaned back, panic resurfacing. What would she do if this didn't work?

When the girls had come home at Christmas, she'd explained that the money their father had left in a special account for their education was depleted. Though she'd invested it and diverted every spare dime of household money toward it, the rising costs of education had vacuumed it up.

And collectively the girls still had six more years of college to go.

Charity had joked that Millie needed to find a rich man, they'd all laughed over the notion, then the girls had given Torrey's book to Millie as a gag gift. She'd flipped through it idly one evening after her sisters had gone back to school. Finding Torrey's style engaging, she'd read the book from cover to cover.

She'd even let herself daydream about how life as the wife of a rock star or a software tycoon would negate her worries about the girls' educations.

But her daydreams hadn't lasted long, for she

knew this was her *real* life—the one in which her own college education had been cut short when her stepfather died; she'd been a sophomore. She and the girls had been given a small monetary gift from his congregation, then had had to move out of the parsonage to make way for the new minister.

She'd rented an apartment and gone to work in the accounts-payable office of Beauregard Boutiques. She was now the accounting manager for all seven stores.

Millie had put the book aside, accepting that while marrying money was fun to contemplate, she hadn't dated even a poor man in more than a year. She was too busy working as much overtime as possible to support her sisters.

Then Beauregard Boutiques was suddenly sold to the Fashion Central Stores, and one day she'd found everyone in the employees' lounge exclaiming over a magazine. When it turned out to be the current copy of *Cigar Aficionado,* she was convinced her co-workers had been through one too many clearance sales.

But the buyer for the lingerie department had held up the magazine and pointed to the handsome dark-eyed man on the cover. "Would you believe this is our new boss?" she'd exclaimed with a giggle that belied her forty-four years. "Rio Corrigan. Isn't he something?"

Millie, finding the face on the cover appealing, had perused the article while everyone else

went back to work. She learned that Rio was
short for Rosario, that his father, who'd taken
over Fashion Central from *his* father, was an
Olympic gold medalist in swimming, and his
mother was a Cuban tobacco heiress.

Corrigan was now president of the company.
His uncles and cousins owned and operated
Contigo Royale Tobacco.

He spent his free time mountain climbing, sky
surfing, white-water rafting and hunting big
game with a camera.

Millie closed the magazine and studied Rosario Corrigan's face on the cover. A man with
a death wish, she thought. Or with something to
prove. But the camera had captured a supremely
confident demeanor that still seemed warm despite a trace of arrogance. A fat cigar was
clamped between shining white teeth.

The headline read Rosario Corrigan, Bachelor
Millionaire.

Then it hit her—twice. Bachelor. Millionaire.

She'd quickly gone over a few of the points
she remembered from Torrey Benson's book.
Show initiative. Be willing to take risks. Go
where the money is.

The last point had quickly deflated her small
burst of excitement. According to the article, Rio
Corrigan lived in San Francisco, where the company's flagship store was located. And this happened to be a month when she barely had money
to keep gas in the car, much less spring for an

airline ticket and whatever clothing and "props" would be required to put her in Corrigan's path.

So she dismissed the notion and went back to work. But she took the magazine with her.

Then three things happened that evening that convinced her Rio Corrigan could very well be her destiny.

First, she'd stretched out in a bubble bath before bed to finish the article on the new owner of Beauregard Boutiques, telling herself it was in her own best interest to know as much about him as possible to ensure that she kept her job. The story mentioned that his parents had retired to Coral Gables, Florida, that his brother had been tragically lost in a plane crash a year before. It also said that he was currently without a serious relationship.

"If I could find a woman," the reporter quoted him, "who could fix the glitches in Fashion Central's new computer system and warm my bed with the same skill, I'd marry her in a minute."

Millie felt as though fate had just taken her by the shoulders and shaken her. She'd shopped for and chosen the computer system Beauregard's used, and she'd supervised the data input herself. It had worked smoothly from the beginning.

But...warm his bed? Her sexual experience had been limited and disappointing. And she'd never been sure whose fault that had been—hers or the uptight former men's-department buyer she'd dated for a year and a half.

No. It was preposterous. She couldn't do it.

Then she'd been listening to the nightly news while getting ready for bed and heard Babs Randazzo, the host of a nationally syndicated daytime talk show, advertise the appearance the following week of Torrey Benson and the *How to Marry a Millionaire* contest. A few details were given, and viewers interested in participating were encouraged to call the studio.

Millie had been stunned. It had to be destiny at work. A rather forceful destiny. But even if she did get on the show and Torrey Benson did give her personal instructions, unless she also gave her several thousand dollars to buy a new wardrobe, travel to San Francisco and frequent Rio Corrigan's hangouts to place herself in his path, she still couldn't do it.

The third thing that happened that evening was the phone call from Kelly Bingham, the store manager's secretary. "I'm sorry to call so late," she'd said, breathless. "But Mr. Lane just called me! He wants you in the store an hour early tomorrow for a meeting."

Millie's heart sank. "Oh, God, Kelly. Has the new regime fired me?"

"No," Kelly replied quickly. "In fact, Mr. Corrigan spoke to Mr. Lane tonight and said he's keeping all of us on."

Millie closed her eyes on a breath of relief. "Then what's the problem?"

"The problem is that Rio Corrigan's coming here!"

For a moment Millie couldn't speak. Then she asked in a thready voice, "Here? To Bridgeton?"

"Yes. Two weeks from today. And Mr. Lane wants everything to be perfect. He needs you to put together a report on..."

Millie didn't hear what kind of report Mr. Lane wanted. All she heard was that the millionaire was coming to *her*—a week after "The Babs Randazzo Show" and Torrey's contest. Destiny was not only at work, it was bulldozing her path and laying down the road.

"I'll be there," she said, then swallowed and added matter-of-factly, "but I'll need next Wednesday off. Family business."

"Ahh..."

"I have to have it, Kelly."

"If you'll spend the next two weeks helping me deal with the stress and extra work brought on by middle-management brownnosing, I'll see you get Wednesday off. Mr. Lane just dictated a memo to me for housekeeping to dust the lightbulbs!"

"I'm your woman, Kelly. Thanks."

Millie had gotten to the show and, not entirely to her surprise given the way fate had taken a hand in this, was selected for the contest. Torrey

Benson, understanding her need to be back at work the following morning, had coached her that night. Vivacious and confident, she had sent Millie home at eleven convinced she could wrest a proposal of marriage from Prince Albert of Monaco if she wanted to.

Watching Mrs. Magruder's tape now, however, gave her a certain distance from the goings-on and made her wonder what on earth she'd been thinking. She saw her chestless self in her clip-back cotton dress looking pathetically out of place next to the host in her Donna Karan suit.

Millie wondered what she had that could possibly appeal to a man who was heir to two fortunes and who jumped out of airplanes.

Her thoughts were interrupted when the remote was wrenched from her fingers and her sisters crowded around her, Charity kneeling at her feet and grinning hugely.

"This is so cool!" she shrieked. "Where are you going to find a millionaire?"

"Wait a minute!" Amy silenced Charity with a glower she then turned on Millie. "What are you *thinking?* You're actually planning to select a rich man and marry him in order to get us through school?"

Millie and Amy had had many face-offs since Millie had assumed parental responsibility for their family. Usually they were in a struggle for control. But this time there was genuine concern in Amy's eyes.

"Yes," Millie replied honestly, "and to secure a few perks for myself of course." That part was a lie, but she needed her sisters' support if this was to work.

Pru hooked an arm through Millie's. "We don't want you to sacrifice love for us," she said gravely.

Millie patted her hand. "That's very sweet, but do you see anyone in love with me? No. And as long as I'm confined to the accounting office in a women's clothing store in Bridgeton, Illinois, you aren't likely to. I'm doing this as much for myself as for the three of you."

The girls exchanged a doubtful look, then Charity asked ingenuously, "Millie, even if you find a millionaire, do you think you can...I mean..." Her eyes went over her oldest sister's short brown hair, her unimpressive proportions.

Millie suppressed a smile and inwardly cursed the Fates that had blessed her with a body streamlined for speed rather than endowed for seduction.

"I have a plan," she said.

"Do you have him picked out?" Pru asked, her concerns swept away by sudden excitement. "A rock star? A baseball player?"

Millie told them about her new boss and reached for the magazine she'd left facedown on the coffee table.

Amy wrinkled her nose. *"Cigar Aficionado?"* Then she noticed Rio Corrigan's face and focused on it with an interested "Oh!"

The other girls crowded closer. They found the article inside and Amy read highlights from it aloud.

Awestruck, Pru turned to Millie. "He's practically begging for a computer-junkie wife. That's you!"

Charity still seemed worried about Millie's qualifications. "But someone to warm his bed! Millie, can you...? I mean, do you...even know *how?*"

The other girls pounced on Charity, who quickly apologized for the question. While they studied Rio Corrigan's face again, Millie conceded privately that Charity's question was legitimate. The man's dark gaze suggested he wouldn't settle for less than what he wanted.

She felt a frisson of trepidation. And a large sense of going into battle without weapon or armor.

But she wouldn't settle for less than she wanted, either. And she wanted to see every one of her talented sisters with a college degree. *She could do this.*

She just couldn't do it the way other women would. She would have to use her own approach.

Torrey Benson had told her to show initiative, after all.

Chapter Two

RIO CORRIGAN shook hands with the buyers and floor staff as the Bridgeton Beauregard's well-meaning but obsequious manager led him from department to department. He distributed smiles, praise for the care they'd taken with this wonderful old store, and reassurance that, apart from bearing a new name, none of the stores would change.

He did all the things his father had always insisted were important and saw everyone around him begin to relax. He was grateful, because that was what he wanted to do himself.

He could almost feel the sun of northern New Mexico on his face. After months of intensive research, study and negotiations to acquire Beauregard Boutiques, and all the agonies the new computer system had caused the acquiring team along the way, he was ready for some downtime.

He had only to meet with the head of the accounting department, then he was out of here.

As Lane led him down the administrative corridor toward the accountant's office, Rio smiled to himself. He imagined C. Brown, who'd signed off on all the reports used in their negotiations, as a sort of Bob Cratchit, devoted to his figures and to the company.

Not that Rio had a problem with that. The man's compulsive attention to accuracy and detail had been the one bright spot in the past few weeks. No matter which way the figures were analyzed, they added up. Every bit of financial information he'd tracked, no matter how obscure, was detailed and justified. Everyone on the team had been impressed—himself particularly.

He admired C. Brown's quest for perfection, and the checking and rechecking it must have required. A fine quality in a boardroom, although in a social situation...well, Rio braced himself to meet with a fussy persnickety individual.

Lane rapped on the door at the end of the hall.

It was opened by a smiling young woman in a soft pink cotton suit Rio recognized from the women's-wear department he'd just passed through. The soft collar of a silky white shirt boasted a small heart-shaped pin with three stones on one side in different colors. A piece of costume jewelry from the store, he guessed.

It occurred to him that he really needed a rest when he looked at a pretty young secretary and saw not her charms but the company's stock.

"Mr. Corrigan," Lane was saying as he drew him into the office, "I'd like you to meet Camille Brown, head of our...or rather, *your* ac-

counting department. Millie, this is Mr. Corrigan, president of Fashion Central."

Rio took the small hand offered him and
looked into a pair of wide hazel eyes. Her face
was pink-cheeked and nicely framed with short
curly brown hair. He was careful to conceal his
surprise. So this was C. Brown. She didn't look
at all persnickety.

"Ms. Brown," he said. "Fashion Central
feels extrememly fortunate to have you on staff.
Your reports certainly simplified our acquisition
of Beauregard. I hope you'll want to stay with
us."

"Yes, of course." She gave his hand a firm
shake, her gaze leveled on his. "I've enjoyed my
work here."

And that was when he saw and felt the subtle
change. Her grip on his hand tightened only
fractionally, but there was an urgency in it, a
kind of…need?

He told himself he was imagining things until
he saw that same urgency in her eyes. They
seemed to be searching his, looking deeper than
an employer-employee meeting called for.

And the color in her cheeks became hectic.
He wondered if he was really that frightening,
or if she was coming down with something.

Millie was on the very brink of losing it. Her
heart was thudding, her knees were shaking, her
mouth was dry. This was it. Do or die. The mo-

ment Mr. Lane left them alone, she was going to propose. But she was scared spitless.

Rio Corrigan was even more gorgeous than he'd appeared on the magazine cover, and even more…magnetic. As his eyes perused her face, she felt drawn into them and powerless to extricate herself.

The grip of his hand was solid, and her world wasn't. She found herself holding on. Clutching. The moment she realized that, she drew back.

"I asked Millie to analyze the last five years' profits," Mr. Lane said, "so that you can compare the manufacturers you use against ours to facilitate any product changes you'd like to make."

Actually the compilation of figures had been Millie's idea, but she was so grateful for the interruption that she couldn't even raise a sense of righteous indignation over Mr. Lane's manipulations for approval.

"Excellent thought," Corrigan said.

"Shall I leave you to look the figures over, then pick you up for lunch at noon?"

Corrigan smiled politely. "Thanks, but I haven't time. I'm flying out of here in a couple of hours." He turned the smile on Millie. "But I would like to take the figures with me."

"No!"

Millie didn't realize she'd made the denial aloud until both men frowned at her. "Ah…I mean, yes, of course," she said quickly, and reached back to her desk for the folder she'd prepared, trying desperately to think how she could keep him long enough to explain her plan. Certainly fate wouldn't block her path now. "I...I just think it's too bad you'll miss the lunch Mr. Lane had planned. Particularly if you'll be stuck with airplane food."

He grinned. "I flew here in our corporate jet, Ms. Brown. Our airplane food is boxed lunches from Guaymas in San Francisco."

She'd have retreated at that point if her sisters' educations weren't at stake. Of course millionaires flew in private jets. Of course they carried gourmet lunches. Of course she was out of her mind to ever think she could pull this off.

But insane or not, she had to try.

The telephone rang. It was Kelly with a crisis, looking for Mr. Lane. Millie handed the manager the receiver. He excused himself to Corrigan and sat at her desk to take the call.

Millie's brain began working. "Can we drive you to the airport?" she asked Rio Corrigan.

He turned away from a perusal of the view of downtown Bridgeton and shook his head. "Thank you, but I hired a car. The driver's waiting for me downstairs." His gaze narrowed on her suddenly and he asked quietly, "Are you all right, Ms. Brown?"

She tried to pretend surprise that he should ask, but was sure she'd failed miserably when his expression didn't change.

"I'm fine, Mr. Corrigan," she said, her voice sounding strangled. "Why?"

He studied her feigned expression a moment longer, then reached down to lift her joined hands in one of his.

She'd linked her fingers to keep from fidgeting and saw as he held them up that her hands were clasped as though forged together, her knuckles white, her short unpolished nails digging into her skin.

He rubbed the thumb of his free hand gently over her knuckles. "What are you worried about?" he asked, glancing at Lane and seeing he was still engrossed in his conversation with Kelly. "The books were in perfect order. You know your job is secure. Is there a problem I'm unaware of?"

This wasn't at all the way she'd hoped it would go. She'd envisioned the two of them closed in her office with time to go over her report, time to show him the computer program she'd implemented, to prove to him calmly and with style that she was the data whiz he needed.

Instead, she probably looked terrified and needy. And with his warm strong hand holding hers, she couldn't think. So she simply answered his question.

"Yes," she replied softly. "There is."

Mr. Lane hung up the phone and stood, his manner a little flustered. "We've just caught a shoplifter in leather coats, and someone has to meet the police. Millie, would you please handle...?"

Oh, no. This was her last chance to...

Corrigan smiled and took Millie's arm. "Actually, Lane, I've asked Ms. Brown to walk me out and fill me in on the highlights of her report. Why don't you meet the police—and please tell your clerks I appreciate their vigilance."

Lane stammered a protest, but Corrigan led Millie resolutely out the door and headed for the elevators.

"I know you're not going to confess embezzlement," he said lightly. "My comptroller says you're not only exceptionally efficient but painfully honest. Even petty-cash accounts balance." He pressed the elevator button and they stood facing each other on the old burgundy carpet. "So what is it?"

She held the sides of her jacket together at her waist as though that could prevent rejection from reaching her.

"It has nothing to do with the store," she said in a breathless rush.

The elevator doors opened to an empty car. Millie stepped in, Corrigan right behind her. He pressed the button for the ground floor.

The doors closed and he placed a hand on the oak railing at the back of the car. She opened her mouth to speak, but nothing came out.

"You need a raise?" he asked.

She shook her head as the car moved steadily downward. "No. It's entirely...personal."

He waited for her to go on.

She didn't know how.

The car moved inexorably toward the bottom floor, toward the street, toward the car waiting to take Rio Corrigan to the plane with the boxed lunch from whatever that place was. The plane that would take him back to San Francisco and eliminate her chance of winning Torrey's contest and getting her sisters through school.

He shifted impatiently. "You've got one more floor to tell me, Ms. Brown."

Millie jabbed decisively at the emergency-stop button. Her mind on how on earth she was going to explain her plan, she forgot to hold on and was thrown against her companion as the car bounced once and jolted to a halt.

He caught her in one arm.

She got an overall impression of muscle and musky fragrance and experienced a sudden vivid resurgence of girlish dreams of a lovers' arms. This *couldn't* be happening to her. She had planned it, but nothing she planned ever worked out for her. Nothing.

But this wasn't for her. It was for the girls. So she forced the words out before she could give herself time to think.

"Mr. Corrigan," she said, her voice a raspy whisper, "I need you to marry me."

She saw the flare of surprise in his eyes. It was followed by a moment's consideration, and then he replied evenly, "Sure. Why not?"

Chapter Three

MILLIE STARED at Rio a full thirty seconds. She wanted to speak, but all her body's processes seemed to have stalled. Had he said yes?

The elevator's emergency phone rang. Rio, still holding her in one arm, reached around her with his free hand to flip open the panel and remove the receiver.

"Yes?"

"Is the car stuck?" a gravelly voice demanded. "My panel doesn't show a problem."

"We stopped it," Rio replied.

"Why? Is there an emergency?"

Rio looked down into Millie's pale face and decided there was. He held the phone between himself and Millie so she could hear. "Of sorts," he said. "But we're fine. We'll be down in a few minutes."

"This is the maintenance manager." The voice was authoritative and obviously displeased. "You listen here! Beauregard does not approve of clandestine meetings in our vertical transportation. No quickies between floors. You free that car right now."

Mortification reactivated Millie's powers of speech.

"Churchill, this is Millie Brown," she said, injecting her own voice with authority. "I'm in the elevator with Mr. Corrigan of Fashion Central, your new employer." There was a moment of silence. "He's checking—" she glanced up at Rio, apologizing in advance for the lie "—the tidiness and safety of the elevator system. He gives you high marks, Church. We'll be down in a few minutes."

"I'm sorry, Millie." The aggressive voice was now penitent.

"It's all right. Go back to work."

Rio replaced the receiver and closed the panel.

Millie pulled away from Rio and stood across from him, leaning weakly against the wall.

"I'm sorry about that." She'd surely lost all hope for the plan, but since she had her millionaire trapped in an elevator, she felt obliged to play it out. "He's a very conscientious employee. Please don't hold this against him."

Rio shook his head and leaned comfortably into a corner, folding his arms. "Of course not. It would be hard to hold anything against a man so alert to the condition of his—" he paused for emphasis "—vertical transportation."

She smiled grimly and tried to relax. If he could take this calmly, so could she. And now that she'd done her worst, the terror she'd felt since she'd made her decision was suddenly gone. She'd been so afraid of his rejection, but now that she knew it was imminent, a kind of numbness was setting in.

"So." She fanned herself with the report she still held. The little cubicle was suddenly very warm. "I guess I'm not your first proposal, judging by how calmly you've taken it."

He pulled at his tie. "I just figured a preposterous statement deserved a preposterous reply. Are you pregnant, Ms. Brown?"

She was indignant for a moment, until she realized her statement could have led someone to that conclusion.

He apologized. "Forgive me, but you said it was a personal problem. Given your demand, I naturally assumed..."

"Yes, well, there's no baby. Unless you consider Charity, who'll probably act like the baby in the family until she's ninety-three."

"Charity?"

"My youngest sister."

"She's pregnant?"

"No!"

Rio found that reply a little snarly, but he had to admit he was now thoroughly intrigued. He was usually good at puzzles, but he had yet to find his way through this one. So far he'd been held hostage in an elevator, proposed to by a pretty stranger and accused of illicit behavior between floors. He couldn't wait to see what happened next.

"I'm sorry, I'm sorry!" Millie put one hand over her eyes and stretched the other out before her in a kind of stopping motion. "Okay, look." She lowered her hands and looked him in the eye. "Can I just tell you what's going on here?"

That sounded promising. "I was hoping you would."

"Okay." She paced three steps across the length of the elevator car, then three steps back. She turned to face him and blew out a breath. "The girls gave me a book for Christmas called *How to Marry a Millionaire*. It was a joke because their college fund was about to run out and they'd kidded me about finding a rich man in a hurry." She shrugged apologetically. "I know that probably isn't funny to you because you *are* rich, but to those of us who aren't, money is often a joke because we need it and usually have little hope of getting it, so we laugh about it."

He was surprised to realize that he'd gotten most of what she'd said. Except for one detail. "Who are 'the girls'?"

"My sisters," she replied with a quick smile. "Charity, Prudence and Amity. Eighteen, nineteen and twenty. An artist, an actress and a writer."

"Ah. Churchgoing parents?"

"Their father was a minister."

"*Their* father?"

She nodded ruefully. "Mine was a math major with a thing for old movies. Garbo movies in particular. That's why I'm Camille and not Faith or Hope or something. Anyway, their father died seven years ago and left them a fairly good college fund, but college is so expensive these days that it's gone now.''

''And your father?''

''Died in a motorcycle accident before he could marry my mother. Her parents were outraged when they learned she was pregnant and tossed her out. The minister took her in, and his young assistant—my sisters' father—fell in love with her.''

A sad little story, Rio thought. And something Dickensian about it—the unappreciated stepchild sacrificed to the needs of her half sisters.

Well. Everyone had a sad story, himself included.

''So they gave you this book...'' he prodded.

''Right.'' She lifted her eyes heavenward, then closed them and shook her head. ''I can't believe that Torrey made it all seem so possible. And that I fell for it!''

She was losing him. ''Torrey?'' he asked.

''The author of the book. Torrey Benson. She was on 'The Babs Randazzo Show' and had this contest where...'' She went on to explain details he couldn't quite connect except to understand that she'd somehow become a contestant.

''You mean,'' he asked, incredulous, ''that in a month's time you're supposed to reappear on the show with a millionaire's ring on your finger?''

She made a face and nodded. ''Yes. It does sound unbelievable, doesn't it? I thought so, too, but then I read that magazine article where you were quoted as saying you were looking for a wife who could make your computer systems work, and I'm really good with ours. And all these other things began to happen that made me think maybe you *were* my destiny.''

Destiny. He knew all about that. It was a trickster that spread pain and sorrow. He couldn't help a stiffening of his spine.

Still, the notion that this pretty but complex young woman considered him her destiny was intriguing and curiously touching.

''See, the girls gave me the book,'' she went on, an awed expression in her eyes, ''but I couldn't get to where the rich men are. Then you bought Beauregard, and Torrey Benson was appearing on a show just a hundred miles from here and had advertised for contestants, I was actually chosen and then—'' she paused and indicated him with a wave of both hands ''—*you* came to *me!* Well, not to me, but to visit the Bridgeton Beauregard! Tell me that isn't destiny!''

Before he could indeed tell her that, she told herself. ''Well, of course it isn't, but that was what I thought, anyway. It was obviously just a curiously related string of events. I'm usually much more logical than this.''

The notion teased him, poked him with a taunting finger. A woman in his life could be a good thing on several levels right now, but he'd pretty much decided there wasn't room for one until he could learn to live with himself again. If that could ever happen.

He looked into her hazel eyes, her peaches-and-cream face, and had to force himself to confront the facts. No. Some things were better left alone.

''Your financial problems and my sudden appearance on the scene just conspired to warp the picture,'' he said practically. ''You can't expect a happy marriage to result from a string of odds and ends coincidentally pulled together.''

Millie met his eyes and saw him for the first time since he'd walked into her office as a man with his own problems, rather than as the man sent by fate to solve hers. His eyes were dark and beguiling, but she could see in their depths that something was troubling *him*. He seemed to need someone as much as she did, though obviously not for money.

''But that's what destiny is,'' she said quietly. ''The coming together of things that otherwise simply wouldn't connect.''

He met and held her eyes. ''Like you and me.''

She felt a weird little charge at that suggestion, a sort of emotional zap.

"Like a man who needs his computer system made workable and a woman who can do that," she corrected. "A woman who promised to get her sisters through school, and the man who can help her keep the promise."

He thought about that for a moment, then gave her a slightly wicked smile. "A modern marriage of convenience? That wouldn't work for me."

She laughed nervously, flustered again. "I know. You also need a woman to warm your bed."

He raised an eyebrow and she explained quickly, "It was in the article. And...I can do that, too." That seemed like a boast, so she added, "And when both our needs are met..." She paused, her color deepening as she heard her own words. He was watching her, his grin widening. "I mean, the data input and the tuition needs..."

"Are you sure?" he said with a teasing smile.

"When those are met," she went on, squaring her shoulders to make her point, "we would divorce. Naturally I'd sign a prenuptial agreement that says I personally want nothing. Oh! And you might have to appear with me on television."

Rio studied her earnest face and the firm line of her chin and wondered where in hell she'd come from. People, particularly young people, didn't sacrifice themselves for others anymore. Yet she was completely serious about doing this.

Of course there could be advantages on her side to this "sacrifice" for her sisters, but she'd just neatly turned them aside.

As a man who'd spent the past year trying to escape his own selfishness, he wasn't sure he could turn her down. He should of course. He'd been looking forward to this vacation with Alex, and having Millie Brown along might upset it.

But he didn't think so.

Heaven help him, he was going to do it. Maybe.

"All right, Ms. Brown." Hands in his pockets, he straightened and looked down at her. "I think the idea deserves consideration."

Relief and disbelief widened her eyes.

"Can you be ready to leave for Taos in two hours?" he asked.

She blinked once, then cleared her throat and repeated, "Taos? New Mexico?"

"I have a vacation place near there. My nephew and my butler are already in residence. We could get to know each other and decide whether or not this is a good idea."

"Nephew?" she asked. "Visiting you, you mean?"

"He lives with me." His expression sharpened. "He's eight. Is that a problem?"

She wasn't sure, but not for the reasons he probably suspected.

"Of course not. But...my vacation isn't until September."

"I'm your employer. I can fix that."

She thought of the myriad details she should be concerned about, then dismissed them in the face of Rio Corrigan's actually considering her proposal. The girls were leaving in two days to serve as counselors at a summer camp, so they would be looked after. And her neighbor would keep an eye on the apartment. Beyond that, well, nothing was more important than Rio Corrigan.

"If you can fix it with Mr. Lane," she said, suppressing a desire to leap and shout, "I'll just go pack a few things."

"All right."

In a dreamlike state, Millie watched him press the first-floor button. The elevator continued its interrupted descent.

"One more thing," he said.

"Yes?"

He reached over, cupped the back of her head and pulled her to him. He kissed her in an analytical exploratory manner—gently, but almost mechanically, as though wanting to gauge what she could bring to the experience.

It was a test she didn't want to fail.

Deepening the kiss seemed too manipulative, so she elevated it from mechanical to personal by touching his face with her fingers.

He warmed to the move instantly, for she felt a subtle responsive change in him. His hand came up to the middle of her back but applied no pressure. His lips moved on hers and she followed, startled by another little jolt of energy, that zap of feeling she'd experienced earlier.

Rio Corrigan raised his head and studied her with a combination of surprise and new interest.

The loud clearing of a throat turned both their heads in the direction of the now open doors. The elevator had reached the bottom floor, and the small crowd waiting for it were smiling at them.

Except for a tall balding man in gray coveralls, the name "Churchill" embroidered on the pocket. He didn't seem to know whether to be angry or concerned.

Rio took Millie's arm and pulled her with him off the elevator.

"Car's sound and safe, Churchill," he said as shoppers moved around them to occupy it. He offered his hand and the maintenance man shook it.

"Was afraid you two weren't coming down," Churchill said.

Rio ran his thumb over his lips, still tingling from Millie's kiss. "Actually," he remarked over his shoulder as he led her toward the door, "for a few minutes there I think we even went sideways."

Chapter Four

MILLIE HAD NEVER SEEN such a sunset. She watched it from the window of the champagne-colored Infinity Rio had collected at the small Taos airport.

Rio pointed out the rugged line of the Sangre de Christo Mountains, dark purple against a pink-and-yellow sky. She stared at the colors, thinking she was seeing things.

"The light's different here," Rio said. "It attracts a lot of artists. Georgia O'Keeffe loved New Mexico."

Millie watched the sky, fascinated. High above, a bright star gleamed like a diamond as sunset began to slip into dusk.

Rio had spent most of the flight wrapping up business details and making last-minute phone calls. She'd spent the time dealing with the nervousness that was setting in now that her plan had met with success. What if she hated his lifestyle? What if he learned that she had tendencies to dweebiness?

She would have to deal with it, she told herself. She should be grateful for the opportunity and not borrow trouble.

Rio turned off the highway onto a narrow road. Groups of bushy little trees dotted the grassy fields.

"Piñon," Rio explained, guiding the car toward a low, sprawling adobe structure. "We have a lot of junipers, too." Then he pointed ahead. "Home."

Millie admired the building's simple lines, so perfectly suited to its setting. An iron gate opened and they drove through it into a large courtyard. The impression of simplicity was replaced instantly by one of luxury.

A long swimming pool occupied the middle of the stone courtyard, and surrounding it were several patio tables and chairs, umbrellas closed now for evening. Distributed among them were padded chaise longues and wooden benches with planters built in at both ends, and everywhere there were earthen pots filled with flowers. Off to one side was an enormous barbecue complete with a counter and wet bar.

Millie wanted to take the elegant beauty in stride but simply couldn't. "Wow!" she said with unabashed amazement. "What a wonderful place to relax."

"I'm glad you like it." He turned to smile at her. She'd been blessedly quiet during the flight from Bridgeton. He'd never known a woman who wasn't full of observations and opinions. This month would be an interesting experiment. "Did you pack a bathing suit?"

She shook her head. "I don't even own one. My youngest sister commandeered mine a few years ago, and I've been too busy to need one since."

"We'll have to rectify that in town tomorrow. Come on. You're about to meet Alex and Gilford." Rio pulled up to French doors where a portly white-haired man and a dark-haired little boy stood.

The moment the car stopped the boy opened Rio's door. "Hi, Unc!" he said. "I can't believe you got here on time! You're always late for vacations. Where's Henry?"

The words were machine-gunned at his uncle while he danced around him, throwing practice punches like some particularly puny flyweight.

"I told you I'd be here before you went to bed," Rio replied.

Millie watched in fascination as he managed to climb out of the car and carry on his half of the conversation while absently dodging and deflecting the blows. "And Henry isn't coming. I'm avoiding work this trip. But I've brought somebody else. No sparring with her until we've assigned her a weight class."

Alex stared with wide brown eyes as Rio reached a hand to Millie and helped her out of the car.

"A girl!" he exclaimed.

Millie couldn't tell by his tone whether he was excited or disgusted.

"A guest," Rio corrected gently. "Millie, this is my nephew, Alex Corrigan. Alex, this is Millie. She's going to spend our vacation with us."

Alex shook her hand politely, then squinted up at Rio and asked candidly, "Is she your girlfriend?"

Rio answered briskly, "Yes."

The boy looked from her to his uncle again, his expression still difficult to define. "Are you gonna get married?"

"Maybe," Rio replied.

And suddenly, although the idea had been hers, although she'd planned and plotted to bring it this far, the involvement of a child in a scheme that would be temporary at best seemed thoughtless and fraught with potential heartache.

She looked at Rio, knowing her expression reflected her concern.

He raised an eyebrow. Then the white-haired man approached, and Rio turned to draw him forward.

"Millie, this is my friend and support, William Gilford. Gil, Ms. Camille Brown. Millie."

Millie's hand was taken in a firm grip. She was smilingly assessed, although there, too, she couldn't tell what he thought.

He rolled his eyes at Rio's introduction. "Actually I'm just the butler," he said in wonderfully British-accented English. "But I do happen to be very good at it. I'm delighted to meet you, Ms. Brown. Welcome." He stepped back to slide open the French doors. "I can offer a cold supper if you're hungry, iced cappuccino if you'd just like something cold, or a margarita if you'd prefer something alcoholic."

"Iced cappuccino sounds heavenly," she said.

He went off to prepare it while Rio led her to an enormous creamy-white bedroom. It was carpeted in white, and the coverlet and draperies were patterned with soft yellow flowers on a white background. A lamp with a yellow shade glowed in a corner, lighting the room against the encroaching dusk. A pot of colorful wildflowers sat on a simple desk in a corner.

When Rio and Alex left to get her bags, she looked around with relief. She'd half expected to be led to Rio's room. She'd proposed, after all, and made it clear that she understood his physical requirements.

But she seemed to be panicking on all fronts. Looking into Alex's bright beautiful eyes had made her aware of what her arrangement with his uncle could do to his young life.

And the physical concession, which had been so easy to make verbally, now made her exceedingly nervous. She wasn't really all that brilliant at it. And she just knew he would be. So the deal could all fall apart when he took her to bed.

Oh, God. She sank onto a yellow-and-white settee. Why hadn't she just thrown herself on the mercy of a loan company?

Rio and Alex were back within minutes, Rio carrying her suitcase in one hand, the hangers of her garment bag hooked over his shoulder by his index finger.

Alex balanced her train case on his head, supporting it with his fingertips.

Millie rose to greet them, opening the wardrobe door so that Rio could put the bags inside.

Alex handed her the train case. "My mom had one like this," he said. "Only it was that cloth stuff with flowers on it."

"Tapestry," Millie said. She remembered that the magazine article had said Rio's brother and his wife had died a year ago in a plane crash. Alex seemed well-adjusted to life with his uncle, but children were good actors. She remembered how long it had taken the girls to deal with their father's death, how often she'd come upon one or the other of them sobbing.

She tweaked Alex's chin. "Thank you for being such a good bellboy."

He looked puzzled. "What's a bellboy?"

"It's a man in a uniform in a hotel who brings your bags up to your room."

"Oh, yeah." He grinned. "He gets a tip, doesn't he?"

Millie laughed. Rio groaned and playfully clamped a hand over the boy's mouth. "Charming kid," he said to Millie, "but a businessman at heart."

"Actually he's right." She gently disengaged

Rio's hand from Alex's mouth, then leaned down to kiss the boy on the cheek. "There. Will that do?"

Alex smiled widely and blushed. "Yeah."

Rio turned Alex toward the door and gave him a little push. "Go tell Gilford we'll be out in a minute."

Alex pulled the door partially closed behind him, then peered around it. "Are you guys gonna kiss?"

Rio took a step toward him and Alex made off with a laugh, his running footsteps audible through the now closed door.

Rio turned to Millie. "You seem nervous suddenly," he said. "Are we not what you imagined?"

She understood the statement, but not the question. "What do you mean? Is who not what I imagined?"

"Me. Alex. When you proposed, you thought I was a bachelor. You didn't learn about Alex until after you'd laid out the plan. It isn't too late for you to find another millionaire, you know. You said you have four weeks until the show."

Alarm made her heart rate accelerate. But if he wanted to back out, he had every right to.

"Do *you* want to change your mind?" she asked. "I mean, I know you haven't made any definite decision yet, but do you want to change your mind about considering it?"

He shook his head. "No. But I thought you might. When I introduced you to Alex, you looked upset."

She sank onto the edge of the bed, overwhelmed suddenly by the enormity of what she was doing, altering the direction of two lives— six lives if you counted Alex and the girls. Seven if Gilford was figured into the equation.

"I suddenly realized what it could mean to Alex—a stranger moving into his life, settling in, then moving out again."

He raised an eyebrow, a faint twitch to his bottom lip. "I don't think it's healthy in a relationship to plan the divorce before the wedding takes place."

She frowned at him. "You know what I mean."

"Yes." He sat beside her, close enough to touch her but not doing so. "And I like that it concerns you. But part of the reason I accepted your proposal was that I hoped you could help me with Alex."

"Of course." She shifted to face him. "I'll do anything. But he seems so well-adjusted."

Rio's expression turned grim. "He's trying hard. He misses his father of course, but in this all-male household, I think he misses most of all the…softness only a mother can provide."

Millie saw in Rio's eyes that he hadn't quite recovered from his brother's death, either, though he appeared to be equally as good an actor as his nephew. Still, his eyes darkened and his jaw stiffened when he spoke again.

"Alex is fine during the day," Rio explained, "but he cries a lot at night and has difficulty sleeping. I put a TV in his room so he can have something to do if Gilford and I don't hear him. That's probably not a good child-rearing technique, but at least it occupies his attention."

"Poor baby."

"Yeah." He stood abruptly, caught her hand and pulled her with him toward the door. "So don't start backpedaling. I'm sure you'll do him more good than harm—however long you stay. Come on. I need caffeine."

Chapter Five

RIO FOUND getting used to Millie's presence almost as easy as Alex did.

He awoke every morning to the sounds of laughter and splashing in the pool, then lay quietly for several moments simply listening to it. It soothed him, even went a little way toward easing the guilt he felt over Ramon's and Margaret's deaths.

He would join Millie and Alex for breakfast under one of the green-and-white-striped umbrellas and listen to Alex's stories about Millie's sisters. Apparently Alex and Millie had time to talk while they swam.

Millie, her hair wet from the pool, her cheeks pink from the sun despite the high-PF sunscreen he'd bought her, would smile at him across the table, obviously pleased with Alex's excitement.

Millie and Alex often took walks until lunchtime, coming back with samples of various plants and wildflowers they'd decided to research and catalog.

Afternoons, while Alex watched favorite cartoons, Millie busied herself with the computer in Rio's office at the far end of the house. It was linked to Fashion Central's system, and she tinkered with the new program that he was having such difficulty with.

Dinners were cheerful affairs where Gilford barbecued and served outside. Alex was animated and full of chatter. Millie, having analyzed Fashion Central's computer system, reported on its good points and its bad.

But nighttimes remained the same as they had for the past year. Alex gave Rio that desperate look when it was time for bed, Rio sat with him until he fell asleep, then awoke in the wee hours of the morning to the low rumble of Alex's television.

Rio would go in to check on him and find that lost anguished look on the boy's face, and know there was nothing he could do for him—particularly since it was his own fault the look was there in the first place.

And Millie slept in the white-and-yellow room his parents used when they visited. Though she'd boldly promised to "warm his bed," she had yet to offer to do so, and he was surprised to find himself unwilling to claim that part of their deal.

At the end of Millie's first week with them, Rio awoke to the sound of the television just after one in the morning and thought it was a little louder than usual. Getting up, he pulled on a knee-length robe and went to check on Alex and ask him to turn down the sound. No need to disturb Millie, he thought.

He felt an instant's panic when he noticed that Millie's door was wide open. He peered in and saw that her covers were thrown back and her bed was empty. Her bathroom was empty, too.

What the...?

Then he heard quiet but definitely feminine laughter coming from Alex's room. He peered around the half-open door and found Alex and Millie sitting cross-legged in the middle of the bed, completely engrossed in a game of fish while an old TV sitcom played in the background.

Millie picked up a card from a pile between them, apparently matched it to the one in her hand and put it down. She raised both hands triumphantly.

Alex frowned at her. "You won *again*. I'm the kid. You're supposed to let *me* win once in a while."

"Ha!" she said in a loud whisper. "You're too smart to need any advantages. Come on. Let's clean up these cards and get to sleep. Your uncle's taking us to Santa Fe tomorrow."

She stretched one shapely leg over the edge of the bed as she scooped up half the cards. Then she stood, straightening the cards, a slender figure in white fleece shorts and a white T-shirt with Marlon Brando's face on it.

Rio caught a whiff of gardenias and experienced ,a powerful… He suspended the thought, trying to analyze it. What was it he felt? He'd been thinking it was simply desire, but as she handed the cards to Alex and walked around the bed to straighten the blankets, he realized that it was more complex than that. It was…hunger. Yearning.

For a man who loved his family but who had always been self-sufficient, the admission was a difficult one to make.

She looked up and saw him standing in the doorway.

"We woke you," she said apologetically, lifting the blankets as Alex put the cards on his nightstand and crawled into bed. "I get too loud when I win."

Rio walked over to the bed, tucking in the blankets on the side closest to him. "I'm used to Alex's television. I just didn't know what to make of your empty room."

"Oh. Sorry." She smiled amiably. "Did you need me for something?"

It occurred to him at apparently the same moment it occurred to her that, considering the circumstances, that was a silly question. And even disregarding the circumstances, there was one obvious reason a man sought out a woman in the middle of the night.

That reason was very much alive in him at the moment. And growing livelier with each heartbeat.

But when Rio pulled up the blankets to Alex's chin and found the boy in tears, such thoughts were forgotten. Alex's crying jags occurred intermittently but often, and he should be used to them by now. Still, they wrenched his insides every single time.

Rio sat beside Alex and pulled him into his arms. He was aware of Millie going across the room to turn off the television, then hovering near him as though wanting to help, but not knowing how.

He rocked Alex and shushed him as he always did, telling him that everything would be all right, that it would get better, that one day soon it would hurt less.

"When you...lean over me," Alex said tearfully, "you look just like Dad."

"I know." Rio rubbed the boy's back. "I can see him in your face, too. It's good that we can be reminded of him, but it's hard not to have him, isn't it?"

"Yeah." Alex's reply was faint and raspy. "And Millie...doesn't look like my mom, but she...she kind of makes it feel like she's here."

Millie knelt on the floor and gazed up at the puffy face on Rio's shoulder. She stroked his hair off his forehead and kissed his cheek, knowing that reminding him of his mother was both good and bad. It might bring back happy memories, but it reminded him of his loss, too.

"Did your mom sing to you when she put you to bed?" she asked.

Alex sniffed. "Yeah. Sometimes. Sometimes she would read."

"Fairy tales?"

"No. Big books. We didn't get to finish *Treasure Island.*"

"Do you still have it?"

He pointed to the toy box under the window without lifting his head from Rio's shoulder. "It's in the bottom. Under the dump truck."

Feeling as though she was on the brink of a discovery that might change this destructive middle-of-the-night pattern, she scrambled to find the book.

Her hand closed over the cold cloth binding in the dark recesses of the chest. As she lifted it out, stuffed animals, small cars and odds and ends of games tumbled into its place.

"Here it is, Alex." She went back to the bed with the book, and sat facing Rio. "Where did your..." she began to ask, then quickly rephrased the question to, "How far did you get into the story?"

"The part where Jim falls asleep in the apple barrel." He pushed away from Rio's shoulder and sat up, sniffing. "But I don't want to read. I want the TV."

Millie caught Rio's eye over the boy's head. His expression was accepting. He'd apparently dealt with this many more times than she had.

But she wondered if he understood what it was all about.

"Why do you like the TV on at night, Alex?" she asked quietly.

"'Cause I like to stay up late."

"Don't you get sleepy?"

"Yeah." He looked at her, then at Rio, and his eyes welled with tears again and his mouth began to quiver. "But when I close my eyes...I can see them. I can hear my mom reading to me. I can feel my dad kiss me good-night." He choked on a sob and leaned against Rio again. "I want the TV, Uncle Rio."

"All right. Millie will put it on again."

She appeared to want to resist, but she finally put the book on the bedside table and turned the television on low. Rio moved the pillows aside and leaned against the headboard with Alex in his arms.

"I'll sit with him for a while," he told Millie. "Thanks for getting up with him."

"He's good company." She blew Alex a kiss. "Good night, sweetie," she said. "I'll see you in the morning."

Rio guessed she wasn't pleased with his handling of the situation. It *was* criminal to allow a child to be up at this hour, using television as a sleeping pill. Alex had to get on with his life. But pushing him faster than he was willing to mend could undermine the sense of security Rio was trying to provide. Hell, he himself was still in pain; it was easy to understand that the boy would still be.

Alex was asleep within twenty minutes. Rio sat there awhile longer, then eased him onto his pillows, covered him with the blankets and turned the television off.

Weary and depressed, he went back to his own room.

He crossed to the bed without turning on the light and was only alerted to another presence by the scent of gardenias. He looked down through the shadowy darkness to see that his bed was occupied. By Millie. He felt the same jolt of yearning he'd experienced earlier.

Could it really be that he wasn't alone in this hunger? Was it possible that she longed for him, as well as his money?

She sat up abruptly, as though she'd only been dozing, and reached for the lamp on the nightstand.

"Close the door," she whispered.

Not your traditional prelude to a night of passion. Still, that didn't have to negate what he hoped she'd come for.

He pushed the door closed.

In the pool of light from the lamp, he saw that she was sitting cross-legged on top of the covers. She patted the area of mattress just beyond her knees. That wasn't so bad....

But the hazel-eyed gaze she fixed on him had more censure in it than sex.

He allowed himself a private sigh.

He sat on the edge of the bed, angled sideways to face her, and tried honesty to forestall her voicing her poor opinion of his parenting. "I know," he said. "He shouldn't be allowed to watch TV in the middle of the night, but I understand his grief, and until you've dealt with a child whose world has been destroyed, I don't think you can understand how fragile he is."

She nodded, but her determination to take him to task apparently hadn't changed. "As it happens, Rio, I have. I dealt with three girls, and I did it twice—when our mother died and when their father died. And I can tell you with absolute certainty, that little boy's going to keep the hours of a vampire until he learns to say good-bye."

Rio looked into her gentle face and saw there for the first time the gritty strength that had brought her this far. He realized how little he knew about her, and yet how comfortably she'd fit into his life.

At least, his vacation life.

At least, until this moment.

"Who saw *you* through school?" he asked abruptly.

She looked startled by the question. "No one. Why? Don't tell me you require degrees for admin—"

"No, no." He cut her off with a swipe of his hand in the air. "I just wondered. You keep talk-

ing about having promised to get the girls
through college, but you never said how you
managed.''

"I didn't.'' She shifted, fussing with the front
of her T-shirt. "I was a sophomore at North-
western when my stepfather died. We had to
leave the house the church provided, so I had to
pay rent on an apartment and buy all the other
things a house filled with girls needs.'' She
smiled ruefully. "And you wouldn't believe
how much growing girls eat. I had to get a job.''

"So, if this happened seven years ago, the
girls were thirteen, twelve and eleven.''

"Right.''

He was amazed. As an adult male he occasionally found his emotional responsibilities to
Alex overwhelming. She'd been a girl of nineteen or twenty with three children to cope with.

"How did you keep your sanity?''

She laughed with real amusement. "I'm flattered that you think I have. Amy would quarrel
with you on that one.'' She sighed and sobered.
"I don't know. The girls all think I'm an alien
because I'm not artistic like they are. But the
advantage to that is that it doesn't occur to you
to agonize over things. You simply pick a course
of action and keep going until you get there.''

"So you made this promise to their father.''

"Yes.''

"How old were you when he married your
mother?''

She smiled. "Minus thirty days."

It was his turn to look startled. "You mean you weren't born yet?"

"Yes. Remember I told you in the elevator that she was pregnant and her parents—"

"Right," he interrupted. "I'm just curious about your relationship with your stepfather. I mean, if he was the only father you've ever known, why do you keep referring to him as the girls' father?"

"Because..." She seemed to draw into herself, fingers locking together and forming a knot at her chest. Deep in her eyes, beyond the strength and the determination, was pain. "He was never able to forget that I was another man's 'love child.' Even though he was the only father I ever knew, I don't think *he* felt like a father until Amy came along."

She shrugged and wrapped her arms around herself. "He was never directly cruel or even unkind, but I always understood that my place in his life was not as his daughter, but as big sister to his real children—to look after them and keep them safe while he was busy with his congregation." She studied the blanket they were sitting on, tracing a fingertip over a broad stripe. "It was weird, really. He adored my mother and seemed able to forgive her, if that's the right word, for having had me, but unable to forgive me for being there to remind him that she hadn't been exclusively his."

She sighed and unfolded her legs, letting one dangle over the side of the bed. "At least, I guess that was the problem. I was never really sure. My mother always tried to make up for what he couldn't give me, but she died when I was fourteen, and then I really became a sort of housekeeper/nanny. But by then I was old enough to understand that I loved my sisters and I *wanted* to be there for them. And their father was a fine minister, but like many men in that position, he was so busy, particularly after our mother died, that all his aid and comfort went to his congregation. So the girls needed me more than ever."

Rio and Millie studied each other in the circle of lamplight. He was astonished by her generosity and her strength. She seemed a little unsettled by the admissions she'd made and uncomfortable with his attention.

"But I wanted to talk about Alex," she said, sitting up straighter, apparently trying to establish a less intimate atmosphere. "I think the TV blots out memories he doesn't want to face."

Rio nodded. "I'd figured that out. But how do you make a child confront loss except to let him do it in his own time?"

"But he'll dodge it forever because it's hard and it hurts. Have you talked to him about his parents?" She hesitated a moment, then added carefully, "Or is it still too painful for you, too?"

It was, and he resented her for seeing it. He'd agreed to bring her here because he'd thought her presence might be diverting, fun. Not because he wanted to deal with old demons.

"I loved my brother very much," he said somewhat stiffly, "and his wife was a great friend. Of course it hurts." He stood, feeling restless and unaccountably angry. He went to the French doors that led onto the courtyard and pushed them open, standing in the doorway with a hand against them, dragging in a breath of clean desert air. "We'll both get over it," he said finally. "It's just a slower process for those of us who don't take that direct route you talked about."

Then to his complete consternation, he felt her hand on his outstretched arm as she came up behind him. She tugged on it gently, pulling it down so she could stand beside him. "He won't get over it," she said, "until he knows you can." She took his hand between her two and stroked it. "I'm sorry. I know I'm butting in, but in this situation, it's hard to know where to draw the line. So I guess it's up to you."

Still edgy, he stepped out into the night, bringing her with him. The stars were bright, and the air carried the fragrant mysteries of the wandering desert breeze. The night was as warm as bathwater.

"I don't want to talk about death anymore," he said, leading her to a plush padded chaise by the pool. He stopped at the foot of it and looked down into her upturned face. Her eyes reflected the big desert moon. "I want to know what you're thinking now about your decision."

Millie didn't have to consider which decision. It was the one that found her at two o'clock in the morning under a bright moon that hung over the Sangre de Cristo Mountains—in the arms of a very special millionaire.

His expression was a potent combination of anger and desire, an alliance she wouldn't have believed possible until this moment.

He wanted *her* but he didn't understand why, and that upset him.

At this point she didn't understand a lot herself. Her knack for analyzing, coordinating, planning seemed to have fled. So it was easy to empathize.

She looped her arms around his neck with no plan of what to do next. She only knew she had to be body to body with him. She didn't stop to consider that straining up on tiptoe and reaching for his mouth with hers would lead him to believe she was willing to go where this night seemed inevitably to be leading.

She didn't try to coordinate thought to action. She simply did what she felt like doing. And that was kiss him, touch him, hold him.

"I think...I was brilliant in selecting you," she said against his mouth as he held her to him and nibbled on her bottom lip. "How do you feel...about saying yes?"

His breath was warm against her face as his lips wandered over her cheek, as he planted kisses along her jaw and over her throat. "I was equally brilliant," he whispered.

She felt the relief of rightness. She'd proposed to him for the sake of her sisters, but during the past week she'd come to see that life with him would do as much for her as for the girls. He was kind, considerate, funny and warm. And before he'd come into her life, she'd been on the receiving end of very few of those qualities.

She'd been right. This was destiny.

His hand went up under the back of her T-shirt, and he placed his warm palm against her flesh. Even as sexual sensation began to radiate out from his touch, she experienced a sense of instant and utter security.

His hand seemed to claim her. And surprisingly she felt no threat to her personal independence in that admission.

Then his hand followed the line of her spine, stroking, exploring, moving gently but possessively over her skin.

He nipped at her earlobe and whispered, "Are you protected?"

She leaned back to smile into his eyes. "Physically, yes. But emotionally I think I'm in trouble."

He kissed her quickly, gently, his eyes dark with intensity. "No, you're not. Trust me."

Then he pulled her shirt off and tossed it near the chaise.

His hands closed over her small breasts and she felt his tenderness and possession all the way to her heart. She shuddered against him and tugged at the belt of his robe.

Loosening the knot, she parted the sides. He was naked underneath.

He wrapped his arms around her and pulled her to him, crushing her against him so that she felt as though they'd dissolved into each other and become some new entity. As they stood entangled, she lost all sense of which limbs were hers, which flesh. She seemed to own all sensation.

Rio tipped his head back with a groan and she looked up to see moonlight on his face.

She pushed his robe off and planted a path of kisses across his chest.

Rio felt warmth begin to radiate from deep within. Warmth that had nothing to do with the fire raging in his groin. This was something apart from lust and passion, perhaps…rebirth?

Its effect was instant and overwhelming. He felt as though it had been dark for a long time. The night had been an enemy since Ramon and Margaret had died—and Alex's experiences with it had only underlined his own.

But now he was no longer alone in it. This

little sorceress, who'd charmed him into such an outrageous deal, was beginning to make him feel as though it was going to be a high-yield venture.

He straddled the chaise and sat back in it, Millie kneeling between his legs. He tugged at her shorts and pulled them off completely. Then he leaned back, bringing her with him.

She opened her mouth on his, swept her hands over his shoulders and chest, followed with her lips as she moved down his body, over the jut of his ribs, into the hollow of his belly. Then she rained gentle kisses even lower, and all thought disintegrated.

He said her name in a strangled whisper. She answered with his.

He pulled her up until she was astride him, his hands cradling the backs of her thighs. Then he entered her and she enfolded him, and life suddenly, finally made sense. Everything that had happened before, good and bad, had been intended to guide him to her—to this.

She moved above him in a shallow circle, running her hands along his arms as far as she could reach, leaning, straightening, little moans of pleasure on her lips.

He moved in counterpoint, pleasure rushing at him like a free-moving comet, and before he could form the thought that she was driving him to madness, the deed was done.

He burst within her, overpowered by the shudders that racked her and so racked him.

Millie heard her own gasps, felt the broadside blow of pleasure that she'd caught only glimpses of before.

He gripped her hands and she clung to his as the pleasure went on and on.

He finally pulled her into his arms and reached down for his robe to toss over them.

His world at last stabilized, Rio expected that feeling of rightness to dissolve, to allow him to attribute it to sensory overload and sentimentality.

But it remained, a radiant glow around the two of them that excluded the old loneliness and the emptiness of the night. Guilt, though, pushed for entry.

He tried to just abide with it as he always did, but now Millie was enclosed in this cocoon with him, and whatever he suffered, she suffered.

He tightened his grip on her and said quickly, before he could change his mind, "I'm responsible for Ramon's and Margaret's deaths."

She raised her head to look into his eyes. He saw the glow of happiness there edged aside by his admission. He felt even guiltier.

"What do you mean?" she asked gently.

"I was supposed to go to that meeting," he said. "But I was late coming back from Boston. I'd met a few college friends for dinner. They remembered that it was my birthday, so they invited some more friends I hadn't seen in years and dinner turned into a party, and when I looked up again, it was hours past the time I should have left for the airport.''

He felt her thumb rub across his cheekbone, but all he could remember was Ramon's impatience when he called him, his accusation that parties and headline-grabbing death-defying feats always meant more to Rio than business.

"It was an important meeting with a major supplier in New York,'' he told Millie. "I think it could have waited a day, but Ramon insisted on going in my place. Apparently Margaret wanted to go with him so she could do some shopping.''

Millie put her hands under his head and looked firmly into his eyes. "I'm sorry. I know how terrible it is to lose someone you love, but their deaths are not your fault.''

"Technically not, but actually—''

"Technically or actually,'' she interrupted. "The article said the plane had engine problems and it went down. Are you taking the blame for the engine problems?''

"The simple truth,'' he insisted, "is that if I'd been home on time, they wouldn't have died.''

"No,'' she said, "you would have. But apparently it was their time and not yours, and you're questioning God. We don't have the right to do that.''

He had to smile at that reasoning. "Yes, we do. We have the right to question everything."

She smiled in return. "Yes. Okay. But we're supposed to believe that He has our best interests at heart."

"Millie, Alex's parents are gone, and look at the state he's in."

"That's only at night, and probably because he's getting your vibes. You're burdened with guilt, and in his young mind, he probably thinks he shouldn't get over it if you can't."

He pulled her hands out from behind his head and kissed them. "That's reaching for an explanation if you ask me."

"Yeah, well, children always reach for explanations because the adult world is so complicated and confusing. After our mother died, Charity was convinced it was her fault because she'd gone to a friend's house to play. She was sure if she'd been home, it wouldn't have happened. But mother had a massive coronary, and nothing would have stopped it."

"Okay, but I'm not a child. I know—"

"You know that you loved your brother and sister-in-law, and losing them was inconceivable to you. But it happened. And because you want to make sense of something so terrible by finding a reason for it, you blame yourself. And guilt keeps them close to you because it haunts you every night. But your guilt haunts Alex, too, so you've got to get rid of it."

He gave a rueful grin. "You know, Millie, you really have a different slant on things. I'm not sure I can ever learn to look at life that way."

She kissed his chin. "Sure you can. You're already considering marriage to a woman who wants you for your money. Give me another couple of weeks and I'll have your brain completely skewed."

"The frightening part about that," he said with a laugh, "is that I'm comfortable with the idea."

"Good." She lay her head on his shoulder, nuzzled her nose into his neck and heaved a sigh. "'Cause I'm comfortable, too."

"Comfortable," Rio thought, didn't even begin to describe it.

Chapter Six

MILLIE HAD NEVER SEEN so many cigars outside of a tobacconist's. She'd come across a climate-controlled vault filled with them as she'd searched Rio's office for the inventory disk she needed to compare Fashion Central's jewelry-department figures with Beauregard's.

"Are you still working?" Rio's voice asked with mild impatience.

Millie looked around to find Rio standing there in khaki shorts and a Chicago Bulls T-shirt. He stopped in the middle of the room when he realized what she was doing. He frowned. "You need a smoke?"

She closed the door, a little embarrassed at having been found exploring his office. "I'm sorry," she said. "I was looking for a disk. Last night you said they were all in the office safe, and I looked at that door and thought..."

"It's all right," he assured her. He reached into the middle drawer of his desk, extracted a key, then fitted it into the bottom drawer of the oak file cabinet. But instead of the drawer opening, the false front of the drawer lifted up to reveal a safe. "This is where you'll find Fashion

Central records that aren't on the desk.'' Then he replaced the cabinet face without opening the safe. ''But you've done enough today. We're supposed to be on vacation, and every time I turn around you're at the computer.''

''*You're* on vacation,'' she corrected. ''The deal was that I would straighten out your computer's snafus in exchange for—'' She stopped. She wasn't sure what was wrong, but since they'd made love a week ago, she didn't seem to be able to say the word anymore.

''Money,'' he finished for her, apparently having no such difficulty. He shifted his weight and folded his arms. ''You were to do that if we agreed to get married. But I invited you here so that we could decide whether or not that was a good idea. And we can't do that if you're locked in the office all the time.''

Millie stared at her sandals. Since that night she felt as though she'd been blindfolded, spun around, then abandoned in an alien world. Everyone was unfamiliar, herself included, and she didn't know what to do.

Rio was no longer simply the very convenient bank account that would help her see her sisters through school. He was the tender and passionate lover who'd cleared away all her doubts about her sexuality in one delicious hour by the pool.

But since then, he hadn't come to her room,

and he hadn't invited her to his. He'd been kind and attentive, but almost...avuncular.

She'd spent the past few days keeping her distance from him, wondering if his behavior meant he'd been unimpressed with her performance, or if he felt the need to pull away from her enthusiastic and effusive reaction to him.

Either way, she concluded, casual sex with Rio was not for her, no matter what was at stake. She simply couldn't be casual about it. But she couldn't afford to lose him, either.

So she was putting together another plan.

"Well?" he prodded.

She went to the computer to save the work she'd done thus far. It also allowed her to turn her back to him so he couldn't see her sudden flush.

"I was thinking we should reevaluate the plan," she said, trying to sound calm. She typed in the command to merge files and save, watching the screen with exaggerated interest while the computer did its work.

Suddenly her high-backed office chair was spun around and Rio leaned over it—and her—his hands on the padded arms. His dark eyes were direct and questioning.

"Why do you say that?"

"Well..." Mercy. How did she put it into words without sounding ridiculous? "Do you think it's really working? I mean, on all... levels? It seems..."

She went on, but Rio didn't hear what she was saying. While women confounded most of his male friends, he'd always felt as though he understood them. Their wiles and schemes were the same maneuvers used in most boardrooms, only they applied them to relationships rather than business.

But Millie was a puzzle. He'd have sworn she'd come alive in his arms that night a week ago, but since then she'd avoided him, and now she seemed to be trying to tell him that their lovemaking *hadn't* been momentous?

He didn't believe it. And he'd never been one to dance around an issue.

"You're saying," he asked directly, "that our lovemaking didn't work for you?"

"No!" she denied with flattering speed and apparent conviction.

She tried to push him out of her way, needing desperately to get out of the chair. He held firm. "Then what is it?"

The muscles in his arms stood out as he gripped the chair, and she knew she couldn't move him until he was willing to be moved. So she subsided and prepared to sell her new plan.

"Actually," she said, "I have a better idea."

He studied her without comment for a moment, then straightened and leaned back against the table behind him. He was clearly skeptical.

"Better than making love?"

She shook her head. "Rio, look," she said

frankly, "I'm trying to save you from gushy feelings."

"You're succeeding very well. But why? I thought feelings were part of the deal."

She frowned at his lack of understanding. "Sex was part of the deal. Feelings...aren't wise in a relationship that isn't destined to endure."

"So, you're talking sex without feelings."

"Yes."

"Then, how come I'm not getting either?"

She pushed out of the chair as though she'd been launched and prowled restlessly around the office, from the French doors to the desk, then off at an angle to a wall of books. "Because...I don't seem to be able to give you one without the other," she admitted, her back to him as she seemingly perused titles. "That's something I hadn't suspected when I proposed."

Rio went to stand behind her. "You're presuming that *I* want sex without feelings."

She turned to face him, her eyes turbulent with complex emotions. "I proposed to you for your money," she said. "Would you ever believe me now if I claimed...love?"

He measured her with a look, then asked carefully, "Are you?"

She opened her mouth as though to reply, but simply stared at him for a long moment of indecision, her lips parted, words he couldn't quite decipher brimming in her eyes.

He stood quietly, resisting an impulse to shake an answer out of her.

She finally walked around him to the climate-controlled vault and opened it. "Actually I have an idea that might take both of us off the hook. May I have one of these? They're supposed to be soothing, aren't they?"

"Ah…" Rio followed her to the vault, trying to hold up his end of what was promising to be a life-altering conversation while still protecting the contents of his stash. "You smoke?"

"Not yet," she replied, pulling out a box of Estrellas and frowning at them. "What are these? What does 'CR' mean?" She picked one up and sniffed it, then made a face. "Smells like tar."

"That's an Estrella Negra," he said, taking the black corona from her, putting it back in the box and replacing it. "CR stands for Contigo Royale. Contigo is my mother's family name. That blend is a little rough to start with. Why do you want to do this?"

"*Cigar Aficionado* said you like to relax with a cigar and a brandy. And I want to relax."

"If you don't smoke, you shouldn't start. A good cigar can seduce you. And you don't want to get hooked on these. The family's out of the smokes business and turning the land to other things."

She was unimpressed with his caution. "*You* ignore the danger." She reached for another box and added almost absently, "Or do you just like to flirt with it?"

Not sure he wanted to get into that, he gently swatted her hand away and reached overhead to the box he kept on hand for his mother.

He opened the cedar box of Magdalenas and offered it to Millie. She selected one and put it to her nose. This time she smiled, looking surprised. "Coffee and cinnamon?"

"Very good." Rio replaced the box, took out an Estrella for himself, closed the locker and with a hand on Millie's back, guided her to his desk. He gestured at the Magdalena. "My grandfather named that blend after my mother when she was a little girl. You're sure you want to do this? Even a mild cigar can upset your stomach when you're not accustomed to—"

He stopped because she'd put the cigar to her ear and was rolling it between her thumb and first two fingers. Her ingenuous concentration made him weak with a strange combination of lust and tenderness.

"Leslie Caron did this in *Gigi*," she said, frowning. "What was she listening for?"

"Freshness." He took the cigar from her and put the tip of it to the clipper on his desk. He handed it back to her. "If it crackles, it's old. But you want to hold any cigar delicately and handle it as little as possible."

"Don't we have to take the band off?"

"Matter of choice. But if you do, wait until

the cigar is lit and warmed up. That loosens the glue so you don't disturb the wrapper.'' When she looked puzzled, he said, ''The outer leaf.''

''Ah.'' She held the Magdalena daintily and put it to her lips. ''Okay. Light me.''

He picked up the lighter off his desk, then hesitated, a little concerned about her embarking on this experiment.

''You know *how* to smoke?'' he asked, sitting on the edge of his desk. That placed them on the same eye level.

The weakness he'd felt a moment ago now seemed to deepen as she took the cigar out of her mouth and unconsciously moved in closer. ''Breathe in, blow out?''

He was sure this would prove interesting. ''Sort of, but take it easy. Breathe too deeply and you'll knock yourself out, but you have to puff to get it going.''

He flicked on the lighter and she leaned into the flame. Then she tossed her head back and puffed valiantly. In a moment the tip burned red.

''Okay, okay,'' he said, clipping the tip off his own cigar. ''Easy now.''

She blew out, then coughed for several seconds. When she stopped, her eyes were watery and her face pale.

''You okay?'' he asked.

She nodded, slapping her chest. ''Think so. It tastes a little like coffee.'' She coughed again and studied the tip of the cigar. "Coffee that's been made in a potting shed."

He lit his Estrella and led Millie to the leather sofa. "You'll get used to the taste in a few minutes. Just go slow. Come on."

She took another puff with less dramatic results. She coughed only once. "We have to have cognac."

"Right." He saw her seated, then placed his cigar in the marble ashtray on the coffee table and crossed to the liquor cabinet for a bottle of Hennessey and two glasses.

He sat beside her, poured and handed her a glass. He smiled to himself when she hooked the cigar in her index finger and slipped the bowl of the snifter between the middle fingers of her other hand.

He clinked the rim of his glass to hers. "To deals made in elevators."

She didn't drink, but studied him warily over the rim of her glass.

"That's what I wanted to talk about," she said.

He felt an instant and surprisingly powerful fear. "I thought you wanted to relax," he said. If she was going to try to back out, he hoped to forestall or at least confuse her.

"I wanted to relax," she said clearly and patiently, "so we could talk."

He turned toward her, dragging on the cigar. The rough woody flavor filled his nostrils, but it didn't relax him. But then, there was more at stake here than even a Contigo Royale could deal with.

She took a deep sip of cognac, grimaced, then drew a breath. She opened her mouth to speak, seemed to change her mind and dragged on the cigar. She didn't cough, but she shifted uncomfortably.

"I was thinking—" she cleared her throat "—that we could bypass the whole marriage thing. You could just...lend me the money for the girls' tuitions, and I could pay you back by giving you twenty hours of overtime a week." Her voice grew quicker and more urgent as she continued. "I've gone over Fashion Central's whole system, and I know I can input Beauregard's programs and make everything work more smoothly. I can even merge the two so you can have an overall picture. Unless there's a reason you really need them separate—"

"Whoa," he said quietly.

She stopped, took another sip of cognac and another pull on the cigar.

"What about the TV show?" he asked.

"I'll just...tell them I failed."

He drew on his cigar, playing for time. "I looked into it," he said finally, "and we're talking about well over one hundred thousand dollars when you consider all three girls. Charity still has a full three years to go. And what if one of them wants to go to graduate school?"

Millie paled.

Rio tried to avoid any betrayal of satisfaction. He sipped at the cognac. "Even considering overtime, do you have any idea how long it would take you to pay me back?"

It had been a rhetorical question, but having come to know her accountant's mind, he should have known better than to ask.

"At standard interest, over ten years," she replied. She put the glass down and considered the cigar with a worried expression.

Rio guessed she was less worried about the cigar than the notion of spending ten years of her life working an extra twenty hours a week. So he eliminated it as an option.

"I'm sorry," he said. "It should only take you a few months to convert Fashion Central's system to Beauregard's."

"But I could do other work," she offered hurriedly.

"You don't want me to eliminate someone else's job so you can work overtime, do you?" he asked, his expression blandly innocent.

"No," she replied grimly. "Of course not."

"Then we'd better stay with the current plan. Only we'll readjust to a little less work on the computer and more time spent on my second demand."

Her complexion had a greenish tinge, and her eyes were wary. "But if I'm feeling things that weren't in the deal, and you're still considering whether or not to marry me..."

He wasn't sure of anything at this point except that after two weeks with her, he didn't think he could be without her. Even if she was mistaking love for gratitude, he'd take it.

He put down his glass and slipped the band with its red-and-gold Contigo Royale logo from his cigar. He pushed the band onto the third finger of her left hand.

"There's a *C* for Camille," he said, pointing to the flourished initial in the logo. "And an *R* for Rosario. Ours must be an old destiny."

Then he kissed the hand he held. "Camille?" he asked. "Will you marry me?"

Her head moved frantically, and for a moment he couldn't determine if it was a nod or a no.

He concluded a moment later that it was neither as she turned very green, put a hand to her mouth and ran from the room.

Chapter Seven

RIO PULLED the Infinity into a parking spot in a trendy mall built to simulate a pueblo. He parked, then walked around the car to open Millie's door.

"I told you I am not going diamond shopping," she said firmly, folding her arms to underline her words, "and that's final."

Rio squatted down beside her seat, the bright rays of the sun putting highlights in his hair. The glint in his eye, she knew, came from stubbornness.

"And I told you that we're going diamond shopping if I have to carry you into the store."

"And I told you I didn't want anything for me," she insisted.

"Right." He reached for her left hand that still sported the cigar band he'd placed there that morning. "But you also told me you have to flash an engagement ring on that TV show."

She drew her hand back, instinctively protecting the band with her other hand. "We'll show them this. They'll probably think it's charming." As she had. God. She was in love! In love. That changed everything. Considering the way she'd made no bones about needing Rio's money, a declaration of love from her now would sound manipulative—as though she'd changed her mind about not wanting anything for herself and was going for an even share.

"It's not too late to decide to give me the loan," she said hopefully. She didn't want to leave him, but this arrangement was now fraught with pitfalls. If she could get out of it, she could approach him simply as woman to man.

But as he reached in to scoop her out of the car, she saw the giant flaw in the alternative plan.

If he were just to lend her money, words of love from her would still sound like manipulation—even if they weren't engaged.

He rolled his eyes. "You're not going to be one of those women who nags, are you?"

She wrapped her arms around his neck and leaned her forehead against his cheek. "No," she said wearily. To herself, she added, *I'm going to be one of those women who loves.*

He bought her a two-karat marquis-cut diamond in a simple setting and insisted she remove the cigar band. He then sent her out to look at sundresses in the window of the shop next door while he had the jeweler replace the battery in his watch.

Gilford had taken Alex to the mall's video arcade, then shopping with his allowance. Rio and Millie met them at the glass elevator that took them to the Mexican restaurant on the third level.

"Look what I got!" Alex said excitedly, waving a videotape of *Toy Story* in Millie's face as they waited to be seated. "It's my favorite movie! Gilly had to give me a loan."

Rio frowned at his butler as a hostess in a colorful skirt and peasant blouse led them to a table.

Gil shrugged. "You'd have held fast against his excitement, I'm sure," he said dryly.

"This kid had all these toys!" Alex told Millie as he slipped into her side of the booth before Rio could. "And they all got together to save this other toy from this mean kid next door who chopped 'em up and made these robot things." He smiled at her. "You know, the toy store has a Buzz Lightyear doll you can buy."

"Really." She grinned at Rio, then feigned interest in the menu. "But do I need a Buzz Lightyear doll?"

Alex gave her a look that told her he knew he was being teased. "I meant for me."

"Oh." She pretended that was news. "You mean in case your other toys need to be rescued from the mean neighbor boy."

"Yeah."

"Our nearest neighbors," Rio pointed out gravely, "are a mile away. And they have two girls."

Alex narrowed his eyes at his uncle. "Girls are even meaner."

"Ah...I'd be careful what I said about girls," Rio cautioned, "especially if you're asking one to buy you something." He indicated Millie with an inclination of his head.

Alex turned to her as she reached over to push his glass of water out of danger, and he noticed her ring.

"Wow!" He caught her hand and moved it so that the facets of the diamond flashed. He smiled at his uncle, then at her. "This means you *are* getting married."

"Yes, it does," Rio confirmed.

Gilford offered quiet congratulations.

"So, are you my aunt or my mom?" Alex wanted to know.

Millie considered that. A glance at Rio was no help. He, too, seemed to be waiting for her answer.

"I guess I'm whichever one you want," she said finally.

The boy leaned toward her and asked with a little smile of apology, "Would you want to be my mom even if I don't want to forget my other one?"

She hugged him to her and kissed the top of his head, giving herself time to swallow the lump in her throat. "Of course I would. And my first official act will be to buy you Buzz Light-year right after dinner."

RIO AND MILLIE argued in a corner of the toy store while Alex gazed at his boxed toy with great excitement. Gilford was busy selecting batteries.

"I want to buy it," Millie said firmly but under her breath, "and I do not want to argue about it."

Rio caught her left hand and held it up in front of her face. "We're engaged to be married. That means we share. That doll's a lot of—"

"No, it doesn't," she interrupted him. "It means I sign a prenuptial agreement and pay for my own stuff!"

"You," he said, giving the wrist he held a shake, "are obsessed with the damned agreement. Okay, buy the doll, because I don't want Alex's excitement dimmed by your neurotic behavior, but when we're home, we're having this out."

"Fine." She yanked her hand away from him and went to the counter, forcing a smile for Alex and the clerk.

WHILE ALEX RAN around the courtyard, Buzz Lightyear held aloft on some secret mission, Millie and Rio argued in the living room. It was decorated in subtle Southwest-sunset colors. Millie was curled in a corner of the plump sofa. Rio, hands in his pants pockets, leaned a shoulder against the molding and watched his nephew through the French doors.

Gilford had diplomatically retired to his rooms across the courtyard.

"I know you're really into keeping books," Rio said, turning away from the doors to look at her, "but this house is not a corporation."

"The deal…" she began stubbornly.

He was across the room in an instant and seated beside her, one hand braced against the back cushion as his body pressed her farther into her corner.

"I hereby dissolve the damned deal!" he snapped in exasperation. "If I hear you quote the terms one more time, I'm transferring you to the shipping department of the store in Nepal!"

"There is no store in Nepal," she said, her throat going dry. His threat was pure nonsense and her denial completely unnecessary, but any threat to the…arrangement rattled her.

He leaned aggressively closer. "I'll build one," he said, "just to be able to send you there."

She began to pull herself together. "You can't dissolve the deal. *I* initiated it."

"Doesn't matter who initiated it. Without me you don't have a deal."

She struggled to think, to prevent her sisters' futures from collapsing. "You just paid an enormous sum of money for a ring."

"That was for an engagement, not a deal."

"Our engagement," she said anxiously, without pausing to think, "was part of the de—"

She stopped, but not in time to prevent most of the word she'd been cautioned not to use from slipping out.

Before she knew it, he was on his feet and marching across the room, and she was being dragged after him. Considering his mood and the lack of a store in Nepal, she was more than a little worried about the retribution he intended. Alex, she noticed, had gone to his room. Her demise would not be witnessed.

Rio strode with her out to the courtyard, stopping on the rim of the high end of the pool. He swept her up in his arms.

She locked her fingers around his neck. "No!" she screamed.

She closed her eyes, expecting to be flung out and into the pool at any moment. "Give me one good reason why not."

"Because I'll get revenge!" she threatened. "You'll always be looking over your shoulder, wondering when it'll happen. You'll never have a peaceful moment."

He dismissed her threat with a laugh. "I never have one now. You fill my vacation with studies and reports and argue with me at every turn. You steal my cigars—"

"You gave it to me," she said.

"Because you were snooping and found my stash."

"I wasn't snooping, I was—"

"Working. I know. Equally offensive." He

made as though to pitch her away from him. The smell of chlorine wafted up, but she held fast.

"No! Wait! We must be able to reach some kind of a de— No! I mean an agreement! A...a...treaty!"

He bounced her once in his arms to resettle her. "I don't think you'd be any better at a treaty than you are at a deal. Your accountant's mentality is forever keeping score, making sure everything stays in its neat little column, concentrating on the fine print and losing all sight of the big picture."

She blinked, honestly confused. "What do you mean? I don't want to take things from you because I don't want you having to spend more..." She hesitated over the word.

"Money," he put in for her a little defensively.

"Money," she repeated thinly, "than you have to because then—"

"Because then," he interrupted, "I might expect more from you than you agreed to give."

"I agreed to give..." Another word she had difficulty saying to him.

"Sex," he provided.

"Sex," she repeated, and swallowed.

"What if I want feelings, as well? What if I want love?"

Everything was suddenly quiet in the encroaching dusk except for the subtle sounds of insects and the lap of water in the pool.

"Then," she whispered, her heart pounding, "you won't get that from me by giving me..."

"Money."

"Yes."

"But you're deliberately staying too far away for me to give you anything else."

Emotion boiled inside her. "I thought...you'd prefer some distance," she confessed. "I didn't think you'd want to know that I was..."

"Yes?"

"Falling..."

"Falling where?" When she hesitated, he made as though to drop her. "Into the pool?"

The look in her eyes loved and rebuked him at the same time. It was so warming, so...telling, that he knew he had her.

"In love," she said, tightening her grip on him, pressing her lips into his neck, then pulling away to adore him with her gaze. "Oh, Rio. This can't happen, can it? I mean...the way we approached it?"

He kissed her soundly. "Of course it can. You're the one who explained it to me in the beginning. It's destiny."

Chapter Eight

"I THINK...IF A MAN declares, ah, his love for a woman," Millie said as Rio kissed her throat, "it's illegal for him to...to toss her in a pool."

He raised his head to look into her eyes. His own were filled with love and amusement. "Well, that's why you're an accountant and not a lawyer. As long as he dives in after her to make love to her, it's within the law."

Everything inside her ignited with the possibility that he intended to do just that.

"Uncle Rio?"

Alex's voice broke their single-minded concentration on one another. Rio smiled ruefully. "Don't think this means you escape your fate," he warned Millie quietly. He set her on her feet and turned to his nephew.

"Yeah, Alex?" His gaze narrowed when he saw Alex standing in the open French doors of his bedroom wearing his Cowboy Bob pajamas. He had Buzz Lightyear tucked under one arm, and Rio noticed with a lurch of his heart that the boy had a book in his other hand. *The* book. He heard Millie's intake of breath. "You ready for bed already?"

"Yeah."

The sadness that usually filled Alex's eyes at bedtime was missing. In its place was a heavy-lidded weariness that filled Rio with parental concern.

He crossed the space between them and lifted Alex into his arms. "You okay?" He put a hand to the boy's forehead, half teasing, half diagnostic. "You and Buzz didn't get space sickness, did you?"

Alex laughed. "I'm just sleepy." He held his book out to Millie, who stood beside Rio. "Will you read to me?"

Rio caught her eye, his concern for Alex turning to hope.

"Yes." Her voice was raspy and a little high. "You bet."

The rocket-shaped bedside lamp was on, spilling light across Alex's bed. Rio placed him against the pillows, then pulled up the thin blanket that was all the warm night required.

Alex patted the edge of the bed. "Millie has to sit here," he directed. When she'd complied, he pointed behind her to the foot of the bed. "And you have to sit there, Uncle Rio, and watch us."

"All right." His throat tight, Rio sat where he'd been directed.

"Do you want me to start the story at the beginning?" Millie asked, smoothing Alex's hair off his forehead.

"No," he replied. "I know that part. I want to see what happens next."

Rio watched and listened in awe and gratitude as Alex, after a year of dark grief, resumed his life with the same quiet grace with which Millie resumed the story of *Treasure Island.*

Alex was asleep by the third page, exhausted from the long months of fighting his loss.

Millie read several more paragraphs, then, certain he was asleep, stood and turned to Rio, her eyes brimming with tears. He took the book from her, placed it on the bedside table and turned off the light.

Alex slept on as they left the room and closed his door.

They held each other in the dark and quiet corridor.

"What happened?" Millie whispered tearfully. "I don't understand."

"I'm not sure." Rio kissed her forehead and tightened his arms around her. "Must have been you. He's not missing his mother's voice anymore now that he has yours."

She kissed Rio's throat. "Maybe he was just ready. I guess the true test will be what he does if he wakes up during the night."

"I guess it will. But for now—" Rio pushed Millie away from him, then bent to put a shoulder under her stomach, hoist her up and carry her off.

She squealed a protest, then, remembering the

boy behind the closed door and the butler across the courtyard, stifled the sound with her hand. "What are you doing?" she demanded in a loud whisper as he crossed the corridor to his bedroom.

He dumped her onto the bed.

She landed with a bounce, which he stopped by leaning over her and kissing her. He straightened abruptly and unbuttoned the sundress she wore. "We were discussing the laws governing women and pools," he reminded her, "but we never reached a conclusion."

He stood, pulled her to her feet and pushed the dress off her shoulders. When it dropped to her waist, he stopped long enough to pull her to him and run his hands over her silky skin.

She leaned into him, feeling a wild new freedom she'd never before experienced. Sensation flashed everywhere he touched, then turned her spine to jelly when he slipped his hands inside her panties and drew them and her dress down.

She kicked them aside and quickly helped divest him of T-shirt, shorts and briefs.

He held her another moment and she clung to him, realizing that this was the first time in her life that she'd felt truly secure. She'd always been self-sufficient, but that wasn't the same as knowing there was someone to turn to if she was ill or tired or if she failed. And strangely, the concepts of freedom and security somehow allied seemed at once paradoxical but comfortable.

"I love you," she said. "And you better love me or we'll be talking about the laws governing *men* and pools."

"Oh, really," he challenged with a grin. "You think you can carry me out to the pool and toss me in?"

"No." She walked toward the French doors and held out her hand. "But I think I can offer you my hand and a come-hither look and you'll be helpless to resist me."

Naked and splendid, he went to her and put his hand in hers. "You're absolutely right."

There were no laws governing pools or men or women, Millie decided later as she and Rio floated across the water, gently propelled by his arms and her feet, their bodies intimately connected.

The stars watched and the heady fragrance of the high-desert night stirred around them as they drifted on their water bed. The night became an unfettered universe completely without restriction.

Millie felt as bound to Rio as if they were tied together, yet she experienced for the first time her absolute individuality. She wasn't a daughter, a big sister or a chief accountant. She was simply and profoundly Camille—a woman.

Rio had never known such exhilaration or such peace. It occurred to him that they were elements that shouldn't coexist in such harmony, much less combine, and yet they did.

As pleasure took control of him, he covered Millie's mouth with his and wrapped his arms around her, causing them to sink into the warm water and down to the bottom of the pool.

She lay quietly in his arms, and he held her there for a moment, enjoying the solitude, the elemental perfection of the silent environment.

Then he put a foot to the bottom of the pool and pushed upward, bursting with her from the water like some new life-form.

She surfaced smiling, her eyes filled with love for him, and he couldn't imagine being happier than he was at that moment.

MILLIE OPENED HER EYES to brilliant sunshine. Morning. And she hadn't awakened to Alex's television during the night. She sat up with a start, turning to Rio and finding a vast and empty expanse of bed. Then she remembered. He'd said he had something to do in the morning.

She pulled on the clothes she'd discarded the night before and ran across the hall to Alex's room. It was empty.

Hurrying to the kitchen, she found Alex seated at the table, working on an enormous waffle drenched in syrup. The boy looked up at her and smiled. "Hi! How come you slept so late? Uncle Rio's been gone for ages."

Millie went to sit across the table from him. "Did *you* sleep well?" she asked gently.

"Yeah," he said. "When I woke up, Gilly

was already cooking breakfast, and he said I couldn't go into the pool until you were up. I think there's a problem in the laundry room.''

All Millie heard was that he'd slept. "So you didn't wake up during the night?''

He cut a wedge of waffle with his fork. "Yeah,'' he said. "Once.''

"What did you do?''

Alex looked at her, obviously puzzled. "I went to the bathroom.'' He stuffed the piece of waffle into his mouth.

So it hadn't been a false hope. Alex *was* resuming his life.

Gilford emerged from the back of the house, his usually impeccable attire drenched, his thinning white hair wet and hanging in his face.

Millie got to her feet. "Gilford!'' she exclaimed. "What happened?''

"The washer, Ms. Brown,'' he replied, going to the phone. "I thought I could fix it, but I obviously overestimated my talents as a plumber.'' He consulted a business card on the corkboard above the phone and stabbed out a number.

"Gilly,'' Alex said, "you said to remind you about picking up Uncle Rio.''

"I know, I know.'' Gilford glanced at his watch. "But I've got gushing water. I'm afraid your uncle will have to wait.'' Gilford turned his attention to the phone as the plumber apparently answered.

"I can pick Rio up while you deal with the plumber," Millie said when he hung up.

"But you haven't even had your breakfast."

"I'll eat when I come back. Where is he, anyway?"

"The little airport outside of town." Gilford turned and hurried back toward the laundry room, Alex in pursuit.

MILLIE DROVE along the road, admiring the occasional piñon and juniper, her heart filled with excitement and the memories of her night with Rio.

The situation she now found herself in was like something out of a fairy tale. A miracle. She'd taken an outrageous chance in the interest of her sisters' futures and found her own future in the bargain.

Love and destiny bloomed in the damnedest places.

She hadn't had time to ask Gilford what Rio was doing at the airport—if he'd taken a brief flight, or if he was just checking on the plane to prepare for one—and she began to wonder where precisely to look for him.

As she drew closer, she saw that the convenient but little-used airport was crowded this morning. She pulled into a parking spot on the far end of the nearly full lot. As she stepped out, a plane flew overheard, dropping several colorful balls.

She looked up at them in amazement, heard a smattering of applause from the crowd gathered in the field just off the runway and watched as the balls plummeted. Suddenly each ball exploded into a parachute, and soon arms and legs were visible to the watcher on the ground. At last the chutists drifted onto the landing strip.

Millie felt a painful and urgent nausea. It was a skydiving meet. No. Rio wasn't skydiving. He couldn't be.

She went to the hangar where he kept his plane and found the aircraft there, but not Rio. She went to the small terminal and found it empty. Everyone was outside, watching the show.

She tapped the shoulder of a tall slender man with a badge that read Manager.

"Pardon me," she said, her throat tight, her heart thudding. "I'm looking for Rio Corrigan."

Without moving his eyes from the sky, the man pointed upward. "You're just in time. Here he comes."

She looked up to see another plane fly over, this time expelling two white balls. But these didn't plummet like the others. One of them seemed to twist and turn in the air, to move almost laterally, to turn and spin and dance.

The other managed to stay with him without doing the complicated moves.

"He and his cameraman were sky-surfing medalists in Rhode Island in '95," the man said.

"Second only to Birch and Greiner. Imagine what he could do if he really had time to give to it. Runs a big corporation, you know."

Everyone, she noticed, had turned their attention to a screen set up in the field. Apparently it transmitted the picture the cameraman captured as he followed Rio down.

Millie thought she was going to pass out. As she watched Rio's body turning and spinning, the manager gave her a running commentary.

"Offspin," he said.

Millie tore her eyes from the screen, unsure which was more difficult to watch—the close-up film of him doing sommersaults in midair or the distant speck whose moves she couldn't see clearly but knew was Rio falling.

"Backspin," the manager went on. "Barrel roll. Wow! Spinning rail grab." Then his eyes, too, went to the sky as the falling forms drew ever closer.

Millie didn't see the skill or the form of Rio's maneuvers but only the vastness of the sky through which he fell. She thought only of the unrelieved solidity of the earth that would receive him.

One shift of current, one tricky crosswind, one wrong move on his part, and the aerial ballet would become a testament to the simple law of gravity.

So. Last night he'd made love to her as though

she was everything to him, and this morning he was back to his old death-defying tricks.

Terror turned to outrage. But she couldn't move until she saw him do one final turn in the air, watched his chute open, then saw his smooth drift downward and his easy upright landing on the target painted on the runway.

The cheers and applause were raucous.

She marched back to the car, fury alive in her and heating every nerve ending.

RIO CONGRATULATED his cameraman, accepted the thanks of the director of the Desert Hospital for Children and declined an invitation to the party that followed.

He'd fulfilled the obligation he'd made months ago. Now all he wanted to do was go home to Alex and Millie and plan the details of the rest of their lives.

He scanned the crowd for Gilford and, when he didn't see him, checked the parking lot. Spotting the car, he headed for it, chute and gear slung over his shoulder.

Depositing them in the trunk, he pulled open the passenger door, apologizing as he climbed in.

"Sorry I'm late, Gilly. We were a little slow getting started, and the—"

He stopped when he confronted not Gilford's quiet gray eyes, but Millie's hazel ones. Her presence in the driver's seat pleased him, until he noticed that her gaze was lethal. For a moment he couldn't understand it.

"Hi," he said carefully.

She responded by backing out of the parking spot with a grinding of gears, followed by a stomp on the accelerator that propelled the car forward like a missile.

He put on his seat belt.

Like a man feeling his way in the dark, he probed for the source of her anger. "I told you before we went to sleep that I had an appointment this morning." He deliberately hadn't been specific about what it was, thinking he might even be back before she awoke. Most people didn't understand skydiving and sky surfing, and considered them foolish risks.

"So you did," she replied stiffly. "You just didn't mention that it was an appointment with death."

She'd been afraid for him. He found a certain unabashed male satisfaction in that. "It wasn't," he said, leaning forward to look into her eyes. He stretched out his arms. "See? I'm fine."

She sent him a glance that felt like a blow. "That's only because I haven't finished with you yet."

There was a moment of heavy silence. "This was a commitment I made months ago," he said reasonably. "Was there something else you wanted to…?"

"I think you made a decision to flirt with

death when Ramon and Margaret died,'' she said, turning with a squeal of tires onto the road that would take them home. "Why else would a man fall from the sky, tie himself to mountains with a rope, go over waterfalls in a boat and intrude on wild animals with a camera? I thought when you proposed to me that you'd dealt with your loss. But I guess not.''

He was beginning to grow impatient. He knew the entertainments he enjoyed were dangerous, but there was nothing psychological about it, and except for this morning, he hadn't indulged in any of them since he'd taken Alex on.

"I did all those things before Ramon died.''

"Why?'' she asked.

He spread both arms. "What do you mean, why? Because they're exciting, invigorating, liberating.''

"You like them because you're defying death,'' she argued. "I suppose when your brother was alive, you did them because men always have to outdo each other. Now you do them to show that, though you cheated death, you don't fear it. Well, maybe you protest too much.''

With her accusation flung in his face like that, he was forced to examine it and consider that it might be true. And that lit a fire under his own temper.

"I love you, Millie,'' he said, his voice barely controlled. "But when I proposed to you, it was because I wanted a wife, not a mother or a big sister. You're not here to tell me what I can safely do and what I can't. Unless you're concerned that I'll croak before you get your tuition money.''

She jerked to a stop on the side of the road, unbuckled her seat belt and turned. Then she slapped him across the face.

She gave it everything she had, but her eyes were brimming with tears.

An answering anger rose in him, but the need to respond was tempered by the genuine denial in that blow. Though her maternal attitude annoyed the hell out of him, she had truly been more concerned about him than his money.

She pulled into the driveway a moment later, swerving around a plumber's van. He wondered absently about it, but his concentration was riveted on keeping his cool.

The moment she switched off the ignition, she turned to him, her chin at a haughty angle. "No, I'm not here to tell you what to do," she said, her voice strained and angry. "I'm here because we made a deal. Apparently last night was just another death-defying game for you. Let's fly in the face of love and see how much we can scare ourselves!"

She stepped out of the car and slammed the door.

That was when he lost it. He hadn't bared his soul to her, made love to her with an intensity that had changed something in him so irrevocably that he'd never be quite the same again, to have her accuse him of playing games with her.

He caught her as she stormed toward the French doors and swept her up in his arms. She cried out and struggled against him, but he turned and headed for the pool.

"I told you not to mention that deal again," he warned as he marched resolutely across the flagstones. "But if I defy death, you defy love. You don't want to come out of your big-sister role because a lover has to share power, and you're too much of a control freak. Well, not this time, darling. Not this time."

Millie couldn't quite believe it when she was dropped into the water. As it closed over her like a warm wet blanket, she remembered the night before. Then, she'd been naked with him inside her as they'd drifted to the bottom of the pool.

Now she surfaced to find Alex bobbing beside her, his wet hair slicked back except for his stubborn cowlick. "Who are they?" he asked.

She forced herself to concentrate on his question. "Who? Where?"

"There," he said, and pointed.

Millie squinted against the morning sun to see three leggy redheads coming through the gate at the far side of the courtyard.

Oh, God, she thought, swallowing a mouthful of chlorinated water. Her sisters were here.

Chapter Nine

MILLIE TREADED WATER in panic. The dunking in the pool had doused her temper and made her realize that fear for Rio had caused her to react like a wild woman. She'd made some harsh accusations. She'd probably killed the deal.

Then she saw Rio, who'd apparently been heading back to the house when he noticed the girls' approach, change direction and intercept them halfway between the pool and the gate.

He was probably explaining to them right now that their tuitions had suffered a fatal setback.

"Who are they?" Alex repeated.

"They're my sisters," she said, swimming for the side of the pool. Alex followed.

She used the ladder while he managed to scramble up onto the side without it. They stood on the flagtones watching as each of the girls hugged Rio in turn, then clustered around him talking and giggling. He must have decided to leave the delivering of bad news to her.

Amy spotted Millie and came running. She hugged her before stepping back with an "Eyuw!" of disgust. "You're all wet. Why are you swimming in your clothes?"

At a complete loss, Millie opened her mouth, then closed it. Alex replied baldly, "Uncle Rio carried her to the pool and dropped her in!"

Millie was horrified to see envy for her and admiration for Rio in the eyes of the sisters to whom she'd carefully fed the principle that every female deserved and should demand respect.

Laughing, Pru and Charity also hugged her.

She introduced Alex and Gilford, whom she now realized had been sitting by the pool watching Alex do laps when Rio had tossed her in. He pretended to be oblivious to her drenched and bedraggled state.

"I suppose she got bossy," Pru said sympathetically to Rio. "She thinks her way is the only way. She's always been like that."

Charity shook her head. "I've wanted to throw her into the pool many times. But we don't have one."

"Well, you do now." Rio pointed to the gleaming water behind him. "You ladies had lunch?"

"No, we haven't," Amy said. "But we didn't—"

Gilford excused himself. "I'll put a salad together and see how the plumber's doing."

"Thank you, Gilford," Amy said. She smiled at Rio. "We didn't intend to impose on you. We just wanted to make sure Millie was okay and—" she put an affectionate arm around Millie, unmindful this time of her sister's clothes ''—that you were okay for her. We didn't know much about you except for that magazine article, and, well, she'd do almost anything for us, and we wanted to make sure she wasn't doing something...you know...awful.''

Millie saw respect in Rio's eyes for their concern. ''Makes perfect sense to me,'' he said.

''How did you get here?'' Millie asked, feeling some of her instincts and brain function returning.

''We drove,'' Amy said. ''We have a week's break between camp schedules.''

''All the way from Chicago?'' Millie demanded. ''Alone?''

''Alone?'' Charity repeated. ''Hell*o-o*. There are three of us.''

''With not one brain or one dose of common sense among you,'' Millie replied, all the horror stories she'd ever heard of young women accosted on the highway coming to mind. She flung out a hand to help make her point. ''I've told you over and—''

''Geez!'' Charity exclaimed, grabbing the hand. ''Talk about a piece of the rock!''

Her sisters closed in to look at her ring, and Millie groaned.

''How long can you stay?'' Rio asked, interrupting their ingenuous admiration.

''We didn't intend to stay.'' Amy hugged Millie to her again. ''We just wanted to look in on Millie, make sure you weren't bad for her, then do some sight-seeing on the way home.''

Rio shook his head. "Well, I have to agree with Millie that I'm not wild about your driving around on your own. As for sight-seeing, there's enough to see around here to keep you busy for a few days. And I'd like some time to get to know you, too.''

"It'll take us two days to drive back,'' Pru said.

Rio dismissed that. "I'll have my plane take you back and have someone drive your car. Then you can stay until the last minute. I'm sure Millie would prefer that.''

The girls' eyes widened in astonishment.

"Your...plane?'' Charity asked in a small voice.

"Right.'' Rio put a hand on Alex's shoulder. "Will you take the ladies to the table and entertain them while Millie and I get changed?''

Alex blushed. "Sure.''

"Good. Then after Millie's had time to catch up on how you girls have been, we'll bring your luggage inside and get you comfortable.''

"Excellent,'' Pru said breathlessly.

Millie saw all three pairs of eyes focus meltingly on Rio as he placed a proprietary arm around her shoulders and drew her toward the house.

"Thank you,'' Millie said stiffly when Rio pulled her into her bedroom and closed the door.

"I appreciate your being nice to them. It never occurs to them to call and let anyone in on their plans."

He walked off as she spoke, and she thought for a moment that he was ignoring her. But he came out of her bathroom with a fluffy yellow towel.

He slapped it into her hands, his manner cool despite the gesture. "Not a problem," he said. "I understand their concern."

He turned to leave the room, but she stopped him with a hand on his arm. "Rio."

He turned back to her, his expression carefully neutral. "Yes?"

"I'm sorry about what I said." Her throat tightened. She'd grown so close to him that this sudden wall between them shaded her whole world. She'd *known* this wasn't wise, that a simple loan would have been safer, but he wouldn't listen. "It was terrifying to see you falling from the sky."

"I was in complete control," he returned stiffly.

She struggled against a resurgence of anger. "You were lucky," she insisted, "that nothing went wrong."

"Oh," he said with feigned lightness, "so since I didn't get hurt, you thought you'd rough me up a little to show me what *could* have happened?"

She dropped her hand and let her anger rise, though this time she controlled it.

"I won't apologize for that. It was a rotten thing for you to say and completely uncalled for. Do you want to apologize for throwing me in the pool?"

"No," he replied, hands going to his pockets as though he was afraid he might be tempted to do it again. "You're a stuffy judgmental little know-it-all sometimes, and a good argument for the return of the dunking stool."

She marched past him and yanked open her bedroom door so that he would leave. "I'd like to get dressed."

"While you're doing it," he said, stopping directly in front of her and looking over her features one by one, "don't forget to put on some manners."

He walked out and she slammed the door after him.

PRETENDING EVERYTHING was storybook happiness between her and Rio was particularly painful for Millie because she got to see up close what a wonderful family the six of them would have made.

As Rio showed the girls the sights—the galleries and studios of Taos, the historical and magical structures of the Taos Pueblo—and took them shopping in Santa Fe, Millie had never seen them so happy.

And she thought she understood what made the difference.

Though their father had genuinely loved them, his attention had always been directed toward his congregation; the responsibility for the girls' safety and happiness had always been in female hands—first their mother's, then Millie's. They'd seldom had a guiding male arm around them, a strong male voice to warn them of danger, gentle masculine laughter to join with their own.

And Rio seemed to be making a point of getting to know the girls and making sure that each of them had a say in the day's activities.

In Taos he'd lingered with Charity when she'd been awed by a particular artist's studio, and he'd asked Gilford and Alex to see that the other girls got to visit what interested them.

In Santa Fe he'd taken Amy to visit a writer he knew while everyone else went shopping, and when they'd all met up again at dinner, she'd been so excited she'd talked for hours.

He'd gotten tickets for everyone to attend a production of *Lost in Yonkers* staged by a well-respected theater company and arranged for Pru to go backstage and meet the actors. Pru hadn't slept all night.

Unable to sleep herself because the arrival of the girls had required that Millie sleep in Rio's bed—unpleasant business when they weren't touching—she had found Pru by the pool at three o'clock in the morning.

"Betsy Richards," Pru said as they sat on the rim of the pool and dangled their feet in the still-warm water, "you know, the actress who played Bella?"

Millie nodded and Pru went on, "She told me..." Pru gasped and put a hand to her forehead. "I still can't believe this, but she told me that if I could come down at spring break next year and audition, they might be able to find a role for me in their summer company."

She hugged Millie, tears in her voice. "Can you imagine? Me, Pru Brown, in a theater company! I can't believe it! Thank you, Millie."

"But, I..." Millie struggled with the knowledge that she should warn Pru that she wasn't sure of the outcome of this engagement. At the moment it didn't look good. But she couldn't find it in her to deflate Pru's beautiful dream.

"Oh, I know you didn't do it directly," Pru said, drawing away and looking into Millie's eyes. At that moment she wasn't the actress, but the young woman inside the actress who worked so hard for what she wanted. "But you always go out on a limb to see that we have what we need and want, and if you hadn't gotten up the courage to ask a complete stranger to marry you so that we could stay in school, you'd have never met Rio, and Charity wouldn't be invited to Arturo Vargas's summer workshop, Amy wouldn't have Baldwin Jones willing to read and critique her manuscript, and I wouldn't have this opportunity with the Santa Fe Repertory.''

And she, Millie, wouldn't have this broken heart. Well. That was a fair trade-off, she guessed, for her sisters' happiness.

Millie saw Pru back to bed, then wandered into Rio's office, thinking she would work on the computer program to while away the time until dawn.

She remembered that Rio had taken a key from the middle drawer of his desk to open the file cabinet door. She pulled the drawer open and pushed aside several sheets of paper to find the drawer organizer in which he kept the key.

Extracting it, she started to push the drawer closed when the name Boston College caught her eye. It was a fax from the school Amy attended.

Curious, Millie picked it up and found that it was a receipt for a year's tuition and room and board.

She stared at it. The receipt delineated every luxury that could be attached to Amy's enrollment. Then she saw that the payment had been made by direct transfer of funds from Rio's San Francisco account.

She replaced the fax, then noticed there were two more. One was from the Art Center of Design in Los Angeles, which Charity attended, and the other from the University of Southern California, Pru's school.

The Art Center receipt was for three years' tuition, paid in full, including all the fees for supplies. The other was for two years, paid in full, also with every amenity the curriculum allowed.

Each receipt was dated three days ago—the day she'd picked up Rio at the airport, shouted accusations at him like a madwoman, then slapped him. She closed her eyes against the memory and leaned her head against the back of the chair, realizing what that meant.

He was giving her what she wanted, but he was going with the loan rather than the marriage. She wasn't surprised, and she didn't blame him, but she felt an overwhelming sense of loss.

She guessed that, though he'd decided he didn't want to deal with her, he'd found the girls deserving of his help. She was grateful for that. And for the financial security he enjoyed that allowed him to add on all the extras to their educational packages. She sighed, thinking it must be nice.

But why hadn't he told her? It wasn't like Rio to leave her in limbo like this. Still, maybe he'd decided she deserved to suffer for a time.

Well, she would suffer. And for a long time. It would be best, she supposed, if she went back to Bridgeton with the girls at the end of the week.

A fist of emotion tightened in her stomach at the very thought. No more midnights in the pool with Rio, no more reading to Alex at bedtime. A sob rose in her throat, but she held it back, conscious of the dark quiet of the house.

She lingered by the door for a moment to remember sitting on the leather sofa with Rio, smoking cigars and drinking cognac. When at last she turned to flip off the light, she saw Rio standing in the doorway in the shorts and T-shirt he'd been wearing to bed in deference to the girls' arrival.

She let her eyes feast on the slightly rumpled sight of him.

Rio didn't like the look in her eyes. It was uncharacteristically defeated. She wore a thin cotton nightgown that fell to her knees and bagged around all the delicious curves he knew were under it.

They hadn't touched each other in days, except for the occasional hand-holding or arm-in-arm stroll for the benefit of her sisters. But he couldn't stop himself from putting a hand to her face now and rubbing his thumb across her cheekbone, wishing he could make her smile.

There hadn't been time to talk about the angry words they'd shouted at each other that other morning, and those words had been between them like barbed wire ever since.

"Are you all right?" he asked. "I just

checked on Alex and he's fine. Everything's quiet from the girls' rooms.''

"Pru couldn't sleep," she said, "so I got up to talk to her for a while, then urged her back to bed. I was going to put in a little time at the computer but—" her voice was tight and breathy "—I changed my mind."

"Come on." He flipped off the light and put an arm around her. "You need to sleep."

He led her down the corridor to his room, wishing he could knock down the barrier between them by making love to her, but accepting grimly that she would probably stick to her side of the bed as she'd done since the girls had arrived.

He pulled back the blankets, and she climbed in with a whispered thank-you.

Millie saw the vague movement in the shadows as Rio walked around the bed and climbed in on his side, careful not to touch her. But the need to touch him was overpowering.

She wanted to make love with him one more time before she left. Not out of gratitude that he'd paid the girls' tuitions, though she was grateful for that, but for purely selfish motives. She would need the memory in order to pick up her lonely life again and go on.

He, though, was probably still remembering the termagant who'd shouted at him and slapped him that morning. He might very well reject her.

The need, she quickly decided, was worth the risk.

She turned toward him and put a tentative hand to his chest. "Rio?" she whispered. The fresh scent of the night rode in on a breeze through the open window.

He turned his head toward her, but made no other move.

Intrepidly she sidled closer and put her lips to his cheek, running her hand over his rib cage, stopping at the waistband of his shorts. "I want to—"

And that was all she had time to say before his mouth covered hers in a kiss that was as hot and desperate as she felt.

He took charge of the encounter with a passion that was both startling and gratifying, considering she'd feared rejection. In an instant she'd lost the gown and was sprawled under him, unabashedly enjoying his ruthlessly tender assault.

Chapter Ten

MILLIE KNEW without even opening her eyes that she was alone in the bed. After last night she wouldn't be surprised if her sensory receptors could track Rio across the globe. He wasn't in the house.

Feminine laughter and Alex's high-pitched shrieks drifted in from the courtyard. It sounded as though they were all playing with Buzz Lightyear. The girls had been spoiling Alex outrageously, and he absorbed their attention with greedy delight.

The morning sunshine burnished all the wooden surfaces in the bedroom, and the fragrant desert breeze stirred everything that wasn't tied down or tucked in.

Millie felt her solitude like a weight. This was how every day would be after she left here. Beautiful probably, but lifeless.

And then, as though the sunny morning had suddenly discharged a lightning bolt, she sat up in the middle of the bed and asked herself why that had to be.

She remembered Pru's words of the night be-

fore. *You always go out on a limb to see that
we have what we need and want.*

She'd launched this plan to marry a millionaire as a fight to save her sisters' educations, and
miraculously she'd won.

Falling in love with Rio hadn't been part of
the plan, and because that had been about her
own needs, she'd been less inclined to fight for
it because...well, she wasn't sure why. Years of
conditioning, she supposed. She was the illegit-
imate one, the one who didn't quite belong. The
one who accepted less.

Well, she wasn't doing it this time. She
couldn't. She didn't think she could survive a
lifetime of the emptiness she felt today. She'd
started this, and even if Rio thought it was finished because he'd paid the girls' tuitions, he
was about to learn he was wrong.

She pulled on a robe and went out to the
kitchen. Gilford was chopping vegetables. He
looked up at her with a smile. "Breakfast, Ms.
Brown?"

"No," she said sharply, then rubbed out her
rudeness with a swipe of her hand. "I mean, no
thank you, Gilly. Tell me." She swallowed,
bracing herself for an answer. "Did Mr. Corrigan go skydiving?"

"No, miss," he replied. "I believe he went to
the mall. He said he'd be home for lunch. Is
there something I can—?"

"No thank you!" she called over her shoulder

as she ran back to Rio's room. Then she changed her mind and dashed back to the kitchen. "Actually there is."

Again Gilford looked up from his vegetables.

"May I borrow your car?" she asked.

RIO HEADED for the mall exit, his purchase tucked away in a pocket, knowing he couldn't go on without Millie. He'd felt a definite farewell in her arms last night, and he intended to make her talk about what that meant when he got home, others eavesdropping or not.

But he'd called her a control freak and tossed her in the pool. What if she didn't want to talk to him?

Well, he had control-freak tendencies, too. He and Millie were going to resolve this, and they were going to do it his way.

He remembered her gentle insistence when she'd encouraged him to stop blaming himself for his brother's death, the sound of her voice reading to Alex, the reorganization of the files on the computer that now seemed to bring whatever information he needed to his fingertips, and realized that she'd given a lot more than she'd gotten.

But he wasn't noble enough to give her her freedom if that was what she wanted.

He was passing the escalators when he recognized a familiar figure in yellow on the upper level. It was Millie, and she seemed to be look-

ing around, searching for something. Or someone. Him?

"Millie!" he shouted, but she didn't hear him
over the din of the midmorning shoppers. He
sprinted to the up escalator.

She was walking away, peering into shops,
standing on tiptoe to see behind displays.

He called her name again and she turned.

He didn't know what to make of the look in
her eyes. It was stricken, anguished, tormented.

And he was the focus of her gaze....

Then she came to him, that expression still in
place, and said simply, "Hi."

"Hi," he replied warily. "Were you looking
for me?"

"Yes," she said. "I...needed some time
alone with you."

A crowd of teenagers jostled them. Women
pushed babies, children laughed, store employees on their breaks wandered by with cups of
coffee. "So you came to a mall?" he asked.

She sighed. "No, *you* came to a mall. I followed you." She took his arm and led him toward the down escalator.

The teenagers were now on it, laughing as
they pushed and shoved one another. Millie
spotted the glass elevator and detoured toward
it, pulling him with her.

It opened as they approached, dispelling two
middle-aged women in broad-brimmed straw
hats.

The doors closed and the car took Rio and Millie up rather than down. Millie didn't seem to notice.

"You know," she said, her expression turning to one of confusion, "when you decided to let...you know, emotions into this relationship, even when I hadn't intended..." She paused, considered, then began again. "I mean, I thought we'd just be able to get married, maybe be friends, I could straighten out your computer and you could give me..."

He had only a very vague idea what she was talking about, but he did know what to say when she paused here.

"Money," he supplied helpfully.

"Money," she repeated with a grateful glance. "But then I got to really like you and then we had..."

Again, familiar ground. "Sex."

"Sex," she said, "and it all—" her eyes brimmed with tears "—it all *changed!*"

The doors parted on what seemed to be the administrative floor, and a man in a suit took one look at Millie's quivering lip and tear-filled eyes and frowned sympathetically at Rio. "I'll wait," he said.

Rio pushed the close-door button. The elevator started down.

"I thought it was wonderful," he said gently.

"It was!" She swiped tears away and sniffed. "But when you let emotions in, you get the bad ones, as well as the good ones. If I have any good quality, it's that I give love easily, but I also have a lot of bad ones and I'm bossy and probably overly protective, and when I'm frightened, I tend to yell a lot. Sort of like Alex and the television.''

That went right over his head. ''Pardon me?''

''The sound makes me feel like I'm not quite so alone.''

She paused to delve into her purse for something she didn't seem able to find. Presuming it was a tissue, he gave her his handkerchief.

She took it with a quick embarrassed glance at him, her lashes wet and spiked. ''Thank you. God, we're in a Capra movie. He slept all night again last night, by the way.''

''Capra?'' He knew of course. He'd spoken to Alex and the girls before he'd left the house.

She glared at him. ''Alex.''

Rio pressed the emergency-stop button before the doors could open on the second floor. Beyond the doors, a woman with a stroller waited and a man with a young boy, both burdened with packages.

''Darling, what's your point?'' Rio asked, wanting desperately for her to get to it so he could take an even breath.

She fluttered his handkerchief in a nervous gesture. ''It's that I *love* you,'' she said, something about the admission making her cry harder, "and I'm truly sorry about the other morning, but I saw you falling out of the sky—"

"Diving," he corrected, feeling his life settle into place. "I was diving."

"Damn it, Rio," she wept, "when you're moving through the sky and you're not in a plane, you're falling! And my nerves can't take that. I'm too...maternal!"

He pulled her to him and kissed her damp cheek. "It doesn't matter because I won't be doing it anymore. I love you, too, and I wouldn't deliberately do anything to hurt you."

"You threw me in the pool," she reminded him, clinging to his neck.

"Well, I was busy letting in some not very nice emotions, too. Anger, disappointment, pride. You had just accused me of making a game out of the most wonderful night of my life."

She leaned her forehead against his chin. "I'm sorry."

"Me, too."

She sniffed and dabbed at her nose with the handkerchief. "And I found the tuition receipts. I thought you'd decided to go with my idea of the loan, after all."

"No way." He framed her face with his hands and kissed her. "We had a deal and you're not welching on me. I didn't tell you about the tuitions because I thought as long as you weren't sure I was going to take care of them, you'd stay with me. After our fight that morning, I thought I needed an edge.''

The alarm bell rang. At least, that was what Millie thought it was until Rio pulled a cellular phone out of his pocket.

"Hello?" he said. He listened, looked momentarily puzzled, then smiled. "Yes, of course. Millie's told me about you. Hold on, she's right here."

Millie put the phone to her ear and heard Torrey Benson's cheerful voice. "Just checking on you," Torrey said. "Making sure you'll be here a week from Wednesday for our return to 'The Babs Randazzo Show.'"

"Ah...hold on, Torrey." She covered the mouthpiece and asked Rio, "Are we going to be in Chicago for Torrey's follow-up appearance on the talk show?"

"Of course." He kissed her forehead.

"Of course," she told Torrey, wrapping her arm around Rio's waist and leaning into him, so full of happiness she could hardly stand up.

"And will you be wearing a diamond?"

"Yes, I'll be wearing a diamond," Millie said, holding her left hand out to admire it. Then she noticed the shake of Rio's head and held the phone against her chest, alarmed.

"I *won't* be wearing a diamond?"

"No." He took a small square box out of his pants pocket and held it open in front of her eyes. "I came to pick this up this morning."

In the box was a gold ring the size and shape of a cigar band and replicating the Contigo Royale logo. She remembered his insisting that she remove her cigar-band ring and his staying behind with the jeweler saying he needed to change the battery in his watch.

"You can wear the diamond on your other hand of course," Rio said, "but you'll have this wedding ring on your finger by a week from Wednesday. We'll see if we can keep the girls a few extra days and get my parents to come."

Millie threw her arms around his neck, laughing, crying, promising.

He held her tightly, laughing with her, kissing away her tears, returning every promise.

Those waiting for the elevator watched the scene through the glass doors and shook their heads, and from the phone Torrey Benson's voice said, "Millie? Hello?"

Dear Reader,

I met my husband, Ron, when I was twenty-one and we worked together at the *Los Angeles Times*.

He was thirty-three, warm, witty and ready to settle down. I was young with big plans to travel and write the great American novel based on what would surely be brilliant observations on my world tour.

Ron proposed marriage on our second date. I declined, explaining my plan and asking that we remain friends.

He promised we would, but said, "I will make myself so indispensable to you that you won't be able to live without me."

After several months of doing precisely that, he took a week's vacation without warning me that he would be gone. It was the longest seven days of my life. When he came home, *I* proposed to *him*.

Sincerely,

Muriel Jensen

ONCE UPON A HUSBAND

Suzanne Forster

"OKAY, CLASS!" Torrey Benson called out to the students in her seminar on flirting. "A handsome stranger gives you a quick once-over that makes you feel like a potted palm. But you notice he's pointing his foot at you. Just a coincidence, or are his Gucci loafers trying to tell you something?"

That question always brought snickers, but Torrey was serious. Foot pointing was rife with unconscious meaning and just one of the many ways that men and women sent nonverbal signals to each other.

One of the students raised her hand. "He wants to race you to the buffet table?"

Another chimed in, "He's channeling Fred Astaire and wants to tango?"

Torrey laughed along with the rest of the group. She wasn't normally a teacher, but then her small assemblage of thirty wasn't a normal classroom situation, either. They were aboard a cruise ship that had just set sail for the Mexican Riviera, and Torrey's class was part of an exhaustive promotional effort for her first book, *How to Marry a Millionaire*. This was the open-

ing session and things had been going swim-
mingly until moments ago, when a latecomer
had sauntered in and took a seat at the back of
the room.

As the students continued calling out answers,
Torrey risked a little nonverbal behavior of her
own. Careful where she was pointing her foot,
she stole a glance at the straggler, who was also
the only male in attendance. He'd attempted to
arrange his lanky muscular body in a chair that
wasn't made for men over six feet, and the impression he gave was one of sprawled grace. But
his posture wasn't Torrey's concern at the moment. He was wearing nothing but swim trunks
and a tank top—and one of *his* bare feet was
pointing directly at her.

"Could mean he wants you to marry him and
bear his children," the latecomer suggested in a
voice almost too soft to be heard.

Torrey heard it, though. She nearly blushed to
the roots of her ginger hair—and not just because he was more right than he knew. He was
also her ex-husband, and his comment was
loaded with private meaning. The shock of having Christopher "Kit" McGrath show up during
her book tour was turning into a nightmare from
which it seemed Torrey would never wake up.

She hadn't seen Kit in fifteen years when he
suddenly appeared in the audience of "The Babs
Randazzo Show," a daytime talk show where
she was promoting her book, and volunteered to

be part of a contest sponsored by her publisher. The rules were simple. Torrey would make herself available as personal coach to each of the contestants, and whoever brought back a millionaire fiancé—or, in the case of a man, a fiancée—using tips from Torrey's book would be featured on a special follow-up show. Now here Kit was, taking her seminar and apparently expecting to be coached, which meant she was trapped with him on a seven-day cruise from Los Angeles to Cabo San Lucas.

At least she could be grateful that "The Babs Randazzo Show" camera crew, who were on the cruise to capture footage for the follow-up show, hadn't come to her class this morning. They would be at the captain's cocktail party tonight, though, and that was worry enough. She hoped Claudia Barnes, her publicist, would be there, too. The poor thing had taken to her bed, already deathly seasick before they were twenty minutes out of port.

"What did that man say?" a woman in the front row asked. "I couldn't hear him."

Kit moved as if to repeat himself, but Torrey was faster than he was—for once in her life. "A pointed foot can mean many things," she informed the class—and him, "but for our purposes, let's just say it means he's interested."

Torrey smiled thinly at Kit as she removed her glasses and tapped them against her lower lip. She didn't really need glasses, but thought they

might make her look more authorlike and, there-
fore, give her some credibility, which she
needed. "That's what you meant to say, wasn't
it? *Sir?*"

"Yeah—" Kit leaned back and grinned
"—that's exactly what I meant to say...
ma'am."

Several of the students were clearly confused
by whatever was going on with their pink-
cheeked instructor and the half-naked guy in the
back row. Torrey could see it in their expressions and the way they craned their necks to
look at Kit. She slipped her glasses back on,
aware that she needed to reclaim their attention
and establish herself as the authority so things
didn't get out of hand.

"Did we go over the body language that says,
'Kiss me, you fool'?" She glanced at her watch
and knew she was hopelessly offtrack. That was
tomorrow's lecture. "Oh, look how late it is!"
she exclaimed. "Let's go over the rules of smiling and then I'll give you your flirting homework."

Lord, but she was rattled. She'd been doing
this seminar the entire tour and hadn't fluffed the
material like this. "The rules are simple," she
assured them. "But they'll allow you to get the
maximum mileage out of your smiles. First and
most important, mean it when you smile. No
halfhearted smirks or sheepish grins. I want
megawatt intensity. Light up the room."

The next few rules had to do with smiling etiquette and the importance of practice. She went over them quickly.

"Be bold," she told them when she finished the list. "Your mother may have told you never to talk to strangers, but she didn't tell you not to smile at them. But more important, be safe. Don't smile in biker bars or dark alleys. And definitely don't smile at anyone who's drooling or reaching inside their clothing."

She barely had the words out when the boat-neck silk blouse she was wearing slipped off her shoulder, revealing a sexy black bra strap. The material was so slippery she fumbled with it for several seconds before getting it back up where it belonged. "Like I just did," she said, flushing with laughter.

As the chuckles subsided, she gave her students their assignment for the day and released them on the unsuspecting world. They were to smile at five strangers and to strike up a conversation with one of them, even if it was just to ask directions. "Cruise staff and children don't count," she told her students as they filed out the door, her ex-husband among them, to her great relief. "And watch where you're pointing your feet!"

A couple of the women lingered and approached Torrey with questions as she was packing up her material. She mustered enough enthusiasm to answer all their concerns, but once they'd left, she collapsed in a heap in the nearest chair. It was criminal the effect Kit McGrath had on her.

She'd run away from their marriage fifteen years ago, determined to put the pain of her unrequited love behind her. Hockey was the true passion in Kit's life. He'd proved that beyond a shadow of a doubt by going on to become a pro player after she left, instead of moving heaven and earth to find her. He'd probably been too busy to even notice she was gone.

She could only think of one reason he was here now after all these years, and that was to ruin her happiness again, whether intentionally or not. She was to be married at the end of the cruise to her CEO fiancé, Steven Gaines. The wedding was a part of the book tour and admittedly a publicity gimmick, but that didn't mean she wasn't completely committed to Steven and to the marriage.

Torrey had met him while acting as a regional manager for his chain of apothecary shops. It was one of two full-time jobs she was working to help pay off the debts of her deceased second husband, who had turned out to have far more liabilities than assets when he died in a freak accident at one of his own luxury-car dealerships.

Rocked by the tragedy, Torrey had plunged into work to survive emotionally, as well as financially—and her dogged efforts had paid off, but not in the way she'd expected. She'd been at a regional managers' conference when Steven had arrived to present her with an award for her region's outstanding sales that year. She'd known instantly that he was the perfect man for her, even if he was nearly thirty years her senior and a lover of all things named Woody, most of which she was woefully unfamiliar with, like Woody Herman and the Woody station wagon.

Fortunately, though, Torrey's hunch about Steven had proved right. He was not only blessed with material wealth, he was a kind and generous man, and when they became involved, he'd offered to pay off her debts. That gesture had moved her deeply, only she hadn't been able to accept of course. It was her responsibility, and a matter of honor at that. But what Steven had inspired without realizing it was the idea for her book, and to her great relief, he'd been completely supportive of her efforts. She doubted many millionaires would subject themselves to a media wedding, except maybe rock stars.

Her blouse had drifted off her shoulder again. Tensing, she yanked the slippery material back up. Perhaps the argument could be made that it wasn't a grand passion with Steven, but where did that sort of thing lead, anyway, except to heartbreak?

"Any idea how to get to the spa?"

Torrey's head snapped up at the question. Her ex-husband was standing in the doorway, smiling at her with such genuine good humor she was confused for a moment. "The spa? Is there a spa on this boat?"

"This *is* the *Love Boat,* isn't it?" His head tilted in the expectant way that had always been dangerously irresistible to her. Or maybe it was the boat that tilted. Whatever it was, Torrey found herself responding. Not only did she want to smile back, she didn't want him to leave quite yet. Just for a moment she wanted to bask in the warmth of that amazing expression.

He was memorable that way, she admitted. When he wanted to, he could make you feel like you were the only other person on the planet. No one else existed when Kit McGrath decided to ravish you with one of his deep penetrating gazes. And when he turned on that slow sexy smile, like a dimmer switch on a floodlight, well, you were enveloped by it. By him. Maybe that was why it hurt so much when he focused the beam on his career and left her in the dark.

"Has anyone told you how great you look these days?"

She shrugged and shook her head, but he wouldn't be put off. "I mean it," he said. "You're so hot you could melt the plastic in my underwear."

Torrey gaped at him. "I beg your pardon?" She was sure she couldn't have heard him correctly, but the twinkle in his eye told her she must have.

"Too bold?" He tucked his hands into the pockets of his trunks and regarded her, all innocence.

"Too bold?" she repeated.

"I'm trying to strike up a conversation," he explained. "You said to be bold."

"Oh!" He was doing his flirting homework, and she just happened to be convenient. She'd thought he was expressing interest in *her,* Torrey Benson. How silly of her. Her energy returned with a whoosh, spiked by anger. "No, that wasn't too bold. I'm sure any streetwalker would have been enraptured."

She rose from the chair, thinking to finish packing her material and get out of there, but the world still felt as if it were tilting, and she had to grab the table to steady herself. Clearly she didn't have her sea legs yet.

"Are you okay?" he asked.

Torrey could hear him coming up behind her. Now that *was* bold of him, especially since she was fondly remembering the knee-to-groin technique from her self-defense class. Luckily for him she was still hanging on to the table.

He touched her arm and sent a thrill zinging between her shoulder blades. When she caught her balance, she turned and found herself trapped between him and the table. "What are you doing on this boat, Kit?"

Her voice rasped with emotion, but she didn't care. She'd been wanting to confront him ever since he'd shown up on "The Babs Randazzo Show" and all but ruined her book tour. "You don't need flirting lessons to meet a millionaire. As long as she was breathing, you could charm her knickers off with both hands tied behind your back and blindfolded."

Garden weeds would have wilted under Torrey's withering stare, but Kit McGrath seemed oblivious to the reaction he was provoking.

"I thought everybody needed their very own millionaire," he protested cheerfully. "You sold me, Torrey. Your book made a believer out of me. You said, and I quote, 'If you want a soul mate, you might as well have a wealthy one.' The good news is I've found her, and she's right here on this cruise."

The boat wasn't rocking anymore, but Torrey was. "You've met your millionaire and she's here on this boat?"

The idea astonished Torrey, although she wasn't sure why. She must have thought he'd entered the contest because of her and never intended to go through with it. She should have known better. Kit McGrath was the most competitive man on the planet. He entered contests to beat the odds, and if he really wanted to meet and marry a millionaire, she had no doubt that he would. But *why* was he doing it?

"You could say I met her," he conceded, "but I didn't make a great impression. That's why I'm here. I need help."

Right, she thought, and Dolly Parton needs a training bra. "What happened?" A secret sparkle lurked in his dark eyes. He lit the room whether he smiled or not, she thought, reluctantly aware of his effortless magnetism.

He rolled his shoulder as if he were about to block an opponent on the ice. "I did some body-checking, got thrown in the penalty box, and I need an assist from you to get out."

The hockey terms made Torrey smile, despite her feelings about the game that had seduced her husband away. "Bodychecking?" She was mildly curious.

"Apparently I trod on her toe in the boarding line and she backed into the guy behind her, because the whole line went down like a row of dominoes. Bubbles sprained her ankle, and to make matters worse, she dropped her designer sunglasses, which got crushed when I knelt to help her up."

Torrey could hardly imagine such a scene. Kit was a good-size man, but he *wasn't* clumsy. He was as graceful as a dancer. Still, there was something about his hockey-playing inclinations that caused accidents. Big ones. No one knew that better than she.

"She sprained her ankle? Then it must be true love," Torrey said, aware of the hurt tone that had crept into her voice. "That's how you and I met in high school, remember? Only I wasn't as lucky as Bubbles."

They'd grown up in the same small town outside of Chicago. Torrey had been a high-school sophomore, Kit a senior, and she'd had a secret crush on him all through her freshman year. When he'd shown up at the locker next to hers, she'd been so startled she'd tripped over his hockey stick and broken her ankle. He'd not only carried her to the nurse's office, he'd asked her to go to a movie with him when she was well enough. Kit McGrath could have had any girl in the school, and some of her friends had unkindly suggested it was a "pity date." Torrey had been too astonished that he'd asked to care.

"You look sad," Kit observed, his voice grainy. "Was it that bad?"

Torrey realized she must have been staring at him with the remembered longing of a fifteen-year-old. And the way he was staring back at her made her think he was remembering, too. He looked sort of melancholy himself, mostly around the mouth. There was the sexy little droop at one corner that she'd always equated with poetic sensitivity. But she wasn't going to tell him. There was no way to know where that line of thought would take them. And she wasn't going to mention the moody cast in his gunmetal gray eyes, either, even though it made her think of a rainy day at the lake. *Lord, the bliss they shared on those stolen afternoons in his parents' ramshackle old cabin at Sumner's Reservoir—*

Her heart chose that moment to tighten painfully, and she hastily changed the subject. "I'm afraid to ask how Bubbles made her millions."

Kit blinked as if he'd been reluctantly yanked from the moment. "She owns a Laundromat franchise chain called Bubbles and Bleach, or at least that's what my intelligence network tells me. She's supposed to be an entrepreneurial genius who made her first million before she was thirty."

"Laundromats? That's not how I was picturing a woman named Bubbles." Torrey had imagined platinum hair, capped teeth—both blindingly white—and a cigarette-girl uniform. Now the uniform was gone, replaced by a frilly blindingly white Betty Crocker apron—and not much else.

From somewhere above them a horn blasted, and the sound startled Torrey. She braced herself against the table just as Kit reached out to steady her. He was going for one of her arms apparently, both of which were behind her back, and his hand grazed several things it wasn't supposed to, including the side of her breast.

He didn't apologize, just glanced at the offended parts of her body as if he wanted to touch her there again. A sharp ache rose in the pit of Torrey's belly. The urgency of it might have been terribly sweet if she hadn't known her need would go unfulfilled. How was it possible that she could still respond so strongly after all this time? She should be over him completely—or at least have developed an immunity, the way you did with mumps and chicken pox.

"So..." He let the word linger for an eternity, and a million ways to fill in the blanks assailed Torrey's mind, none of which were safe to dwell on. "Can I count on you for some private coaching?" he asked.

"You don't need private lessons, Kit. Just send her some flowers and offer to carry her around in your arms until her ankle's healed." *I guarantee she'll fall in love with you just the way I did.*

The tightness in her chest made Torrey turn her back on him and begin shoving papers and books into her tote bag in a mad desire to be anywhere other than near him.

"You agreed to coach the contestants, Torrey, and I take coaching very seriously." He moved in so close that the heat of his breath tickled her nape and whispered along the gaping neckline of her blouse. Why had she worn the impossible thing? At least she knew it wasn't for him. She hadn't realized he was on the boat until he showed up at her class this morning.

"You'll do fine," she said dismissively. "Just show her your hockey scars. She'll swoon. I'm sure they all do." She'd heard about the groupies that hung out at the games in hopes of partying with the players afterward. She could imagine them drooling all over Kit. And him loving it.

"You made a public promise," he reminded

her, "and one way or another, you're going to keep it. Even if I have to take the matter up with your publisher."

"Are you threatening me?" she exclaimed softly. She whipped off her glasses and whirled to confront him.

"You bet, baby. You bet."

Baby? He'd never called her that before, not even in their most intimate moments. She slipped her glasses into their case, dropped them into her tote and hooked the strap over her shoulder. Fresh air had suddenly become a necessity.

What she didn't realize as she headed for the door was that she'd left a sheaf of papers behind. Nor did she see her ex-husband pick up that sheaf and smile. If she had, she would have known that her narrow escape led to a blind alley.

"SCORE ONE GOAL for the challengers," Kit murmured as he settled on the edge of the table and watched his ex-wife disappear through the doorway. The neckline she kept yanking up had fallen off her shoulder again, and it gave her the look of a woman who hadn't quite managed to get herself dressed following one of those spontaneously steamy interludes that happened too seldom in life, as far as Kit was concerned.

"Torrey, Torrey, you slay me," he whispered. She'd always been inadvertently sexual, seemingly with no idea of the appeal of her disordered clothing and startled responses. But the catch in Kit's throat wasn't from laughter. It was from times long past his ex-wife clearly didn't want to acknowledge, much less remember. She hadn't been in any hurry to escape their afternoons together when they were kids, as he recalled, at least not at first.

She'd grown up a lot in a decade and a half. She hadn't changed, though, not in the important ways. On the surface she was sleeker and more sophisticated, a look designed by her publicity machine, he imagined. Her casual tumble of red-gold hair had been tamed some and her features expertly made up. But she still had an air of calamity about her, and her big amber-colored eyes harbored the same questions he remembered from high school: *What do you want with me, Kit McGrath? What do you really want?*

Maybe that was why he'd been so taken with her. She hadn't pretended to be anything other than what she was. No artifice, no facade of sophistication. The word "cool" wasn't in Torrey's vocabulary. She was warm and real and available, as bewildered as the questions in her eyes and not afraid to let her vulnerability show.

Too bad he'd had blinders on in those days and hadn't been mature enough to deal with her questions or her vulnerability. He'd had very little idea what he wanted with Torrey Benson beyond the obvious stuff most teenage boys

wanted. But that had changed. A lot of things had changed. He knew exactly what he wanted now, and in fact, he'd already said as much. Luckily for him, she'd been too shocked to take it in, or she would have dived off the boat and swum for shore by now.

"Oh, yeah," he said, looking over the papers she'd left behind, "this *must* be my lucky day." It was a list of the unconscious signals men and women send each other when they're sexually attracted, and she'd even included the hidden meanings in a number of seemingly innocent gestures.

He perused the list with a chuckle. Her answer to the foot-pointing question was in there, but she'd fudged a little earlier on what it meant. "'When a man points his foot at a woman,'" he read aloud, "'he's not only expressing his desire to take her to bed, but his availability to do so.'"

He held the papers aside and saw that his bare foot was still pointed at the door she'd disappeared through. No wonder she was nervous. If his toes were telling the truth, she was lucky to have made it out of the room. "Smart move, Torrey," he murmured, continuing with the list. Her research might give her the home-ice advantage, but from now on, she wouldn't be the only one who knew what this body-language stuff meant.

Kit stood up and shifted his shoulders again,

working out some of the kinks that years of rough-and-tumble professional hockey had put there. Her class notes ended up rolled like parchment and secured in the waistband of his trunks. If Torrey Benson thought he had a hidden agenda, she was right. He had plenty of interesting surprises in store for his runaway bride. Before the cruise was over he was not only going to rock the boat, he was going to rock her world.

TORREY WAS FEELING uneasy about that evening's captain's cocktail party before she even got there. She hadn't seen any sign of the film crew yet, but they were supposed to be there, filming Torrey, her students and the party. Still, she might have skipped it had her publicist not threatened her life if she didn't attend. Claudia was still dreadfully sick and confined to her stateroom after a visit from the ship's doctor, whom Torrey had insisted on calling. Otherwise, organizational genius that Claudia was, she would have escorted Torrey personally and made sure everything ran smoothly.

However, an even more compelling reason to attend the party was the curiosity factor. Torrey was burning with it. She had to find out who Bubbles was.

The Promenade deck was already milling with passengers when Torrey arrived, but she spotted Kit immediately, mostly because he was wearing clothes. No one could carry off wrinkled summer linens the way he could, she admitted, recalling the jacket and slacks he'd worn at their nuptials, a rushed affair in a roadside wedding chapel. Not exactly formal attire, but he'd looked gorgeous. Breathtaking.

The sigh welling in her throat made Torrey realize how mixed her emotions were. She'd told him once that his body was made-to-order for a Greek toga. It was true, but she probably shouldn't have gushed all over him. Those were the days when she didn't know better than to worship at his feet.

A waiter came by, offering exotic-looking drinks on a tray. The one Torrey picked tasted like fermented fruit cocktail, which wasn't necessarily bad, except that it was probably strong enough to double as barbecue starter. She took a sip and ducked behind a huge potted palm. Two of her students had shown up, and Torrey didn't want to be seen yet. She needed a little more time to check out the situation.

Kit was behaving oddly. He'd stopped a waiter and pointed out a group of passengers chatting near the railing, but the woman he'd sent the waiter to approach didn't seem like Kit's type at all. That couldn't be Bubbles, Torrey thought. The object of his desire looked to be at least twenty years his senior. Granted, she was petite and curvaceous, but—and Torrey didn't want to be unkind—her hair was titian red and massively coiffed, and the colorful sarong she wore made Torrey think of one of Bob Hope's road movies. Perhaps the most interesting fashion statement were her mile-high "chickadee" wedgies, which were all the more extraordinary because of the flowered Ace bandage wrapped tightly around her ankle.

No wonder she'd fallen, Torrey thought. You could throw out your back on those things without ever taking a step.

Torrey's curiosity mounted as the waiter whispered something to the woman, who glanced Kit's way with a smile that definitely signaled interest. Kit held up his drink and nodded. Bubbles blushed and toyed with the glittering diamond pendant that hung around her neck. Forget the road movies, Torrey thought. This was a scene out of *Body Heat*. The sexual signals were zinging like lightning. Torrey could almost smell ozone from all the electricity crackling in the air. And Kit's sandled foot was pointed straight at Bubbles!

No way, Torrey thought. Millionaire or not, this couldn't be the woman Kit had singled out, unless he'd developed an Oedipus complex. Torrey felt an immediate twinge of guilt and mentally shook herself. She wasn't usually so catty, and it disturbed her to think that she might be jealous after all these years. She was just startled—and wondering if her ex needed to go for a thorough checkup.

A group had gathered nearby, affording Torrey some cover, so she decided to risk coming out from behind the plant. Another waiter darted by, offering flambé rum drinks that flared like torches and huge fishbowl concoctions with everything but goldfish swimming in them. Torrey declined, but noticed that her own drink was half-gone. She'd been so deep in concentration she hadn't even realized she'd been sipping it.

Kit had begun to make his way through the throng toward Bubbles, who'd turned as if to welcome him with open arms. Meanwhile, the waiter who'd been the go-between appeared with a gleaming silver ice bucket and a dripping magnum of champagne.

Bubbles for Bubbles? How very clever of him.

Torrey felt stab of pain and plunked down her drink on the buffet table. Nice touch, she thought bitterly. She couldn't remember him ever doing anything so splashy or romantic for her. He must really be smitten. But was it with Bubbles—or her millions?

A tickle along Torrey's upper arm alerted her that the strap of her sundress was slipping. Her clothing was going AWOL again! She'd seen a gadget in a magazine ad called Strapmate, which was designed for the fashion-impaired, women like herself who had trouble getting themselves dressed and staying that way. She should have ordered it, especially since a fallen strap, if intentionally left that way, signaled that you wanted to be undressed the rest of the way. It was an interesting thought, but not the vibe she wanted to send under the circumstances. Not that anyone was receiving. Certainly not her ex-spouse.

She crushed the strap in her hand, thereby giving her entire outfit fair warning. Behave or else.

"Ms. Benson, there you are!"

Vicki Tyler, one of Torrey's students, had spotted her and was jumping up and down—to report a success story, judging by the grin on her face.

"Did you see me flip my hair at that man?" Vicki asked. "I didn't think I did it right, but look. He's smiling!"

"Good for you, Vicki." The young woman had apparently used one of the signals Torrey had taught her in class. For women, smiling, flipping the hair, solitary dancing and leaning toward a man were all invitations to approach.

Torrey was genuinely pleased, but she needed to extricate herself. She couldn't afford to miss a minute of the Kit-and-Bubbles show. "Now that you've got his attention, why don't you take the next step and strike up a conversation?"

Vicki nodded, caught up in the possibilities. "Maybe I'll use one of those great lines from your book like 'Your eyes should be registered as lethal weapons.'" She thanked Torrey and headed off, practicing the line and reaching inside her blouse to fiddle with something in the vicinity of her shoulder pads.

I should have told her about Strapmate, Torrey thought, silently wishing her luck.

Torrey moved in cautiously for a better vantage point. Kit and Bubbles had made contact and were already in animated conversation. He was certainly doing well with *his* flirting homework, Torrey thought.

Their laughter reached Torrey, but not their words. Still, it was a dismayingly intimate sound, and Torrey winced as Kit raised his champagne flute in a toast, then finessed the move by catching hold of Bubbles's bejeweled hand and bestowing a kiss on her fingertips. The teacher in Torrey was impressed. The woman in her was aghast. What in the world was Kit thinking of! This Bubbles person was much too old for him. Who cared how much money she had?

Torrey was well aware that the gap between her age and Steven's was probably larger, but that was different. They were compatible. Just because she'd never heard of Artie Shaw and Steven thought U2 was a spy plane rather than a rock group didn't mean they weren't simpatico in the important ways—whereas these two were completely wrong for each other. Anyone could see that.

With a despairing sigh Torrey realized what she was doing. She was in hot mental competition with Bubbles, and that made no sense at all.

She, Torrey Benson, was engaged. The man of her millionaire dreams was waiting for her in Cabo San Lucas, and their plans included a big media wedding as the grand finale to her book tour. There wouldn't be just one bottle of champagne. There would be cases of it, probably Dom Perignon, knowing Steven. And of course there were those debts Torrey had to pay off, too, a staggering amount she'd kept secret even from her publishing company for fear it would shake their confidence in her. Yes, *everything* hinged on the success of this book tour, including both her personal and professional reputation if she couldn't get herself solvent *and* marry her millionaire. She had to remember that.

A combo had assembled on a small bandstand, and the vocalist, a Latin balladeer with a sensual style worthy of Julio, had begun to sing "Malaguena." Torrey knew it was time to make an exit, but turning her back on Kit and Bubbles was like trying to drive by a car accident without looking. Impossible. The urge to take a parting glance at the lovebirds was overpowering, and at the last minute, she did. Just a quick peek.

Her mouth fell open when she saw what was happening, what was *about* to happen.

A disaster.

Kit was refilling the champagne glasses, and Bubbles was living up to her name, laughing and hiccuping giggles like a carbonated beverage. They were having far too much fun to notice the waiter coming up behind Bubbles with the tray of flambé drinks. Unfortunately the man was a walking torch. Worse, the sheer breadth of Bubbles's hairdo alone made her a fire hazard, not to mention the hairspray. With every bob of her head, Bubbles risked ignition, and no one, including the waiter, who was busy serving the drinks to another party, had noticed.

No one but Torrey. And she couldn't get a word out of her mouth. Stunned, she saw a poof of smoke rise from Bubbles's hair. "Fire," Torrey whispered. "Fi-i-i..." She couldn't manage more than squeaks, and by now smoke was pouring from Bubbles's beehive like Vesuvius about to erupt. Torrey veered back and forth, up and down, looking for an opening, but the milling crowd had her blocked. She couldn't get free and she couldn't shout.

This was unbelievable! There was a human Fourth of July fireworks in their midst, and everyone was too busy to notice, including Kit, who was staring so deeply into Bubbles's eyes he didn't see that she was going up in smoke.

"Fire!" The cry broke from Torrey's throat.

Heads bobbed around, startled.

Kit was the first to react. He plucked the champagne bottle from the bucket, grabbed up the bucket itself and doused the flames—and his companion—with the icy water. Bubbles's eyes nearly bugged out of her head. Her mouth dropped open with a soundless gasp as glacial streams drenched her hair and face, and ice cubes slid down her sarong.

Kit took command immediately. "Turn around," he ordered. Bubbles's hair was still smoldering like a wet campfire, and he apparently wanted to make sure he'd put it out. But the woman he was trying to rescue was as rigid as the ship's smokestack.

"Make up your mind!" she wailed. "Do you want to cripple me or drown me? Which is it?"

"You're on fire." But his attempt to turn her bodily resulted in a right hook. Hers. She would have connected, too, if he hadn't ducked.

"Pervert!" she spluttered. Water flew in a rooster tail as she stalked off, barely evidencing a limp and spraying everyone she passed, including Torrey. She trailed smoke like a Blue Angel jet.

That was when Torrey saw the talk-show camera crew, and they were hot on Bubbles's vapor trail. It was the same three men who'd been with Torrey the entire book tour—an aggressive young producer named Bruno, who set everything up, a minicam operator and a sound man. They'd recorded the entire fiasco and weren't done yet, Torrey realized.

This could be her dreams going up in smoke right along with Bubbles's. If the camera crew hadn't yet figured out that Kit was one of the volunteers in the *How to Marry a Millionaire* contest, they soon would, and his performance didn't reflect terribly well on the tips in her book. She was supposed to be inspiring people to marry millionaires, not maim them.

Yet, despite the awfulness of it, Torrey had to admit to some grudging sympathy for Kit. The flames did appear to be out, but Bubbles clearly had no clue she'd actually been on fire—or that Kit's motives were noble. She apparently thought he was a total crazy who was trying to kill her.

Meanwhile, Kit had spotted Torrey and was walking her way. He heaved a frustrated sigh and hesitated beside her, staring at the wet exit path and lingering haze that Bubbles had left. "See, Teach?" he said under his breath. "I need help."

This was true, Torrey thought.

"LET'S DO SOME role-playing," Torrey suggested for the benefit of the camera crew. Bruno and his boys had been waiting for her in the classroom when she arrived that morning, and she wanted to give them something memorable for the show.

"Vicki," she said, volunteering her most animated student, "let's show them some of the sexual signals women send to men. Would you come up to the front and help demonstrate the shoe fondle? You can be the girl and I'll be the boy."

Reputed to drive men wild, the shoe fondle

was a technique Torrey had discovered while researching her book. A woman dangles her shoe, preferably a high heel, from her toes, while slipping it on and off occasionally. It was believed to be the "naked thrusting" motion of her foot that was so highly appealing to the opposite sex.

"Could I make a suggestion?" Vicki asked as she joined Torrey. "Since we have a real-live guy right here in the class—" grinning, she pointed out Kit "—wouldn't it be great if he and I could demonstrate?"

No! Torrey thought, but Kit was already making his way toward them, and Torrey could see the gleam in the producer's eye. Bruno loved the idea. There was virtually nothing Torrey could do, and it probably would make for better television, unless Kit decided to be perverse.

Unless? she thought moments later. *Of course* he'd decided to be perverse. She wasn't sure what he was up to, but anyone watching would have had to assume he hadn't heard a word she'd said during the sessions. If anything, he seemed flustered at Vicki's coy toe-wagging gestures, and the more Vicki encouraged him, the more wooden he got. Vicki finally flipped her sandal off in her enthusiasm, and Kit's response was to suggest she try a smaller-size shoe.

The class roared, but Torrey was humiliated. What was wrong with him? All she could do was pray they didn't use the footage.

"Looks like I need some practice," Kit suggested, giving the camera a sideways glance. He swiped the dark hair from his knitted brow in a diffident gesture that threatened to melt every feminine heart in the room—except hers. "Fortunately Ms. Benson here has volunteered to coach me."

He indicated Torrey with a nod of his head.

"That's right," she cut in quickly. "Mr. Mc-Grath is one of the volunteers for the contest Tower Books is sponsoring, and I'll be giving him individual attention. Lots of it." She smiled wanly.

"I'd like to film that," the producer said.

"Certainly," Torrey agreed, but panic nearly prevented her from getting the word out. She would have to set something up to keep Bruno happy, but not before she had a chance to talk to Kit privately.

"Mr. McGrath will be getting my crash course in remedial social skills ASAP," she promised with a bright smile. "We'll have him ready for polite company in no time."

TORREY HAD ONLY to enter Kit's stateroom the following evening to know that she wasn't living right. She was housed on a lower passenger deck, where the staff had their rooms. Not that her room wasn't nice, but Kit had a luxury suite on the uppermost deck, and it was sumptuous, a pasha's palace compared to hers.

The centerpiece of the salon was a huge white

crescent-shaped couch piled high with pillows in brilliant hues of blue and green. An entertainment center in black ash stood against the far wall running flush to the open balcony doors, and to Torrey's right was a wet bar on which sat a gleaming gold bucket of ice that held several bottles of Möet Chandon.

"Can I get you something to drink?" Kit asked, indicating the champagne.

"What's the occasion?" The place looked suspiciously like a bachelor's lair, and Torrey was immediately on guard. She could hardly believe she was meeting her ex-husband on the sly in his stateroom, anyway, even though she had good reason. A more public place, and the camera crew would have been all over them.

Besides, she had to do whatever she could to prevent another catastrophe like... Well, take your pick, she thought—either the fiasco at the captain's party or the nightmare in her classroom.

She cringed to think what would happen if Kit continued to fail so publicly while under her tutelage. Every one of his disasters could easily be showcased on "The Babs Randazzo Show" when this was all over. Who'd want to buy *How to Marry a Millionaire* then? Torrey also needed to keep her own wedding plans on track, and to that end, counseling Kit on how to win Bubbles back seemed a wise move.

Still, she couldn't believe she was here. With him. Alone.

"Hungry?" he asked, indicating the small feast laid out on the coffee table. "Shanghai-duck tamales? Braised oyster mushrooms? Fresh strawberries with whipped cream?"

"You certainly went to a lot of trouble," she said. "What's this all about?"

Not only was his suite a surprise, but tonight's fashion statement was a far cry from the shorts and tank tops he hung out in most of the time. He was wearing an elegant long-sleeved turquoise silk shirt with a cleric's collar, sand-colored slacks and woven leather sandals. Set off by his dark hair and tan, it was a great look, one that conveyed all the casual sophistication of a world traveler.

"I just assumed we'd be doing some role-playing and I should think of you as Bubbles," he offered by way of explanation.

Torrey wanted to laugh. "If I were Bubbles, you'd have a cocktail toothpick in your eye by now. She probably has a contract out on you, Kit, and you're planning to win her over with finger food?"

He lifted a dripping magnum of champagne from the bucket. "I guess this wasn't a good idea, either?"

"Are you familiar with the term 'emergency room'?"

Kit seemed surprisingly unconcerned about

the bad news she was giving him. She wasn't just telling him to abandon his plan, she was saying he'd better watch his back in the meantime.

With a mysterious smile, he drew two glasses from the ice and filled them, then replaced the bottle. "It's going to be fine, Torrey."

"What's going to be fine?"

He crossed the short distance and handed one of the glasses to her, then clinked the rim with his.

"To old times," he said, his voice stirringly husky. The only thing he didn't do was kiss her fingertips, and she felt a little flutter of relief at that.

When she didn't join him in the toast, he took a sip and gazed at her a moment as if studying the changes in her features. Still holding her gaze, he took another sip. Was he remembering the eyelids he used to kiss shut? she wondered. The lips he'd once tasted, the neck he'd nuzzled? *The body he'd made shudder with ecstasy?*

Torrey set her glass down without touching the champagne. The flutter in the pit of her stomach was no longer about relief, and alcohol didn't settle right when she was this nervous.

"You'll have to trust me on this," he said finally, "but there'll be no trouble winning Bubbles over. I know a little secret about her."

"A secret?" Torrey was startled. She hadn't

thought his lingering gaze had anything to do with Bubbles. ''What kind of secret?''

''Well, now, if I told you that, it wouldn't be a secret, would it.''

''It had better be a pretty good one.''

His smile darkened with intrigue, and his laughter was so full of infectious devilment, she couldn't help but wonder what he was up to. Kit was one of the most competitive men she'd ever met, and if he'd made winning over Bubbles a mission, then Bubbles was going to be won over. He'd always had the ability to make it seem as if he could pull off miracles because he knew something no one else did. That was why he was a great hockey player. He was able to psych his opponent out.

A bitterness rose in her at the thought of some other woman getting this new and improved Kit McGrath, a man who from all appearances was ready for a full relationship. Torrey had no doubt that once he'd focused all of his passionate drive on captivating and capturing a woman, she wouldn't have a chance.

''If you've got the Bubbles thing figured out,'' she said, ''then I don't understand why you need me.''

''Some remedial help, just like you promised. These disasters I've been having are undermining my confidence, and I'm not taking any more chances. I could always fill her stateroom with flowers, but with my luck she'd be allergic.''

"You have a point."

"I need some practice courting a woman—and you need a contestant who will do you and your book proud on 'The Babs Randazzo Show,' right?"

Again he had a point. She certainly couldn't afford any more disasters. Still, it was hard to imagine Kit McGrath suffering from a lack of confidence with women. When he'd put his mind to it, he'd been wonderful at making Torrey feel special, even back in high school. She could admit now that the conflicts that led to her running away were probably as much her fault as his, though she didn't want to get into that with him now. Some water was better left under the bridge.

"Just for the sake of argument," she said, "let's assume Bubbles doesn't go for your throat the next time she sees you. What's your next move?"

"If she's receptive, and I have reason to think she will be, I thought I'd invite her here, create a mood."

There was a remote-control device on the occasional table next to Torrey. Kit picked it up and pressed a button. Torrey heard the rush of ocean waves, and suddenly the room was awash in the rich briny scents of the sea. A cool breeze caressed her shoulders, and she looked up to see a panel opening in the roof. The result was a star-studded sky equal to the brilliance of Tiffany's finest. Diamonds on black velvet, Torrey thought, more impressed than she wanted him to know.

"Pretty," she said, "but a little too Hollywood perhaps. The mood you want to create is one of intimacy."

"Intimacy? Coming right up." He hit another button, and the lights dimmed slightly. Music began to play, something soft and dreamy, probably by Kenny G.

She smiled. Men were so gadget-oriented. They'd rather play with remotes than with their mates, and this one seemed to be no exception.

"I was thinking of intimacy in a more personal sense," she explained. "For example, you could ask her to join you on the couch and then tell her you don't have to look up to see the stars. You can see them reflected in her eyes. That might go over a little better than 'You're hot enough to melt the plastic in my underwear.'"

"Even if it's true?" A smile quirked at the corners of his mouth, and his hand dropped to his belt as if he could offer proof. This time his gaze was both personal *and* intimate, and she had the distinct feeling he meant her, not Bubbles.

She wanted to smile back, but it seemed safest to keep a grip on her responses tonight. Make that a hammerlock, she amended. In her most teacherly tone she said, "After what happened to Bubble's hair, I think it best to keep all references to heat at a minimum, don't you?''

Undaunted, he tossed the remote on the table, took Torrey's hand and led her to the crescent-shaped couch. She knew before she sat down that it was going to be like floating on air currents. She could almost imagine a fashion model draped across it, and though she'd certainly never considered herself in that league, she knew the couch's lush white silk fabric was the perfect compliment to what she was wearing.

She'd picked an outfit she considered safe—not too sexy, but not demure, either. Bronze silk palazzo pants and a matching cropped top with a deep V-neck that buttoned up the front. Her sandals were all delicate gold straps, revealing bright splashes of coral polish on her toes.

She sat down a little left of center, intending to leave a comfortable space between them, but he didn't join her immediately. Instead, he poured her a fresh glass of champagne.

''Maybe this will help,'' he said as he handed the flute to her. ''You seem a little tense.''

And you don't, she thought, *for a man who was so flustered this morning.* But she put the crystal to her lips and drank, almost as if she'd been challenged.

Though she wasn't much of a drinker and had never really understood what the fuss over champagne was all about, the wine was delicious. It streamed down her throat, little bubbles bursting and tickling, cool yet warm, and had the odd effect of making her want to smile.

Perhaps she *was* smiling, because he seemed to be enjoying looking at her. Even in the low-lit salon, she could see the dark sparkle in his eyes, and their gazes connected for a moment as if they shared some private joke.

"Lovely," she admitted, meaning the Möet. "And you were right. It does, well, help."

"Good," he said. "That's important. I want this to work."

"This?"

"The evening, the talk show, all of it. It's important to you, isn't it?"

"Oh, yes." After a few more sips, Torrey would have been quite willing to admit on Bab's show that champagne was lovely if they'd let her. And it did seem to have the paradoxical effect of invigorating and relaxing you at the same time. If anything was making her tense, she realized, it was that Kit was still standing.

She patted the couch, amused at how flirtatious the gesture seemed. She might be getting a little too relaxed. "Aren't you going to sit down?"

"Actually I had something else in mind." He indicated her champagne flute, and she relinquished the glass with a certain reluctance, aware that she probably shouldn't have any more. But instead of refilling it, he set both their glasses on the table.

She was startled when he knelt by her feet. "What are you doing?" she asked as he slipped one of her sandals off.

"Something I've wanted to do since you walked in here." He cradled her bare foot in his hands. "May I?"

"May you...what?"

"This." He rolled a thumb over the ball of her foot, making a circle, lightly at first, just a whisper of sensation, then with a little more pressure. "I used to be pretty good at this, remember?"

Torrey's tummy flutters were back—and threatening to braid themselves into plaits and coils. She didn't doubt for a second that he was still *very* good at it. Her feet were the most sensitive part of her body—well, the second-most sensitive part—and his foot massages used to melt her like snow in a mountain hot spring. They were always the prelude to a night of passion.

"No, I don't think— Oh!" He'd delved into the curve of her arch and was applying just enough pressure to make her swoon.

He hesitated as if willing to back off if she said the word, and Torrey felt a sharp welling of disappointment and relief at the same time.

"You can stop me anytime," he assured her. *Stop,* she thought, but didn't say it. It was already too late. It had been too late the moment he'd knelt in front of her, and he knew it. Stopping this man was like stopping the tides from ebbing and flowing. She'd never been able to do it before, no matter what he was bent on. Why should she think she could now? And anyway, she told herself, it was just a foot massage. They weren't doing anything wrong, for heaven's sake.

He slipped off her other shoe, then, sitting on the couch, lifted her feet and cradled them in his lap. "This used to work wonders when you were tense, as I recall."

"Wonders...yes." It came back to her in a whoosh what great hands he had and how much he'd seemed to enjoy touching her, even casual touching. There'd been so little physical contact in Torrey's life before Kit. She was an only child, raised by a single mom, and Vera Benson had not been demonstrative. But Kit had exuded a male warmth and sensuality that caressed her like bathwater. She hadn't been able to get enough of it, even when he was just playing eensy weensy spider with her fingers or stroking the pulse point on the inside of her wrist.

Now he was running his knuckles the length of the instep of one foot, and ripples of pleasure made her belly tighten. Lord, massages were wonderful, full of marvelous contradictory sensations, as paradoxical as champagne. A warmth seemed to be building in the crease his knuckles made. Lovely, she thought. Almost too lovely to be borne.

Kit looked up, his head lifting slightly, his lashes lowering with curiosity.

Was she making noises? She certainly wanted to. The moan that filled her throat was musical, like a violin whose strings were being plucked, and the pressure to release it was almost overwhelming.

"Feel good?" he asked.

Heaven, she thought. Seventh or eighth at least.

"Don't hold back, Teach," he persisted in a low sexy voice. "Tell me how I'm doing here, would you? I need feedback."

Deadpan, she tilted her hand back and forth. "So-so."

Soft laughter told her he was a man who knew a faker when he saw one. "Apparently you need my magic-fingers Freddy Kreuger massage."

"No, no, no," she assured him. "This is fine— Ohhh, my!" Her back arched with pleasure.

He'd found a sweet spot in the center of her instep and was going for it. His thumbs probed deeply while his fingers stroked, first stimulating, then soothing. A flood of pleasure shot straight up her spine. She'd heard that parts of the foot corresponded to organs of the body, and if that was true she knew exactly what organ he was stimulating now. Yes, it was possible to make love without taking off your clothes. Torrey Benson had only to take off her shoes—and Kit knew that, too.

Apparently he hadn't forgotten that time on their honeymoon when he'd massaged her sole while doing wicked things to her toes, and she'd...well, suffice it to say she'd put a certain actress in a certain restaurant scene in a certain movie to shame—and Torrey hadn't been playacting. She'd fought for breath like the victim of an asthma attack. That wasn't the only time it had happened, either, but she didn't want to think about that now. It might happen again!

"Too hard? Too soft? Just right?" he asked.

Too wonderful. She was starting to question how she could ever have left a man with hands like his. His gifts weren't limited to the hockey rink, but the last thing she wanted to do while receiving a foot massage from her ex-husband was call up those memories. "Maybe we should get back to the remedial social skills?"

A dark eyebrow lifted in surprise. "You're not enjoying this?"

"That's not what I said."

"We can't have that." His tone was rich with irony.

"I *am* enjoying it, really."

"I thought so." Studying her expression, he worked along the outsides of her foot toward her toes, rotating his thumbs in wider and wider circles and deepening the pressure as he reached the ball. He was approaching the place where her nerves were ultrasensitive—the delicate crevice at the base of her toes. The slightest touch there, even the zing of a thumbnail, was wildly stimulating.

It wasn't just what he was doing, she realized. It was the way he was watching her, with the dark fascination of a researcher who took some private satisfaction in her responses. He wasn't dispassionate, though. It would have been a mistake to assume that kind of detachment. His focus was deep and penetrating as he began to stroke outward from the center of her foot in a fanlike pattern.

Torrey had never wanted to groan with pleasure so badly in her life. She could feel tension building within her, and it was a vibrant living thing.

"Is that better?" he wanted to know.

"Define 'better.'" She laughed helplessly. There was no point in lying. Her cheeks were hot and she could feel prickles of warmth mottling her throat. The skin of her throat and chest always got blotchy when she was aroused. Hopefully he didn't remember that detail.

"This," he said huskily, "is better." A smile flickered as he brought her foot to his mouth and kissed her instep lightly. Odd little thrills rolled up Torrey's leg, robbing her of strength and draining her of the will to resist. Her muscles and nerves went slack with pleasure. No more, she thought. No more. But it *was* too late. He was just beginning.

He kissed a path up her sole like a caressing breeze, and the ball of her foot was all taut tingling curves as he feathered it with his lips. Suddenly his tongue darted into the sensitive crevice at the base of her toes, and Torrey sagged backward, catching herself with her elbows.

This man would be the wrack and ruin of her. He'd seduced her into running away from home with him at sixteen—or was it the other way around? Well, however it happened, he'd destroyed her life. He broke her ankle and her heart with that silly hockey stick of his. And look what he was doing to her now!

He was tormenting her with pleasure, running his demon tongue along the crease of her toes and even slipping it between them. He had to stop. He simply had to or something embarrassing was going to happen. Her body was alive with sensation from her toes on up.

"Was I right?" he wanted to know as he caught the ball of her foot between his teeth and bit down lightly. "Better?"

"Champagne pales," she assured him, utterly sincere. Her mouth was so dry she could hardly speak. Her clammering heart seemed to have taken up permanent residence there, which didn't help. "Can we stop now?" she pleaded. "We're supposed to be helping you learn to court women."

"I'm a fast learner." He drew one of her toes into his mouth and sucked on it lightly. The gentle pressure pulled at Torrey's senses and lit her nerves like fuses. By the time he'd worked his way down her toes to the smallest one, her entire body had seized up and she was in big trouble. There was only one way to go now, and she couldn't let that happen.

"Don't you think we—" She tried to pull back her foot, but he wouldn't let her.

"Yes, I do," he said, looking up. "I definitely do." Torrey braced herself against the next blast of feelings, determined to block them. She had no idea what to expect, but somehow she had to resist him. And more important, resist herself. Her body was going crazy.

He did nothing except look at her for a moment, a slow searching gaze that caressed her from the top of her head to the foot he was holding. And then he placed another kiss in the curve of her instep and sent her over the edge.

Her stomach muscles locked violently, and deeper still another part of her sent out pulse after glorious pulse. Rapture flooded her, the color of a sunrise. A deep shudder rocked through her, and she fell backward into the cushions, unaware she'd cried out.

Kit was quiet for a moment, but she could feel his presence, and she heard the concern in his voice as he spoke. "Are you all right?"

She shook her head slowly, unable to move

from the pillows and not wanting to speak for
fear she'd gasp. Finally, when she could manage
it, she lifted her head and croaked, "I'm never
wearing sandals again. From now on it's Doc
Martens. I'll even wear them to bed."

"I guess that means you're *not* all right?"

"I'll be fine once I find out where my pulse
took off to. It headed for parts unknown about
fifteen minutes ago."

He was cradling her foot in his lap and lightly
stroking the top. It felt so good Torrey wanted
to cry. She really did.

"Is there anything I can do to help?" Kit
asked. "Would you like more champagne? Min-
eral water? A tranquilizer?"

"You've done plenty," she said with bitter-
sweet conviction. She could only hope against
hope that he didn't actually know what he'd
done to her. No man should be able to give a
woman a peak experience by touching her foot.
It just wasn't fair!

She struggled to a sitting position, repeatedly
refusing his offers of help. It took her several
moments to clear her head, but putting her feet
solidly on the floor helped, as did bending over
to strap on her sandals. Once she'd taken those
steps, she was out of the woods and back on the
path to restoring her sanity.

"Does this mean the lesson's over?" he asked
as she tweaked her palazzo pants into shape.
"I'm supposed to capture the heart of a million-

aire with only one weapon in my arsenal—foot massage?''

That possibility had never dawned on her. She glanced up at him, startled at the thought. ''You're not planning to try this stuff on Bubbles, are you?''

''You're the teacher. Should I?''

''I don't think her heart will hold out.''

ICE. KIT NEEDED some ice to cool himself down. A long gleaming stretch of it and a pair of blades to work off this energy.

Steam. That was what the ice would be the moment he made contact with it. That was how hot he was. For her.

He threw off the sheets and crossed the room naked and aroused, bathed in chilly ocean breezes. It was freezing. He'd opened the entire suite to the night air, but the problem was his thoughts. They were burning him up inside.

Kit McGrath had brain fever. He was obsessed with feminine body parts. His mind was cluttered with them, all delicately arched and gracefully shaped. All sexy as sin.

All feet.

Her feet. The seat of her passion apparently.

Kit wanted to laugh as he stood at the open doors to his private balcony and stared at the sparkling star-sheened ocean. He might have if he hadn't known that laughing would hurt like hell. That was how tight he was. How hard. Over a woman's feet. He could see them, feel them, taste them. And he could still hear her breathless reaction when he'd done all those things.

Don't hold back, Teach, he thought, remembering what he'd said to her at one point in the evening. *Don't hold back.* And she hadn't. He'd seen her eyelids quiver and her body jerk. She'd come unglued right there in front of him. Trembling and gasping and trying desperately to cover it up.

If she'd known how impossible that was, she wouldn't have bothered. There was nothing she could hide from him. He'd lived with her for more than a year in wedded bliss, all things being relative, especially the bliss. He knew her secrets. Like Achilles, her feet were her downfall, but she had others, clothing being one. Try as she might, she couldn't seem to complete the dressing process, which made her vulnerable to anyone who might decide to lend her a helping hand.

Again the urge to laugh welled in his throat. Most men preferred undressing women. He got tremendous satisfaction out of buttoning, snapping and zipping them up, at least one of them. Sagging slips, upturned labels, forgotten price tags, bra straps. He loved that stuff.

But he wasn't exactly impartial to the other stuff that made her unique, either. It had been years since he'd seen her, but it was all stashed away in the data bank. Whether blessing or curse, he could remember nearly every smile, every tear... Not to mention her vulnerability. When she wanted something, when she needed it, she couldn't hide. She wasn't able to conceal her desires like most people. She wore them on her unbuttoned sleeve.

Only one thing about her had caught him off guard. Her beauty. Not that her features were perfect. She still had that goofy little wobble in her smile and a visible bend in the bridge of her nose. Her eyes were odd, too, a smoky shade of amber when they should have been gray or blue, and you had to stare at her awhile to figure out what was wrong. But she *was* beautiful. And she was every inch a woman. He should have seen that before.

Aware of the damp chill in the air and the steam heat in his veins, he supported himself with a hand propped high against the door frame. At least steam would clean the pipes, he told himself. Luckily she couldn't have known what effect she was having on them. His pipes.

Starlight sheened the rigid muscles forged by years of athletic competition. He should be shivering and shriveled, but the cold felt like a balm to his overstimulated condition. His body was primed for action, and it wanted the games to begin. Hell, he could have played hockey without a stick.

"That will be *your* downfall if you're not careful, McGrath," he announced, a warning directed at the offending part of his anatomy. The rising ache in his groin was sublimely uncomfortable. He'd never been so aroused for so long without relief, and he didn't see any coming his way.

Glittering waves lapped gently along the boat's prow, but the sound did nothing to soothe him. He was supposed to get *her* hot and bothered, not the other way around. He wanted Torrey Benson eating out of his hand, even if he had to go by way of her feet to do it.

He released a crack of pained laughter. He was a man with a fever. A man with a plan. And he was going to get what he came for before Torrey Benson caught her balance and figured out what was really going on. Otherwise he'd be burning up inside for the rest of his natural life.

THE TELEVISION CREW didn't show up for Torrey's class the following morning. They were doing pickup shots around the cruise ship, clips of sea gulls in flight, couples around the pool and towel-draped bodies in the sauna. The other missing party was her ex-husband, and Torrey was nearly crazy with relief on both counts. Maybe Kit had found her wanton display as offensive as she had. Or maybe that was all he'd wanted, to reduce her to a puddle of passion and move on to bigger game, like Bubbles.

Torrey could hope.

The lecture she'd planned was called "Exer-

cising the Love Muscles," but first she wanted
to hear how her students had been doing with
their homework assignments. "Good morning,
everyone!" Her voice rang with false confidence. "Anybody have a success story to
share?"

Vicki's hand shot up. "I've been having too
much success," she announced. "One of the
men I smiled at followed me into the john and
offered to hold my purse while I...you know."

"Polite of him," Torrey allowed, reasonably
certain she hadn't heard the whole story. "Is
there any chance you did anything other than
smile, Vicki?"

"Oh, yeah, absolutely. I used one of the pickup lines from your book and, zowie, did it work.
I had to fend him off he got so amorous. He was
bird-dogging me around the buffet table, waving
a tamale and telling me how hot he was."

Delighted laughter rose from the class, but
Torrey was growing uneasy. "Which line was
that?" she asked.

"Well," Vicki said proudly, "I sidled up to
him at the bar, leaned over and whispered in his
ear, 'The word for today is legs. Let's spread the
word.'"

A gasp went up and then the small assemblage
broke out in uproarious applause. But Torrey's
heart sank. She had listed the "best" and the
"worst" pickup lines in the book, but her students seemed to be confusing the two lists. Kit's

melting-underwear remark was another case in point.

"Class, class..." She was trying to get their attention when the door at the back of the room opened. The woman who swished in could have entered herself in the Rose Parade as a small float. Not that she was a large woman. In fact, she was petite. She was simply flowers from head to toe. Her sarong was a tropical-jungle print, and several gaudy antheriums were stuck about her bouffant hairdo. Even her sandals were adorned with blossoms. Bubbles herself had joined the flirting class.

"Please, have a seat," Torrey said with a smile that was warmer and more welcoming than she felt. She nodded toward a chair at the back of the auditorium-style room. The passengers were supposed to have signed up for the classes in advance, but there was no extra fee and technically the sessions were open to all, so Torrey had little choice but to be gracious.

Only a handful of Torrey's students noticed Bubbles as she took a seat and began to arrange her flower garden. The rest of them were having too much fun comparing the dreadful pickup lines Torrey's book specifically told them to avoid.

"'Wanna go play Twister naked?'"

"'My friends call me Orange. Wanna squeeze me?'"

"'That must be a mirror in your pocket because I can see myself in your pants.'"

"Class!" Torrey had to raise her voice to be heard above the commotion. "Sorry to be a kill-joy, but that's the 'worst' list you're reading from. Those lines are the no-no's." When she had their attention, she picked up her copy of *How to Marry a Millionaire* and began flipping through it. "Let's all turn to chapter five and go over the 'best' list."

She was about to read one of her favorites when the door opened again. This time it was Kit, and for some reason everyone turned to look. Not because of his appearance, Torrey realized, though he looked disgustingly fit in his black workout pants and tank top. It must have been the expression on her face that made their heads swivel.

Torrey's gaze flicked from him to Bubbles and back to him.

Kit's gaze flicked from Torrey to Bubbles and back to her.

She felt like a mouse caught in one of those nasty spring traps. Not only did she have to deal with the man who'd made love to her feet the night before, she had his target millionaire mate right there in the room. And Torrey didn't share Kit's confidence about winning Bubbles over. Still, there was *something* to be grateful for, she reminded herself. No TV cameras were present.

If Kit sensed Torrey's apprehension, he gave

no sign of it. Very much the strategist having a leisurely look at the playing field, he paused by the door to size things up before entering.

Alerted by the sudden silence, Bubbles stopped arranging her flower garden and looked up.

She spotted Kit immediately and, to Torrey's surprise, smiled and patted the chair next to hers. Bubbles was inviting him to come sit down? But the last time she'd observed these two lovebirds, the body language had been unmistakable. Bubbles had been taking a swing at him.

Bewildered, Torrey looked down at her notes, trying to remember what today's lecture was. Love muscles. She was going to talk about how to strengthen them. Could there possibly be a worse topic.

She glanced up and saw that they were all watching her.

"If you want physical health, you have to exercise the muscles of the body," she said, picking up her notes and reading directly from her material. She didn't dare do otherwise. She could barely keep a thought in her head. "If you want emotional health, you have to exercise the muscles of the heart. How many of you have ever sent yourself a love note and flowers?"

Torrey glanced up to see Vicki waving her hand. "Chocolates," she said. "I send myself a box of Godiva truffles every year on the anniversary of my gallbladder operation."

"Good for you, Vicki." Some instinct told Torrey to move on quickly. "How many of you believe there's an incredible relationship in your future? That someone special is already out there waiting for you, wondering where you are at this very moment?"

Apparently Kit believed it. He was so busy laughing and whispering with Bubbles, he seemed to have forgotten he was in a classroom. Whatever grudging sympathy Torrey might have felt for his predicament was history. He gave a woman about the same amount of attention he did a hockey puck, just long enough to score. Somebody ought to warn poor Bubbles what she was getting into.

"N-e-x-t." Torrey spelled out the letters with military briskness. "How many of you are willing to let go of whatever isn't working and say *next?* Next boyfriend, next life lesson, next golden opportunity?"

Me, she thought, raising her hand. *Next husband! One who hates sports and is too much a gentleman to take advantage of a woman's instep.*

Inspired by her example, the rest of the class raised their hands, too, all except Kit and Bubbles, who were too busy playing touchy-feely games. Kit seemed intent on identifying all the various flowers in Bubbles's garden, and she seemed more than happy to let him play groundskeeper.

The rest of the lecture went badly. It was difficult convincing people they should practice loving themselves and others unconditionally when you were speaking through clenched teeth and with the snap of a drill sergeant. Somehow Torrey made it to the end of the session, and as she wound things up, she realized she'd learned something today even if her students hadn't. She'd put a lot of miles and time between herself and Kit McGrath, but that was all it was. Physical and temporal space. Emotionally she was still as stuck as the day she tripped on his hockey stick and fell head over heels in love with him. It really was time to say *next*.

"Your homework for today," she told the class, "is pure self-indulgence. I want you to set aside ten minutes for uninterrupted relaxation. Choose whatever method you prefer—meditation, alternate-nostril breathing, a massage or a sauna at the spa. The goal is to pamper yourself."

Torrey pretended to be busy with her papers as the class filed out, Kit and Bubbles bringing up the rear. But as they approached the door, she overheard Kit say something to Bubbles about meeting her later. Bubbles blew him a kiss and left.

Torrey braced herself as Kit came sauntering up to her, looking impossibly pleased with himself. And why wouldn't he be? Knocking over two women in less than twenty-four hours was pretty good scoring.

She was very aware that he'd paused to check her out, especially her wraparound skirt and blouse, as if he expected to see inside-out pockets or material coming apart at the seams. Fortunately she'd taken extra care this morning.

"Something wrong, Teach?" he asked. "You don't look happy at the progress your remedial case is making."

"I'm thrilled. See?" She bared her teeth in a smile, not caring that he knew how upset she was. "That's what 'thrilled' looks like." She gathered her materials together and thrust them into her tote bag. "You're making so much progress you should be teaching this class, Romeo."

She left him standing there with a startled expression on his handsome face and went off to indulge herself in ten minutes of total relaxation. Or die trying.

"CLAUDIA, ARE YOU SURE there's nothing I can do?"

Torrey hovered over the bed of her fallen friend, deeply concerned about her condition. Claudia had valiantly shepherded Torrey through every glitch during the promotional junket until this ordeal. She was a dynamo among women. Torrey had rarely seen her sit down, much less take to her bed, but Claudia was violently indisposed this trip. She still couldn't keep anything in her stomach, and green was definitely not her color.

"Actually there is something," Claudia mumbled. "You could kill me and get it over with."

"Can do," Torrey said cheerfully, hoping to get a smile out of her friend. "But who'd plan the burial at sea? Nobody, but *nobody,* has your organizational skills."

Claudia moaned and turned her face into the pillow.

Torrey, who normally was pretty good with people not named Kit, was at a loss. She'd been on her way to the sauna to try out her own homework assignment, but she'd wanted to stop in and see how Claudia was doing. In truth, she'd come for selfish purposes, hoping to find the courage to confide the mess with her ex-husband to Claudia, who had no idea Torrey and Kit even knew each other. Torrey sorely needed to get it off her chest, and Claudia was a whiz at damage control. But she couldn't say anything now that Claudia's condition had worsened. She didn't want to make her friend any sicker.

Torrey picked up a bottle from the bedside table and rattled it. "More motion-sickness pills?"

"Can't keep 'em down, thanks all the same," Claudia mumbled. "That nitwit ship's doctor should have prescribed suppositories."

Torrey took some encouragement from the

sarcasm that had crept into her friend's tone. "Should I call him again?"

"Call that horrible little man? He had the nerve to ask if I might be pregnant, and you can guess what he suggested then. It also starts with a *P*. Pelvic exam! Don't let him near me, Torrey. Promise you won't."

Torrey volunteered to stand guard at the door if necessary. Feeling helpless, she gingerly suggested an acupuncture technique she'd heard about for nausea, but Claudia pulled the covers over her head and burrowed like a hibernating animal. The pathetic sounds emanating from the bed made Torrey think that the best thing she could do was leave her friend in peace.

As Torrey rose, she saw the pitcher of water with a slice of lemon floating in it. She was a dabbler in natural medicine, and sometimes the old-fashioned remedies worked when nothing else did. "You know, something as simple as sucking on a lemon has been known to cure—"

The bedcovers flew off and Claudia sprang up, a shade of green that was beyond description. "Torrey, get out of here before I lose another motion-sickness pill! Go bother people who want to marry millionaires!"

This is why I'm not a nurse, Torrey thought. With a vague promise to check back later, she crept out the door.

TORREY WASN'T A FAN of saunas. She found them too hot and confining to be truly relaxing, but she wasn't taking her chances with another massage. If her feet were still that sensitive, there might be other parts of her body that were, too. She wouldn't be dealing with Kit of course, and the massage therapists in the spa were trained, but still, the potential for embarrassment was ever present.

That was how she'd come to be lying naked on a bench made of wooden slats, with nothing but a towel draped over her dripping torso. Fortunately the ship's sauna was so small it could only accommodate two or three people at once, and she happened to be alone in the little square box of a room at the moment. Alone and sweating profusely.

It was a cleansing thing, she told herself, feeling beads of perspiration trickle over her closed eyelids. She merely needed to visualize all the stress and toxins streaming from her body through her pores, making a new woman out of her.

Torrey was imagining being a warrior squaw enduring her first purification ceremony when the door opened and she heard someone enter. She didn't dare look. Her eyes were already stinging from the salt, but all her other senses were alerted to the intrusion.

When she heard the person stretch out on the bench opposite her and release a satisfied sigh, she relaxed, too. At least it wasn't someone who

wanted to chat about vitamin supplements and
workout sessions, which was pretty much the
conversational fare in health spas these days.

Still, it wasn't the same as being alone, she
soon realized. She was very aware of the other
presence and couldn't seem to get back into the
visualization mode. After a few more moments
had passed, she decided to call it quits. She used
a corner of the towel to wipe her face and eyes,
but as she sat up to wrap the thick bolt of terry
cloth around her, she realized she couldn't make
out much more than blurry images.

Knotting the towel above her breasts, she tip-
toed her way to the door to let herself out. A
twist of the doorknob told her something was
wrong. It nearly came off in her hand. She tried
again, not wanting to disturb the other occupant,
but the knob wobbled around without catching.
She was going to have to butt the door with her
shoulder, and that would be noisy.

As she turned to explain, she got a glimpse of
a body that nearly made her eyes bug out. A
totally naked and totally astounding body
stretched out on the bench. There was a towel,
too, but it was covering the person's face.

"Oh, my God!" Torrey gasped, averting her
eyes. She was afraid to believe what she'd just
seen. The heat must have cooked her brain cells.
It couldn't have been— Could it?

Afraid to move, she could hear considerable
fumbling with the towel and then several sec-

onds of pregnant silence. "Isn't this the men's sauna?" a male voice asked sheepishly.

"*Kit?*"

"Torrey?"

"What are you doing in here?" She choked out the question, still afraid to turn around. "Are you decent?"

"No—" he laughed "—but I've got the towel around me now."

She whirled, breathing furiously and absently aware that she was endangering the security of her own towel. "How could you have mistaken this for the men's sauna? It says 'women' right there on the door. If I could get it open, I'd show you."

"Sorry." He shook back a thatch of dark damp hair and fought off a grin that threatened to break his jaw if it ever got loose. "I guess I wasn't paying attention. You know how I am."

Did she ever. If he'd been paying attention fifteen years ago, they might still be together. But right now she could do just fine without his attention, especially in this tiny room with both of them sweltering hot and nearly naked.

He'd changed in ways that only a lover would notice, she realized, reluctant to admit the awareness, even within the privacy of her thoughts. He seemed bigger and stronger, more heavily muscled through the shoulders and neck, but it was probably the close quarters. He certainly had more scars. She counted three on his chest alone and one on his left biceps, and there was a nasty diagonal slash across his belly that looked awfully fresh, like it might have happened not long ago. Worse, it cut low, to parts below his towel line. It was even possible it ran all the way to his—

"See anything you like?" he asked.

Hip, she thought. All the way to his smart-aleck hip. "The outside of this room—that's what I'd like to see. The door is jammed. I suppose *that* was an accident, too?"

He never answered the question, but he took a moment to look into her eyes, as if he'd spotted something utterly intriguing in their blazing amber depths. And then he glanced down at the loosening knot in her towel, which she immediately covered with her hand.

"Let's see what we can do about that," he said.

"My towel?"

"The door first, then we'll see about you."

In your dreams. She moved aside to give him room to work, and while he was tinkering with the loose doorknob, she quickly untied the towel and mopped her face again. At least she had an excuse for being so flushed. *It was hot.*

"What did you do to this thing?" he asked.

"Me?" Rushing to get herself back together, she protested, "I didn't do anything to it. It was working perfectly fine when I let myself in."

"Well, it's broken now." He turned around with the knob in his hand.

"No kidding." Torrey was aware of an odd mixture of feelings as she realized they were trapped in the sauna. Indignation and dread, laced with a strange rising excitement. What surprised her was the latter. She had the same tight throat and startled pulse she'd had when he'd picked her up after she took a nasty spill on their first ice-skating date. They'd been kids, and he'd pressed a breathless kiss to her tearful mouth.

She'd been dripping with perspiration then, too, though it'd been the middle of winter. And she had never wanted that kiss to end. Her wildly racing heart had told her how much she loved the crush of his arms and the glorious heat of his embrace. It had felt as if his passionate concern for her safety was penetrating to the very center of her being, and the answering need that had risen inside her had been frightening, a harbinger of doom, she now realized. No one should ever be that vulnerable to another human being. Or that much in love. It was inviting devastation.

The situation could not be more different now, she reminded herself. Her throat might be tight and her pulse might have that same high hollow percussion, but she wasn't a desperate clinging vine of a teenager anymore. She didn't have stars in her eyes or hunger in her heart. If she had anything in her heart at the moment, it was the desire to stop the perspiration that was trickling into her cleavage.

He smiled at the clumsy knot she'd made with the sodden towel. "You do need help," he said, his voice softening to a husky growl. "You need a valet."

"You mean a maid."

"I mean someone to get you dressed and keep you that way until it's time to undress you."

"I can dress myself just fine, thank—"

"Really?"

His hand flicked out so quickly she didn't know what had happened until she saw her towel fall away. When she attempted to grab it, he was already there, covering her exposed breasts with the terry cloth and neatly tucking one end of the towel into the other as if she were a bed to be made up with military corners.

His fingers left faint marks on her overheated skin. He'd touched her, *was* touching her!

"There," he said, stepping back to inspect his handiwork. "Now you don't have to worry about flashing anybody. Not even a hurricane could rip this baby off you."

Torrey's voice was low and it shook so hard she could barely make herself understood. "You don't have the right to worry about my clothing, Kit McGrath," she said. "Much less touch it— or me! You lost that privilege a long time ago."

She turned her back on him, wishing there was somewhere for her to go. How could she possibly humiliate herself any more than she already had? By crying, she thought, tears welling.

The slat benches were stacked up three deep and arranged in tiers, like stair steps. They were her only refuge, she realized. But the floor was slippery and her foot hit a slick spot as she moved toward them. The rest of it happened so quickly she would have been on the floor if he hadn't caught her.

How could she have forgotten about his reflexes?

He gripped her gently by the shoulders, steadying her as she lurched backward. When she didn't move or try to break away, he drew her close enough to breathe an apology against her hair. "You're right," he said. "You're absolutely right, Torrey, and I'm sorry."

Now her heart was beating wildly. Painfully. Dear God, what was he doing? He had to stop! The solid strength of his hands swept her back in time and held her in memory's embrace. She was that girl again, lying on the ice one second, scooped up into a boy's arms the next, a boy whose voice was so choked with passion and concern that she didn't want him to let go of her. Ever.

Kit, she thought, *Kit, if you knew what you did to me that day, if you knew what you're doing to me now...*

Longing. It flared through her with frightening force, even more frightening than all those years ago. Life had promised her everything then, that she could love and be loved to distraction, that all her needs would be met by this one man. Now she knew what could happen when you held nothing back, how hope could rip through your heart and leave it in tatters, how love could bring you to your knees.

With a ragged sigh, she wrenched herself free and sank onto the bench, defeated. All those years, all that hurt, and she hadn't escaped any of it. She was still in love with him.

He knelt beside her, his hands clasped in his lap in a seeming effort not to touch her. "I meant it, Torrey. I am sorry."

Torrey shook her head, needing distance. She couldn't handle the emotional proximity any better than the physical. "It's all right."

"No, it isn't. This isn't a sporting event and you're not the opposition. I'll admit I was trying to make a point, but I didn't have to be a world-class jerk about it."

"Point taken," she said, unable to hide the shakiness in her voice. "To be honest, I'd forgotten how fast you are. Those reflexes of yours, they're...amazing."

His eyes darkened, and she could only imagine what thoughts were going through his head.

"I think we need to talk," he said. "Don't you? We never had that chance..."

Because I ran away, she thought. *Because I*

want to run away now. "It's awfully late in the game to call a time-out." Her voice was edged with a hurt she couldn't conceal, and she knew it must be making her sound bitter. "Why don't I just concede the match and get it over with? Wouldn't that be easier all the way round?"

He was quiet for a moment. Finally his shoulders moved and he exhaled a heavy breath. "Maybe the smartest thing to do right now would be to get us out of this room."

He was giving up? So easily? Why wouldn't he fight for her? Why hadn't he come after her? The pain in her heart made Torrey want to lash out. That was what he'd done before. He'd let her go. That was why she couldn't forgive him. He would fight to the death to win a hockey game, but he wouldn't fight for her.

"That would be the smartest thing," she agreed, her voice in danger of cracking. "Why don't you concentrate on getting that door open, and once you have, do you think we could manage not to see each other again? Ever?"

TORREY HAD SEVERAL dresses under consideration for the nightclub excursion that evening, but a glance in the mirrored doors of her closet told her it had to be this one, the marigold yellow halter dress with its snug-fitting smocked top. The neckline was cut dramatically low, but what really drew the eye were tantalizing glimpses of her suntanned legs through the sheer ankle-length skirt.

The cruise ship had docked that afternoon in Puerto Vallarta, and tonight's excursion was her class's field trip. Her students would actually get to practice their flirting skills with civilians on dry land. Torrey would be along to supervise of course, and the camera crew would be there to record the event on tape for the entertainment of the masses. Torrey hoped it wouldn't be too entertaining.

Of course she wanted to be dazzling for the cameras, but that only explained part of her obsession with grooming. She was hoping to drop a certain someone in his tracks when he spotted her. Kit hadn't come back to class or made any attempt to see her since the disaster in the sauna, and Torrey wanted, just once, to make him feel a pang of regret over losing her. Yes, it was a childish impulse, even counterproductive, she knew that. But if every relationship had pain, then it should be shared equally, and he hadn't had his quota yet. That was why she had to be devastating tonight.

She wanted to make him sweat, too. Bullets.

She smoothed a finger over the arch of her eyebrow, congratulating herself on her look. She'd slicked back her hair in a very tight French knot and secured an exotic pink orchid above her ear. It wasn't at all like her, much too sophisticated and sensual, but apparently her ex-husband liked bold fashion statements, or he wouldn't have picked a woman like Bubbles.

She only hoped she could carry it off. She didn't have the best of luck with regular clothing, much less something this Mata Hari-ish. Just once Torrey hoped the gods of fashion would cut her some slack. Was that too much to ask? Just once. Tonight.

She stopped by the dresser on her way out, where there was a huge bouquet of exotics. Steven had sent them with a note saying he was counting the moments until she arrived in Cabo San Lucas for their wedding tomorrow. From another man—from Kit—it might have been a very passionate sentiment, but Steven wasn't a passionate man. He was an *appropriate* one. Which was exactly what she liked about him.

He always did the appropriate thing—flowers on the occasions that called for them, a lovely personal gift on her birthday. His gestures of affection weren't just thoughtful, they were reassuring. She could count on them, on him. There was nothing reassuring about Kit McGrath, however. He was as likely to forget your birthday as not, then kidnap you and hold you hostage, torturing you with all kinds of exquisitely sensual delights, until you "forgave" him—or died of pleasure trying to resist.

She touched the orchid in her hair, reminding herself that it was one of Steven's flowers. Tomorrow she would become his wife in a gala wedding ceremony that would be taped and ultimately seen across the country. But that wasn't why she was marrying him. She was marrying him because he was exactly what she needed—someone solid and stable, a boulder in the gravel pit of life.

She smiled at the analogy. Most important, though, Steven loved and accepted her the way she was. He didn't feel the need to embarrass her in public situations, torment her with foot massages or "fix" her clothing. And he didn't inspire those terrible surges of feeling that left her gasping. Torrey had had her fill of passion, quite frankly. It was dangerous, and with the wrong man it could be deadly. The warm cozy glow Steven inspired was better any day.

THE EMBARCADERO was one of those theme nightclubs where the decor reminded you of an elaborate ride at Disneyland. This one could have been Pirates of the Caribbean, Kit had decided, except that a plaque in the *entrada* claimed the entry was made from the hull of an original eighteenth-century man-of-war. The fishing nets and ship parts hanging on the walls looked weathered and worm-holed enough to be authentic. At any rate the place was the showpiece of one of Puerto Vallarta's largest hotels, and it had atmosphere to spare.

Kit sat at the El Capitan bar, sipping his second Scotch neat and watching the band set up at the far end of the spacious cocktail lounge. A large expanse of gleaming ship's-wheel tables and glowing lanterns filled the space between the bar and the hardwood dance floor, which could be seen through the dangling beads of an archway that was nearly as wide as the room. Kit had come early, knowing this was where Torrey was bringing her class, but even two drinks hadn't prepared him for the sight of his ex-wife as she entered the lounge.

He wouldn't have recognized her if she hadn't been with her students. The sleek hair, sensual flower and revealing halter-top dress lent her the regal air of a flamenco dancer. She looked perfectly put together and invulnerable in every way. And God, how he ached to mess her up. Why was that? he wondered. He'd caught the brass ring he'd been reaching for. He should have been happy to see her reaching for hers. She'd worked hard, and now everything she wanted was within her grasp, a new husband, a career, a whole new life, none of which had anything to do with him. She'd put up the barriers; why couldn't he leave them intact?

He finished the Scotch. The truth was he didn't know the why of it. He didn't have an answer. He just knew he couldn't. Perhaps he hadn't appreciated her when he'd had her, but God, he'd barely been eighteen at the time. Too young to appreciate anything except the outrage he felt when he found out that she'd lied to him, that she wasn't pregnant and their rushed marriage had been a sham. All her efforts to explain had fallen on deaf ears. All he could think about was what he'd given up for her, the chance of a lifetime, a shot at the pros, probably the only one he'd ever get.

Sure, he'd been a self-centered bastard. He hadn't realized how selfish until it was too late, but she'd been wrong, too. She hadn't trusted him enough to let him go after his dream. She hadn't believed he would come back for her and make her a part of it all. Or she simply hadn't thought he was worth the wait.

Well, Kit McGrath *was* back, fifteen years later and a great deal wiser. Back to do what he should have done then.

TORREY NOTICED KIT coming toward her out of the corner of her eye and quickly checked her outfit. Everything looked fine. No tags, no straps, and she wasn't wearing a slip. Hopefully the orchid was still in place and didn't look as if it were growing out of her ear.

She'd had her eye on him all evening and was aware of his brooding interest in her. She'd seen him with Bubbles earlier, but they'd only spoken briefly, and then Bubbles had wandered off with a group of Torrey's students, apparently to check out the dance band. Other than that, he'd been watching Torrey like a hunter, waiting for the quail to break into flight.

Torrey wanted to do just that. If he kept looking at her like that, he was going to burn a hole in her, the way a magnifying glass did when it concentrated sunlight. Fortunately several of her students were crowded around her, scoping out the male possibilities and discussing flirtation strategies. She was glad to have them for protection.

"You look ravishing," Kit said as he walked up to her, apparently not caring who heard him. Something in his voice made the group go silent and fall away from Torrey, although they were glancing at each other in barely suppressed delight as they did so. Torrey could hear their whispering and buzzing as they huddled a few feet away. The only one with the nerve to hang around was Vicki, and when Kit cut her a look, she excused herself and backed off, too.

"I said you look ravishing," he repeated.

He clearly wanted her to acknowledge his compliment, but Torrey had no intention of doing so, no matter how powerful the impulse was to give him what he wanted. He looked pretty ravishing himself.

"Where's Bubbles?" she asked, her voice artificially bright.

Kit's shrug was so offhand it sent an anticipatory thrill through Torrey. Was it wishful thinking, or had he lost interest in the Sudsy One?

The way he was looking at Torrey now made her want to turn her back to him and check herself out again. Was she coming out of her dress? Getting blotchy? She sensed that he was dying to touch her, to rearrange her and leave his mark of ownership on her in some way. Or at least his seal of approval. Mostly he looked like he wanted to pluck the flower out of her hair and toss it away.

"Trouble in paradise?" she asked.

"Not that I know of," he said, slipping his hands into his pockets and hunching his shoulders. "Bubbles met someone who installs salad bars in Laundromats so you can graze while your underwear is being fluff-dried. They're talking business."

Torrey continued to hold out hope. "She met another man?"

He shook his head. "Bubbles only does business with women. She doesn't think men understand the potential of clean laundry as a healing power in our lives. It's part of her charm."

Despite everything, Torrey found herself laughing. Bubbles *was* quite a character. Torrey loved people, the quirkier the better, and she didn't like feeling jealous and possessive, especially of a man she had no claim on. Besides, she herself was getting married in less than twenty-four hours. She kept forgetting that.

"I'd like to dance with you," he said.

"Interesting way to ask," she replied, determined to be sardonic. Her mind was screaming no, but every part of her body wanted to leap at the chance. And if her breasts weren't blotchy before, they were now. She could feel the heat.

Torrey nearly gasped when he laced his fingers through hers as if he meant to dance right there. He was just so damn sure of himself. He always had been, and it was easy to mistake that for arrogance. He knew what he wanted and spared nothing to get it. He'd never believed that life owed him anything and had worked ceaselessly to realize his dreams. She admired his drive. She only wished their relationship hadn't been sacrificed in its name.

"I'm not here to dance," she informed him. "This is the high-school prom, and I get to be the chaperon who makes sure her kids don't get into trouble."

"Your kids are all in there dancing," he pointed out, turning her around so that she could see her students had abandoned her. "You taught them well. Now let them flirt till they drop. It's your turn, Ms. Benson. Besides, if you'll remember when we were in school, even the chaperons got to dance. That's the best way to keep an eye on the students."

She couldn't argue with his logic, so she decided to ignore it. "Apparently I didn't teach *you* well. You're supposed to wait for signals, you know. A man should approach a woman only when he's received clear signals that she wants him to."

"What kind of signal is it when a woman

sneaks peeks at a man all evening long?'' His hand tightened around hers, and he urged her toward the dance floor as he spoke. "Or when her breath goes shallow and her pupils dilate while she's talking to him?''

"My pupils aren't dilated!''

He laughed. "Who said I was talking about you? That was hypothetical. What about a woman's pulse? When that goes wild, what does it mean?''

"It could mean she's about to kill him.'' Her moist palm was the equivalent of a lie-detector test, but by that time they were on the dance floor, anyway.

"You're on 'Candid Camera,''' Kit whispered.

She followed his gaze and saw the talk-show camera crew. They were cruising the dance floor, interviewing Torrey's students, and the deer currently caught in their headlights was Vicki, who looked a little rattled by the questions she was being asked. Torrey had been interviewed extensively earlier and was reasonably pleased with her performance, but she'd mistakenly thought the crew had packed up and left for the night.

"Let's get this over with,'' she told Kit, meaning the dance. The path of least resistance was the only road open to her now. If she fought her way to freedom, it would almost certainly end up on network television, and that would look especially dubious with Kit being one of the contestants.

"Smart woman," Kit crooned, drawing her into his arms. "I always said you were a smart woman."

He'd said nothing of the kind that she could remember, but it wasn't worth the risk of an argument, and he knew it. He could virtually get away with murder as long as the TV cameras were around. She wanted to accuse him of planting them, but she didn't think even *he* could have arranged that.

The band was deep into a medley of Sam Cooke songs, and though Torrey had never been crazy about rhythm and blues, after rocking lazily with Kit to a torchy rendition of "Baby, Won't You Please Come Home," she was willing to change her mind. Maybe it was the setting, *maybe it was the man,* but she could feel the lush raunchy tug of the saxophone and the sultry twang of the guitars, and she liked the way they made her want to move.

Hiding in the crook of Kit's shoulder, she saw Bruno and his crew leave the room and knew she was out of immediate danger, but still she continued to sway to the rhythm of the music and with the movements of Kit's body. She could have pulled away from him, but she didn't. There was something about being with him she loved. What was it? The way he felt was an obvious reason, an ocean of muscled heat and brawny power. But more significant was the way he made *her* feel—warm and smooth and mellow all over, as liquid as the raspberry center of her favorite kind of chocolates. He made her feel good.

"I knew it," he whispered in her ear.

"Me, too," she murmured.

He pulled back to look at her. "You did?"

"Hmm?" She had no idea what he meant, but she'd been thinking about how it didn't seem as if any time had passed at all, how they could be back in the high-school gym at a sock hop with their shoes kicked off and probably lost forever, and their arms flung rapturously around each other. Had he ever loved her? she wondered. Really loved her?

"I knew this would feel right," he said. "Like yesterday."

She nodded, but didn't look at him, secretly glad his thoughts were running along the same lines as hers. "It wasn't all soft music and slow-dancing," she reminded him, sotto voce. "And anyway, you can't go back."

"It wasn't all bad, either. There was some good stuff between us, lots of it as I recall."

Gradually Torrey realized that the music had stopped and the other couples had moved off the floor. Several of her students were watching them and seemed to enjoy this chance to glimpse the master in action. Only she wasn't sure who the master was—her or Kit.

"Look around," she whispered. "We're the main attraction."

That possibility seemed to amuse him. "Then maybe we should give them something to watch," he suggested, toying with the halter strap of her dress.

Suddenly he caressed her face and tipped it up with his hand. Lord, he was going to kiss her. His dark eyes sparkled with sexual intention, and Torrey's stomach did a back flip at the mere thought. Kiss Kit McGrath? It hardly mattered that they had an audience. Just the prospect of something that intimate boggled. "No, please!"

She shook her head reprovingly and stepped back. "Have you gone nuts?" she said, glancing around, her voice a barely discernible hiss.

The band had begun to play again, providing a much needed distraction. Couples were starting to move back onto the floor and a choice had to be made. Finally Kit gave her a nod of great reluctance. "Okay," he said, "but let's get out of here."

She felt a sharp tug on her hand, and the next thing she knew they were heading for an exit. Kit flung open the door when they reached it and led her outside to a grottolike rock garden. A weathered wooden bridge spanned a pool full of fish.

The breeze was cool and laden with moisture. Torrey shivered, rubbing her bare arms. She was so relieved to be out of the spotlight she didn't even protest when Kit plucked the flower from her hair and tossed it away. She had a feeling he'd wanted to do that all night.

"Better," he said. "You look more like Torrey now."

"And less ravishing?"

"It isn't flowers that make you ravishing, it's your..." He looked her over as if trying very hard to decide. "Your perfect white teeth and clear eyes."

"You make me sound like a beast of burden."

Her perfect teeth chattered on the last word and he gathered her in his arms. "Come here, you," he said, his voice textured with grainy laughter. "You're freezing."

She snuggled into him, reveling in his heat and knowing how crazy it was to indulge herself this way. But the pleasure she felt was beyond description. She really didn't know what was happening, except that she was getting in deeper by the second. This was not an innocent reunion, not the way she felt.

"Let's get you warm all over." He pulled off his jacket and draped it around her shoulders, then tilted her face up to his and kissed her lightly. "Ravishing, Torrey, that's the right word for you. And you know what happens to ravishing women."

Her eyelids fluttered open. Even if she hadn't known, she wouldn't have had to ask. The imprint of his lips sizzled like fireworks on hers, and the answer was right there, burning hotly in his gaze. He'd not only meant it when he said he wanted her warm all over, he planned to accomplish it in ways that had nothing to do with his jacket.

She must have drawn back because his hands curled into the lapel of his jacket and pulled her toward him. She glanced up, startled at the force in his touch. Desire stirred in the silvery depths of his irises. Dangerously sexy, it filled her field of vision.

"I don't have to look up to see the stars," he told her. "I can see the Milky Way. It's right there in your eyes."

Torrey was still feeling woozy, but she vaguely remembered hearing that line before. The warmth fled her body in a headlong rush, and suddenly she was cold, very cold. Nothing could have warmed her at that moment, not even the heat in his gaze. He'd just repeated the line she suggested he try on Bubbles, which made her wonder about the sincerity of everything else he'd said. Was that what this evening had been about, more role-playing for his assault on Bubbles? Or maybe it was some kind of elaborate joke, only she wasn't sure who the target was.

He must have sensed the change in her, because when she stepped back, he let her go. "What are you doing here?" she asked him. "Why aren't you with Bubbles tonight?"

"I told you—she's talking business."

"But you would have been with her otherwise?"

He shrugged, a response so nonchalant she didn't know what to make of it. Clearly it was time to voice the suspicions she'd been harboring since he'd walked into her classroom. "This isn't about Bubbles, is it? You're not serious about her or the contest. This is about me, about us and what happened—"

He cut her off. "I don't do anything I'm not serious about, Torrey."

"Then what is it about her? What are you after? Her money?"

He seemed surprised she'd asked. "I thought you'd be proud."

Now she was stunned. She kept waiting for him to laugh, to let her in on the joke, but he didn't do either. "Kit! She's twenty years your senior. Have you thought about that? She's old enough to be your mother, and you're marrying her for her money."

"Yeah, isn't it great?"

"It's disgusting." Was that a sparkle in his dark eyes?

"If that's true, I owe it all to you, Torrey."

Suddenly it hit her what he was doing. He was trying to make another point, only this one was about her book, her message and maybe even her philosophy of life. "That's not fair," she protested. "I don't advocate marrying people only for their money. My book talks about caring and companionship, the importance of a life-long partnersip. It talks about love, Kit. Maybe you should read it again.''

''I'm intimately familiar with what your book says about love, Torrey Benson, bestselling author.''

''Then why don't you practice it? You're supposed to be going after a millionaire you're in love with—or could be.''

''Why do you assume I don't love Bubbles?''

''You *do* love her?''

''Oh, yeah. Definitely.''

She *had* to ask. Her head began to swim and her stomach to churn. She felt as if she were back on the boat with a bad case of motion sickness. Poor Claudia. She hadn't been nearly sympathetic enough.

''You'll have to excuse me,'' she said. ''I'm not feeling well. It must have been something I ate.'' She wasn't sure she could make it off the bridge, but she had to get out of here, and quickly.

''Torrey? Wait.''

She fended off his attempt to detain her and hurried back the way they'd come. Only she didn't go inside. Instead, she stumbled through the rock garden toward a gravel path that led around the side of the hotel. She had no idea where it would take her, but anything was better than a frantic dash through the nightclub.

Her heels sank into the gravel, making it nearly impossible to run, and her heart rocketed out of control. But she could hear him behind her, and desperation drove her into flight. She rounded the corner of the building, ran several yards and ducked into a causeway where some construction was being done on a separate wing of the hotel. A rickety framework of scaffolding rose toward the balcony that was being renovated.

Torrey spotted an extension ladder and figured if she could climb it and pull it up after her, Kit wouldn't be able to follow. It was a reckless move, but physical safety didn't matter to her at the moment. It was her emotional safety she was concerned about, and she simply couldn't deal with Kit right now.

He called her name and she knew she'd been spotted.

The skirt of her dress snagged on splinters and caught under her feet as she labored up the rungs. It was a nightmare. The ladder was almost as shaky as the scaffolding, but she had to keep climbing. There was nowhere else to go.

"Torrey, stop!" he shouted. "It won't hold you."

She was already two-thirds of the way up and probably twenty feet off the ground, far enough to hurt herself badly if she fell. The ladder creaked and groaned with her weight, and the scaffolding swayed precariously. But she was nearly there, and anything was better than the humiliation of climbing down with him waiting for her at the bottom.

"Torrey! Come back down!"

Fear and fatigue were already taking their toll. Her muscles were burning with the effort to struggle upward and keep her balance. She grabbed the next rung, heaved herself up and tore a strip from her skirt. Despairing, she realized her beautiful dress was going to be in shreds by the time she reached the top. She gathered the material up, but there was nowhere to secure it, and finally there was nothing she could do but let it catch and tear. At least her legs weren't being sliced up.

The closer she came to the framework, the more wildly it swung, and she was afraid the ladder might be dislodged. To her horror she realized the rungs were rotting. Kit was right. They weren't going to hold. Desperate, she lunged for the scaffolding and the ladder fell free, clattering to the ground.

Kit was beneath her instantly, shouting for her to drop.

"Let go," he yelled. "I'll catch you."

Torrey let out an anguished wail and tried to pull herself up, but it was impossible. She didn't have the upper-body strength, and the scaffolding was bobbing like a trapeze.

Kit was below her, his arms outstretched, but she might as well have been jumping off a cliff.

Nothing had ever looked farther away to her than he did. It had to be thirty feet to the ground, and the surface was a gravel pit of razor-sharp rocks. She was afraid to trust that he would actually catch her. Or even that he could.

She tried once more to drag herself up. Her fingers had clawed their way into the splintery wood, but her arms felt as if they were going to be ripped out of their sockets.

"Torrey! For God's sake! Please—"

With a horrible cry she let go and dropped. The seconds of free fall were the most harrowing of her life. She could feel the impact long before she hit the ground. What flashed before her eyes was not her life, but her limbs. She could hear bones cracking and shattering. Tendons snapping. Tissue being crushed into pulp. She could feel herself flying into pieces, thousands of them.

"Ahh!" A wrenching force knocked the wind out of her as she was snatched out of midair. Kit had caught her. He had reached up for her and literally dragged her into his arms.

"Hang on," he said as he stepped backward to catch his balance.

She clung to him, shaking and stunned, still imagining what would have happened if he hadn't been there. She would be dead or crippled, surely.

"God, you scared me!" The words rushed out of him as he hugged her close and turned with her in his arms, triumphant and obviously deeply relieved. He was holding her so tight she couldn't breathe, but his whispered passion made her feel as if she *had* hit the ground. "I don't want to lose you, baby. Not this way. Not ever," he breathed, almost incoherently. "I love you."

Nothing could have revived Torrey faster than that. She was quaking from head to toe and not sure she'd heard him correctly, but she had to know what he said and, more important, what he meant.

His eyes were ablaze with an odd mix of emotions as she looked up at him. But he did look suspiciously like a man in love. He had all the passionate concern of the boy who'd picked her up off the ice and kissed her tears away. Maybe more.

"You said you loved Bubbles," she managed to rasp out.

He looked a little startled, then kissed her nose and grinned. "What's not to love? She's a great lady."

"Kit McGrath—" she narrowed her eyes in a glare, which took all the energy she could muster at that moment "—I don't find this amusing anymore. Did you or did you not say you loved me? And if you didn't, why did you come back into my life? Was it to pay me back or to *get* me back?"

His smile faded into something much more

intent, a hotly penetrating stare as he perused her features. He seemed to be reflecting on her searching gaze and her pursed mouth, on the nose he'd just kissed. "And just what would you do if I said it was to get you back?" he asked.

Her heart squeezed painfully. "What about Bubbles?"

"Never mind about her."

"But you—"

"You're evading, Torrey."

"*I'm* evading? That's all you've done is evade."

"Are you going to answer the question?"

"First, I'd ask you why you waited this long to decide you wanted me back." Answer that, hot shot.

She could remember the details of their split as vividly as if it had happened that morning. They'd had a terrible fight over his obsession with hockey and her obsession with him. He'd been invited to tryouts in Canada for a major-league team, and she was secretly terrified that if he went she would never see him again. He was in a wounded rage because she didn't understand his dream of playing pro and because she'd lied to him about being pregnant. She'd truly believed she was pregnant right up until they'd eloped. She just couldn't bring herself to tell him when she discovered she wasn't, because she knew he wouldn't have understood about *her* dream. Him.

Lord, she'd been such a child in those days, such a desperate creature. She'd made so many mistakes.

"I thought I was doing the noble thing," he told her. "When I got home from tryouts and you were gone without even a note, I went straight to your mom's place. She blasted me into the next week for 'stealing' her sixteen-year-old daughter and ruining her future. She told me to leave you alone because now you had a chance for something better, a chance to meet a professional man who could give you a decent life."

He was still cradling her in his arms, only now he was walking toward the gravel path that led back to the rock garden. "What could I say, Torrey?" he wanted to know. "I had nothing but a dream and some athletic talent, and we couldn't live on that."

Torrey was shocked but not surprised. Her mother had never told her about any conversation with Kit or even that he'd come looking for her. Vera Benson had had grand plans for her only daughter, and Kit wasn't part of them. Vera had been abandoned by the man who'd fathered Torrey, and she'd raised her daughter alone. Their lives had always been a struggle, but Vera's goal was for Torrey to marry well and to live the life that she, Vera, had always dreamed about.

Funny how dreams could get you in trouble, Torrey thought.

"She never told me," Torrey explained. "I didn't know."

"Would it have made a difference?"

"Then? Yes, definitely."

He shifted her weight in his arms, not holding her quite so close as he gazed at her. "And now?"

The answer that lodged in Torrey's throat was far too risky to reveal under the circumstances. She could hardly believe that she was entertaining the possibility of giving it all up for him, especially when there was still so much she didn't know about his motives. She would never know if he'd really done the noble thing, waiting fifteen years to come after her, or if his timing had more to do with the fact that he knew she was about to marry another man. Was this the old Kit McGrath, the fiercely competitive man who simply wanted her because someone else had her?

No, she wasn't going to tell him the truth— that she still loved him. Frankly she didn't trust him enough to risk being in love with him. There was something he wasn't telling her, some secret agenda he hadn't revealed, and she was afraid it had to do with their past and his unresolved anger, even if he didn't know it himself. But that aside, she still had a book tour, a career, a fiancé and an imminent wedding to worry about.

Imminent? She gasped softly. "I'm getting married tomorrow!"

His expression turned stoic. With elaborate care, he set her down on her feet, steadying her as she wobbled. "I guess you've answered my question," he said.

"TORREY, SHOULDN'T YOU be in your own stateroom squeezing into your wedding dress and veil, instead of sitting here with me, huddled in your ex-husband's jacket? You look sicker than I do, hon."

With that pronouncement, Claudia grabbed a mirror from her bedside table to inspect herself. She pulled down her lower lid to check the color and drew up her lip to check heaven only knew what.

Torrey was reminded of visits to the vet's office with her beloved late basset hound, Bosco, but didn't say so. "Squeezing into what veil?" she mumbled, wishing the situation was that simple. "I'm not wearing one."

She would have liked nothing better than to go to her room, put on her white lace sheath, get hitched and be done with it. No regrets, no doubts as she strolled arm in arm into the sunset with Steven. Instead, she'd had a tormented night, slept not a wink and then dragged herself to Claudia's room at first light.

Luckily her friend was much improved, because Torrey had no choice but to tell her the awful truth. She'd confessed everything, and to her relief, Claudia had taken it all in stride, probably because the publicist's solution was simple.

"You're going to marry Steven, that's all. If not for love then for money, *our* money. Tower Books is not shelling out a fortune for a promotional tour that ends with a gala wedding to have you jilt the blushing millionaire bridegroom on network TV."

Torrey had sighed and nodded.

"See how easy that was?" Claudia had said, laughing.

Ever the organizer, Torrey thought now. But to be fair, Claudia knew better than anyone what was at stake. The cruise ship had dropped anchor in the harbor of Cabo San Lucas some time during the night, and Torrey was due to be ferried to shore and then limoed to the chapel in less than an hour, with a busload of her students and the TV crew in tow.

"It was weird last night, Claudia," she said, still stuck in the revolving door of Kit McGrath. "There was a moment when it felt like he might even be planning to kidnap me from my own wedding or something. You know, the way the real love of your life shows up just as you're about to marry the wrong guy and won't let you go through with it. Remember Katharine Ross in *The Graduate?* How Dustin Hoffman was pounding on the church doors to get to her?"

"That could be interesting for ratings," Claudia said, glancing up from the mirror. "And as long as Kit's a millionaire, it might work. Is he a millionaire?"

"Claudia, Kit is a *contestant*. He's supposed to be marrying a millionaire."

"Right. Never mind. You'll have to marry Steven."

Torrey let out a sigh of despair that went completely unnoticed by her friend. She was talking to the wrong person if she wanted to get to the heart of the problem. And maybe it was too late for that. Maybe what Torrey Benson wanted didn't matter in the grand scheme of things. There was more to this situation than her future happiness unfortunately. Lots of futures hung in the balance. Hers was only one of them.

"Besides," Torrey said, forcing resolve into her voice, "Steven doesn't play hockey, and he's a wonderful man—warm and giving and so very accomplished, the CEO of a worldwide chain of apothecary shops. If for no other reason, I have to do it for Vera, my mom."

"Right you are, Torrey. *There's* a reason to spend the rest of your life with a man."

Torrey shuddered, but as she reached to draw Kit's jacket around her, she stopped short. "I'm wearing his coat, Claudia," she said. She unfolded her legs, sat up, pulled off the coat and gaped at it.

"I told you that fifteen minutes ago."

Torrey patted the pockets and realized she not

only had his coat, she had his wallet. "I have to return this," she said. "It's a sign."

"It's not a sign," Claudia protested, rising from her pillows. "Let a steward return it."

"What about the money in his wallet? The credit cards?"

"Leave the wallet with me and he can come here to get it."

Torrey rose slowly, clutching the coat to her chest. "I couldn't ask you to do that."

"I'm happy to do it. It'll save you time, so you can hurry and get dressed. Torrey! Hurry up and get dressed!"

"Where are you going?" Claudia called after her as she started toward the door.

"To hurry up and get dressed," Torrey said. She felt like a robot, programmed for self-destruction.

"No, you're not! You're going to return the coat, damn it!" Torrey swiftly let herself out of the room, Claudia's prophecy ringing in her ears.

TORREY KNOCKED on Kit's stateroom door, praying he was in, praying he wasn't. If he wasn't, it was a sign. If he was, she didn't know what it meant.

No answer. Her heart plummeted and she turned to walk away. Fine then, good, she told herself. She would do the right thing, what she was supposed to do. She would make everyone happy, especially her mother.

A ship's corridor left something to be desired in the way of aesthetics, she decided, feeling as listless as the beige walls and utility carpet. She'd taken only a few steps when she remembered Kit's jacket. She wouldn't be able to return it later and he would certainly need his wallet.

No more incentive was required.

His stateroom was empty. She discerned that from the oppressive quiet as she let herself in a moment later. The door had been locked, but not bolted, and she'd used the little trick with a credit card that Claudia had taught her when they'd locked themselves out of their room in a Des Moines motel.

Torrey laid Kit's coat across the bed, then looked around for some paper to write him a note. An old-fashioned maple secretary desk occupied one corner of the room, and as she circled the couches to get to it, she noticed something lying on the floor.

Gasping, she came to a swift halt. It was his hockey stick, the very same one she'd tripped over the day she'd broken her ankle. She recognized it by the chipped yellow paint and battered shaft.

This *was* a sign. How could she ever forget that hockey stick?

Something told her to get away from the

thing, that it might leap up and attack her as it had before. But as she scrambled backward, she felt the rug slip out from under her feet. She was going to fall, anyway!

She twisted toward the couch to catch herself, but a wrenching pain shot up her leg and she landed heavily on her side. The impact knocked the breath out of her, and when she tried to push herself up she was overcome by dizziness.

How am I going to walk down the aisle? she wondered as she slumped to the floor and lay there. A horrible sensation gripped her neck and shoulders and crept downward. Icy chills brought gooseflesh to her skin, and static burned through her thoughts like a bad phone connection. She'd never passed out in her life, even when she'd broken her ankle, but as her vision began to fade, she knew there was a first time for everything.

A sign?

SHE HAD NEVER LOOKED more beautiful. Her ivory sheath was made of Chantilly lace and lined with the lushest of satins. Her chignon was abloom with delicate pink-tinged roses, and like the buds, her own heart, her bride's heart, was opening, unfurling, with love.

The aisle of the church seemed to stretch forever in front of her, but at its end, waiting at an altar festooned with flowers, stood the man who was to be her husband. His back was to her, and the sight of his powerful shoulders, draped in the midnight blue lines of a morning coat, made her mouth go slack and her thoughts swirl with anticipation. This was the way it should be. This was the wedding she'd always dreamed of.

But as she reached the altar and whispered the name of her groom, the man who turned and held out his hand was Steven Gaines.

"No!" Torrey screamed the word with all her might and fought to get free of the weight that was holding her down.

Her eyes flew open and she saw a man looming over her, felt his hands on her wrists and his body pinning hers. Pain flared hotly from her ankle as she tried to move, sending spears of fire into the aching muscles of her calf.

"Kit?" She gasped out his name. "What are you—"

"Easy, Torrey, easy," he said, gently but firmly trying to keep her where she was. "Hold still. You're hurt."

"Let me up," she insisted. "Where am I?"

"You were screaming. What was it, a dream?"

A dream? She fell back onto the pillows and realized she was lying on a bed. Kit's bed. As he released her and sat down beside her, it all began to filter back. She'd fallen in his suite. She was still in his suite. Had she missed the wedding? Her own wedding?

"Hey, stay down!" he said as she struggled

to sit up. "You hurt your ankle. I've got some ice on it."

"You did this on purpose," she accused. Emotion nearly strangled her. "You booby-trapped the place with that hockey stick!"

He started to laugh, then thought better of it. "Torrey, be reasonable. I didn't know you were going to be here. I was out looking for you."

"Looking for me?"

"Yes, I went to your cabin, hoping to…"

He hesitated, seeming reluctant to finish the thought, so she filled in the blanks. "Get your jacket back?"

"My jacket was the least of it." He tried to touch her face, smooth her hair, but she wouldn't allow it.

"The water taxi, the limo…" She made another attempt to sit up, and this time he let her. It was the pain that made her drop back down. "My wedding! Is the taxi still here? Is there still time?"

He heaved a guilty sigh, caught her flailing hand and brought her fingers to his lips. "The taxi's gone, Torrey. It left about fifteen minutes ago."

"Without me?"

"Bubbles went in your place."

"What?" The word shot out of her like a body from a cannon. "Bubbles is being ferried to my wedding? Why?"

"I asked her to entertain your fiancé, Steven

whatever-his-name-is, in case you didn't make it. They're the same age, so they should have plenty in common, and Bubbles is a hoot at any age. He may not even notice you're missing, Torrey.''

She stared at him, cautiously mouthing the words ''In case I didn't make it?''

Music played softly somewhere in the suite. It was turned down so low Torrey couldn't be sure, but it sounded like ''Baby, Won't You Please Come Home,'' the same song they'd danced to at the nightclub.

Her heart began to beat oddly as Kit went quiet. The dark sparkle of intrigue in his eyes that was his trademark had ignited into something hotter, deeper.

''I was hoping you might have a change of heart,'' he said. ''Especially after I told you what you do to *my* heart.''

Torrey looked away instinctively, not wanting him to see her startled smile or how helpless she was to control it. *A good line,* she thought. *I taught him well.*

One possible explanation for the bizarre situation was beginning to seep through her confusion—that Kit had never intended to let her go through with the wedding. He was not going to let her marry Steven Gaines. She'd had a hunch all along that Kit was holding something back, and she was right.

''What's going on, Kit?'' she demanded to

know. "Who is this Bubbles woman, and what is she to you?"

He'd apparently thrown on a polo shirt when dressing, because the collar was turned up on one side, giving him an air of haste and dishevelment she couldn't help but hope she was responsible for. Frankly it was adorable, but she had no business making observations like that when she didn't know what he was up to.

"Promise you won't get upset?" he said, leaning into the jeans-clad knee he'd drawn up to anchor himself. "I don't want you hurting yourself any more than you already have."

She crossed her heart, the one he'd hoped he might change. "Tell me what's going on. Tell me everything."

"Bubbles is my aunt and she owns a Laundromat in Azuza—one, not a chain. She's the one who wants to marry a millionaire, so it was easy to convince her to take the cruise. She wasn't thrilled about having to pose as the woman of my dreams, but she did a great job, at least I thought so."

"She had me fooled," Torrey murmured, wondering if she was in shock from the fall. Bubbles was his aunt, and the whole thing was an elaborate charade? The outrage she should have felt didn't seem to be forthcoming. She was mystified at the lengths Kit had gone to. What were his motives?

"Why in the world did you do it?" she asked.

He was staring at the inseam of his jeans and rubbing his thumb along the ridge. "To get you back. I would have done anything to get you back."

When he glanced up at her, the desire in his eyes took her breath away. In her weakened state, that look alone could have done her in. But she had to keep a clear head. She couldn't be seduced by smoldering passion again. Passion was the thunder and lightning that lit the horizon, then vanished when the storm was over.

"Did it occur to you that you might have come to me and told me the truth?" she inquired. "Exactly what you're telling me now?"

"Many times. But you would have dismissed me if you hadn't been forced to deal with me, and I think you know that, Torrey. I had to find a way to make you spend time with me, to make you remember what you didn't want to remember."

"Which...was?"

"That we were perfect for each other from the first, only one of us didn't know it at the time."

You, she thought. *You're the one who didn't know it.* But she could see by his expression that he had already accepted full responsibility. She let out a sigh that was laden with conflict and confusion. What was she supposed to do now? This was her wedding day. "Oh, Kit—"

Her entreaty was interrupted by a thunderous pounding on the double bedroom doors. It sounded as if someone had forced his or her way into the suite proper and was now trying to break down the bedroom doors, which were apparently locked.

"Torrey ! Are you in there?"

"Claudia?" Torrey struggled to sit up, but only managed to get to her elbows.

"Who's Claudia?" Kit rose from the bed.

"The publicist from Tower Books," Torrey explained. "You'd better let her in."

"Torrey, are you in there? *Answer me!*"

"Hold it down, would you?" Kit called out as he approached the doors. "Torrey's fine."

"She's in there? Torrey? Torrey, are you all right, darling?" One of the doorknobs began to crank as if Claudia was trying to twist it off. "What have you done to her, Kit McGrath? Kidnapped her? You've taken her hostage, haven't you."

Kit glanced at Torrey with a questioning look. Clearly he thought he was dealing with a nutcase.

Torrey herself had planted the hostage notion in Claudia's head, but the mention of it now gave her an idea. An outrageous idea to be sure, but outrageous was better than nothing. She nodded at Kit, signaling him to go along with it, then whispered the words. "It's in my book."

It took a moment, but then his perplexed frown became a grin.

"*Torrrrrey!*"

"She can't answer you," Kit called back. "She's bound and gagged on the bed."

Claudia's gasp was audible, probably throughout the ship. "I'm calling the captain!"

"I wouldn't if I were you," he warned.

"And why not?"

"Because I'm just following the instructions in a certain book that was published by Tower," he explained. "Chapter ten, page 315 of *How to Marry a Millionaire*. You're familiar with that chapter, aren't you, Claudia?"

The pounding ceased. "What are you talking about?" she demanded.

Kit winked at Torrey. "Let me refresh your memory," he continued. "It says and I quote, 'If all else fails, you could always kidnap your millionaire and hold him for ransom, only don't give him back when you get the money.'"

"That was meant as a joke!" Claudia insisted. "Even our legal department laughed. This is blackmail! You let me in there, damn it. Now!"

"Let her in," Torrey said, surprised and pleased that Kit remembered the exact page number of the kidnapping ploy. Of course it was intended only as a humorous aside, but it seemed he might even have considered it. "No wait! Find something to tie me up with first."

Kit complied with a swiftness that made Torrey wonder where he'd learned to tie knots. Boy Scouts, she hoped.

Claudia was pounding up a storm by the time

he got the doors open. She burst in, wearing a floral bathrobe that clashed with the chartreuse hue of her skin, her hair in wild disarray.

"Are you all right, darling?" She rushed over to Torrey, who was propped against the headboard, her wrists loosely bound with the terrycloth tie from Kit's bathrobe, her ankles with a king-size pillowcase that was more tucked than tied. The ice compress had been temporarily removed.

"I'm fine," Torrey assured her weakly. "But maybe you'd better listen to his demands."

Claudia whirled on Kit. "Tower Books does not negotiate with terrorists."

Kit's scowl silenced her. "There's only one thing I want, Claudia, and she's right there on my bed."

"Well, you can't have her! You do realize what you've done, don't you? My company has invested a fortune in this tour. Why, Torrey's wedding alone—"

Kit dismissed her concerns with a wave of his hand. "I'll take care of the expense, whatever it is."

"You will?" She looked him over, scrutinizing his clothing, the sumptuous suite. "I guess you must do awfully well, Mr. McGrath. Pro sports, is it?"

"Not anymore—a sporting-goods chain."

"Really? How lovely for you." Her brows knit in thought. "Then why this outrageous scheme to get Torrey back? You're probably a millionaire in your own right, so if it's not her money you're after, then what?''

Torrey might have been offended by Claudia's line of reasoning if she hadn't been so pleased that the publicist was leaping to take the bait. She could see the wheels beginning to grind.

"It's Torrey I want, Claudia. She happens to be a millionaire, but it's not about money, as her book points out," he explained patiently. "It's about love. I couldn't love her more if she had all the wealth in the world. And if she had nothing, I'd still spend the rest of my life trying to win her back.''

Torrey beamed. The room positively glowed with her joy, which Kit caught and reflected with a secret smile.

Claudia barely noticed. She was tapping a finger against her lips and nodding. "I think this could work," she said. "I really do. It might not even matter that Torrey's left her fiancé at the altar. No, actually this is better.''

Her eyes lit up with enthusiasm. "You two are better!"

A moment later Kit politely but firmly escorted the publicist from the bedroom. "One of you *is* a millionaire, right?" Claudia asked Kit as he shut the door behind her and locked it.

When he turned back to Torrey, it was with the promise of sweet and terrible pleasure in his dark gaze. Torrey let out little gasp of delight. The man who had taken her hostage had something forbidden in mind, she realized. His eyes had a gleam that made her think of dark nights and demon lovers. But it was where the gleam was pointed that alarmed her the most.

"Kit? Why are you looking at my feet like that? Kit!"

"Your ankle," he assured her, settling himself by her loosely bound feet. "I have to see how it's doing, don't I?"

Feigning innocence, he let his gaze run up her body to her flushed face, her parted lips...to the pink glow mottling her throat. The low sexy growl in his voice sent a shiver of delight through Torrey's body as he dropped to all fours and began to move up the bed toward her.

"On second thought," he said laughing, "maybe this time I'll start at the top."

Epilogue

THE SET OF "The Babs Randazzo Show" was decorated like a wedding chapel, and standing in the midst of the flower arrangements and candelabras was Babs herself in an ivory Armani suit and a headpiece with a pouffy net veil, which she kept blowing out of her eyes.

"Are you as excited as I am?" she asked the audience.

A rousing "Yes!" came back.

"Then let's ring those wedding bells! It's time to announce the results of our Millionaire Mating Game. Last month Torrey Benson, bestselling author of *How to Marry a Millionaire,* visited our show and picked three volunteers from the studio audience. The lucky ones were sent on a quest to meet and marry a 'mogul' using the tips from Torrey's book."

Babs held up a copy of the book long enough to let the camera zoom in on it, then walked over to the couch and breezily seated herself.

With an engaging wink she drew her skirt up and snapped the lacy white garter on her thigh. "They say all's fair in love and war and, folks, this contest proves it. You're not going to *be-*

lieve what happened to our intrepid contestants.''

Three Western Union telegrams lay on the table in front of her. She scooped them up and waggled them for the benefit of the camera.

"The good news is all three of our contestants fell madly in love with millionaires and are *already* happily married. The bad news is they're so happy they're not coming back to the show. They've extended their honeymoons indefinitely!''

A camera panned the audience for reaction as Babs read the first telegram.

"'Babs—Sorry we can't be on the show. We're honeymooning in the south of France. Tyler wants to open a Golden Key Resort here. I want to close the bedroom door. Pleasure before business, right? Emilie.'''

The camera caught smiles, laughter, and more than a few wistful expressions in the audience. "Oooh...the Riviera!" one woman murmured, just loud enough for a mike to catch it, while the woman beside her countered, "Oooh... pleasure before business!''

Babs turned to the telegram from Millie and read, "'Babs— *bonjour* from Paris! We're sorry to miss the show, but we can't get my sisters out of the shops on the Champs-Elysées. Rio's nephew and butler out of the *pâtisseries* and my new in-laws out of the Folies Bergère! Not that Rio and I are anxious to leave, either. He and I are escaping to a villa tomorrow while his parents ride herd on the others. We look forward to a little time alone to treasure the wealth of our love—a relationship that began because of money and is now beyond price. Please give our love to Emilie and Christopher and of course to Torrey. Best, Millie and Rio Corrigan.'''

Babs grinned at the audience. ''Does this show know how to come through for its guests or what?'' The audience erupted in cheers.

She waited for them to quiet. ''I'll bet some of you are wondering why Torrey Benson, the author of *How to Marry a Millionaire,* isn't here. And so were *we* wondering. Torrey was supposed to join us for this show, but couldn't because she married one of the contestants herself.''

There was an audible buzz of disbelief.

Babs began to laugh. ''It's true. Torrey married contestant number three—that hunky ex–hockey player, Kit McGrath—and they're currently honeymooning in Fiji.''

She snapped open the last telegram, preparing to read it. ''Here's what the passionately happy couple have to say: 'Help, Babs! We're being held hostage on an island paradise. They don't get your show here in Fiji, and they won't let us go until they do. Pray for cable. Meanwhile, they're forcing us to lie on the beach and drink piña coladas. It's torture!'''

Bab's voice rose over the laughter. ''How

about that, folks? Isn't love wonderful! Let's hear a round of applause for our three courageous contestants and their millionaire mates.''

There was a great outbreak of clapping and cheering, which Babs joined in herself. As the clamor began to subside, she raised her hand to get their attention.

''I know you're all as disappointed as we were that our contestants couldn't be here, but we have a surprise for you. We have a replacement contestant, one of Torrey's protegées who's freshly married to her own millionaire, and we'd like to bring the newlyweds out now.''

Trumpets and fanfare preceded the appearance of a handsome older couple beneath a bower of red roses. As they descended a short flight of steps, Babs grabbed a mike and went over to greet them.

The bride was an organdy explosion of flowers from the veil that floated around her enormous titian chignon to the pansy-dotted pumps that adorned her tiny feet. Appliquéd daisies ran riot, covering the sweetheart neckline of her dress, and her bouquet of lilacs was almost too cumbersome for her to manage.

The bride's tall striking husband, on the other hand, was the picture of restraint in his immaculate white morning coat and vest. A single pink carnation and fern sprig adorned his buttonhole.

The couple were an odd match, to say the least. The situation might have concerned Babs if the man's expression hadn't been a dead give-away to his inner state. A big goofy grin lit his handsome face as he looked into the camera.

Babs sighed with relief. The groom was a happy camper.

"Ladies and gentlemen," she announced, "it's my pleasure to present the former Bubbles Cavanaugh and her husband, Steven Gaines, now Mr. and Mrs. Gaines.

"Congratulations!" she said as she joined the beaming newlyweds. "Bubbles, that's an amazing outfit. But I have to ask. Are you wearing the traditional garter? How about a peek?"

"Oh, sorry!" Bubbles exclaimed. "I'm not wearing a garter, but will this do?" She lifted her skirt, revealing the flowered Ace bandage wrapped around her ankle.

Babs touched her arm in concern. "Are you all right?"

A giggle of delight escaped the bride. "Couldn't be better," she explained. "It's just that I was wearing this when I met Steven, and he's such a sentimental softie he thought it would bring us luck."

Babs glanced over her shoulder at the camera and grinned. "Is that sweet or what?"

"Anyone can wear a garter," Steven ventured proudly. "No offense, Babs, but my wife is a woman who needs to express herself uniquely through fashion. The moment I saw Bubbles I thought of a gift basket in one of my apothecary shops, filled with flower soaps and tied up with ribbons.''

Laughter filled the auditorium and it took Babs a moment to get control. "How did you two meet?" she asked, extending the mike to Bubbles, who blushed prettily but didn't seem to know what to say.

"Bubbles was my angel of mercy," Steven explained. "She showed up at my wedding bearing the news that my fiancée wasn't going to make it. *Ever.* Bubbles spent all morning trying to console me, then kiddingly offered to stand in for Torrey if it would help. You should have seen her face when I took her up on it. I guess you could say she wrapped my broken heart in her flowered Ace bandage.''

Babs turned to the camera. "It's true, folks. Bubbles and Steven were married in Cabo San Lucas in a wedding ceremony that was originally planned for Steven and Torrey, but that's a whole different show.''

Bab's theme music began to play, signaling a station break. There was a flurry of activity on the set as she led the newlyweds to the couch and seated them. Once they were back on the air, she turned to the bride.

"Bubbles, can I ask what attracted you to Steven? Was it his understated elegance?''

Bubbles gazed at her groom fondly. "Oh, sure. That and the fact that I liked his Woody.''

"His *woody?*''

"She loved my Woody," Steven corrected.

"It's true." Bubbles's sigh shook her daisy appliqués. "He showed me a picture, and it was mad passionate lust at first sight. I couldn't wait to try it out."

"Would you like to see it?" Steven asked Babs.

Bab's producer was making frantic throat-cutting gestures.

"I don't think…" Babs started, but Steven had already pulled a snapshot from inside his jacket.

Babs took it gingerly, then gasped. "Oh, that kind of Woody!" she said, staring at a picture of an antique station wagon. Falling back into the couch cushions, she waved the picture at the audience and laughed weakly. "It's a car, everybody."

The music started up, and to Bab's shock, she realized they were going to a commercial break again with or without her.

"Wait!" she cried, throwing up her hands helplessly. "We didn't find out where our newlyweds are going on their honeymoon. The Flower Forest in Barbados, I'll bet."

Bubble's giggle was infectious, carrying over the announcer's voice as the guest promos for next day's show began to run. "Maybe we'll stop there on our way back," she said. "Right now we're off to Fiji to rescue Kit and Torrey. It's a tough job, but somebody's got to do it."

Dear Reader,

If you've ever read a romance novel where the secretary is secretly in love with her boss, then you're already familiar with the premise of my own personal love story. My aeronautical engineer husband, Allan, was my boss back in the seventies, and I knew the minute I stepped into his office that he was the one. Dark wavy hair, mysterious brown eyes, thickly lashed, and an intriguingly sexy smile. How could he not be the one!

But as it turned out, his good looks were only a very small part of what made Allan such a special man. I'm not sure what finally caused him to notice me as a woman, as opposed to his efficient Girl Friday. He claims it was the morning I wore a miniskirt, which was the style of the day, and spilled a cup of hot tea in his lap. I was so embarrassed, I murmured unintelligibly that it was *his* fault, that he made me nervous. Perhaps it was the heat of the tea rather than the heat of the moment, but he did look at me in an entirely different way.

Shortly afterward he received a promotion. Brokenhearted, I helped him clean out his desk. Little did I know the move would allow him to pursue me in a way that he'd felt inappropriate as my boss. And pursue he did! When he appeared at my desk one day to ask me out, I was speechless for several reasons. First, he asked for two dates at once. He wanted to see me on Tuesday *and* Saturday. And since he knew I was a divorced mom with a toddler, who "worked hard for the money," as the song goes, he wanted to be sure that dating him would not be a financial burden and that my child would be well cared for. So he insisted on paying for the baby-sitter.

Was this a man straight out of my dreams?

Our courtship began the moment I said yes, and it was a

whirlwind affair. By that time he had decided that *I* was the one, and, since he was a goal-oriented man, nothing was going to deter him in his quest. I know you'll agree with me that I had to marry him, especially after the way he proposed to me. I'd started jogging to tone up and lose weight, and he gamely joined me at a neighborhood high school one day. Afterward, we were resting on the bleachers. I was flushed bright red, dripping wet and wearing no makeup when he slipped the most beautiful ring I'd ever seen on my finger. "I want you to know that there is never a moment when I don't think you're beautiful," he told me, "and never a moment when I don't love you. Please say you won't jog with anyone else but me."

Dear reader, how could he *not* be the one?

Sincerely,

Suzanne Forster

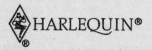

MILLION DOLLAR SWEEPSTAKES
OFFICIAL RULES
NO PURCHASE NECESSARY TO ENTER

1. To enter, follow the directions published. Method of entry may vary. For eligibility, entries must be received no later than March 31, 1998. No liability is assumed for printing errors, lost, late, non-delivered or misdirected entries.

    To determine winners, the sweepstakes numbers assigned to submitted entries will be compared against a list of randomly, preselected prize winning numbers. In the event all prizes are not claimed via the return of prize winning numbers, random drawings will be held from among all other entries received to award unclaimed prizes.

2. Prize winners will be determined no later than June 30, 1998. Selection of winning numbers and random drawings are under the supervision of D. L. Blair, Inc., an independent judging organization whose decisions are final. Limit: one prize to a family or organization. No substitution will be made for any prize, except as offered. Taxes and duties on all prizes are the sole responsibility of winners. Winners will be notified by mail. Odds of winning are determined by the number of eligible entries distributed and received.

3. Sweepstakes open to residents of the U.S. (except Puerto Rico), Canada and Europe who are 18 years of age or older, except employees and immediate family members of Torstar Corp., D. L. Blair, Inc., their affiliates, subsidiaries, and all other agencies, entities, and persons connected with the use, marketing or conduct of this sweepstakes. All applicable laws and regulations apply. Sweepstakes offer void wherever prohibited by law. Any litigation within the province of Quebec respecting the conduct and awarding of a prize in this sweepstakes must be submitted to the Régie des alcools, des courses et des jeux. In order to win a prize, residents of Canada will be required to correctly answer a time-limited arithmetical skill-testing question to be administered by mail.

4. Winners of major prizes (Grand through Fourth) will be obligated to sign and return an Affidavit of Eligibility and Release of Liability within 30 days of notification. In the event of non-compliance within this time period or if a prize is returned as undeliverable, D. L. Blair, Inc. may at its sole discretion, award that prize to an alternate winner. By acceptance of their prize, winners consent to use of their names, photographs or other likeness for purposes of advertising, trade and promotion on behalf of Torstar Corp., its affiliates and subsidiaries, without further compensation unless prohibited by law. Torstar Corp. and D. L. Blair, Inc., their affiliates and subsidiaries are not responsible for errors in printing of sweepstakes and prize winning numbers. In the event a duplication of a prize winning number occurs, a random drawing will be held from among all entries received with that prize winning number to award that prize.

5. This sweepstakes is presented by Torstar Corp., its subsidiaries and affiliates in conjunction with book, merchandise and/or product offerings. The number of prizes to be awarded and their value are as follows: Grand Prize — $1,000,000 (payable at $33,333.33 a year for 30 years); First Prize — $50,000; Second Prize — $10,000; Third Prize — $5,000; 3 Fourth Prizes — $1,000 each; 10 Fifth Prizes — $250 each; 1,000 Sixth Prizes — $10 each. Values of all prizes are in U.S. currency. Prizes in each level will be presented in different creative executions, including various currencies, vehicles, merchandise and travel. Any presentation of a prize level in a currency other than U.S. currency represents an approximate equivalent to the U.S. currency prize for that level, at that time. Prize winners will have the opportunity of selecting any prize offered for that level; however, the actual non U.S. currency equivalent prize if offered and selected, shall be awarded at the exchange rate existing at 3:00 P.M. New York time on March 31, 1998. A travel prize option, if offered and selected by winner, must be completed within 12 months of selection and is subject to: traveling companion(s) completing and returning of a Release of Liability prior to travel; and hotel and flight accommodations availability. For a current list of all prize options offered within prize levels, send a self-addressed, stamped envelope (WA residents need not affix postage) to: MILLION DOLLAR SWEEPSTAKES Prize Options, P.O. Box 4456, Blair, NE 68009-4456, USA.

6. For a list of prize winners (available after July 31, 1998) send a separate, stamped, self-addressed envelope to: MILLION DOLLAR SWEEPSTAKES Winners, P.O. Box 4459, Blair, NE 68009-4459, USA.

HARLEQUIN® Temptation.

and

HARLEQUIN®

I N T R I G U E ®

Double Dare ya!

Identical twin authors Patricia Ryan and
Pamela Burford bring you a dynamic duo of
books that just happen to feature identical twins.

Meet Emma, the shy one, and her diva double,
Zara. Be prepared for twice the pleasure and
twice the excitement as they give two
unsuspecting men trouble times two!

In April, the scorching **Harlequin Temptation** novel
#631 **Twice the Spice** by Patricia Ryan

In May, the suspenseful **Harlequin Intrigue** novel
#420 **Twice Burned** by Pamela Burford

Pick up both—if you dare....

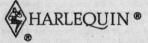

HARLEQUIN®

You are cordially invited to a
HOMETOWN REUNION

September 1996—August 1997

Bad boys, cowboys, babies. Feuding families,
arson, mistaken identity, a mom on the run...
Where can you find romance and adventure?
Tyler, Wisconsin, that's where!

So join us in this not-so-sleepy little town and
experience the love, the laughter and the
tears of those who call it home.

WELCOME TO A
HOMETOWN REUNION

Daphne Sullivan and her little girl were hiding
from something or someone—that much was
becoming obvious to those who knew her. But
from whom? Was it the stranger with the dark
eyes who'd just come to town? Don't miss
Muriel Jensen's *Undercover Mom,* ninth in a
series you won't want to end....

Available in May 1997
at your favorite retail store.

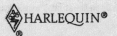

HARLEQUIN®

Look us up on-line at: http://www.romance.net

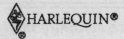

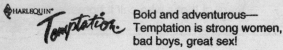